PILGRIM STATE

PILGRIM
STATE

JACQUELINE WALKER

SCEPTRE

First published in Great Britain in 2008 by Sceptre
An imprint of Hodder & Stoughton
An Hachette Livre UK company

I

Copyright © Jacqueline Walker 2008

A CIP catalogue record for this title is available from the British Library

HB ISBN 978 0 340 96078 3
TPB ISBN 978 0 340 96079 0

Typeset in Sabon MT by Hewer Text UK Ltd, Edinburgh

Printed and bound by Clays Ltd, St Ives plc

Hodder & Stoughton policy is to use papers that are natural, renewable
and recyclable products and made from wood grown in sustainable forests. The
logging and manufacturing processes are expected to conform
to the environmental regulations of the country of origin.

Hodder & Stoughton Ltd
338 Euston Road
London NW1 3BH

www.hodder.co.uk

To all my mothers . . .

PROLOGUE

DEMETER

Let me tell you how it really was, because this is my story . . .

In the beginning there was the Earth and the Mother, and the Earth was in light and in darkness, and the darkness was good, always good.

I am Demeter. It was from me that life first came, the wetness of it all, fecund and ripe and sweet. It was my hands stirred up the dark Earth, dipping my fingers in its dried-up places, feeling its salt against my feet, the bones of its stones, of my Earth, mine, Demeter, Goddess and Mother.

And the people of the old days knew me and honoured the beauty of my work, they praised the fruits of my belly and listened when I spoke because I am the Child Maker, the Crop Giver, the Mistress of the Flowers. From me came the deep mysteries, now barely remembered, of the fields and the workings of the moon, of the flood and the blood of women, and from my blood came Persephone, my daughter, who was all the beauty and love I ever needed. And by the time I had finished with it, the Earth was as good as any god-given heaven, everything growing in plenty and the women of the people united, no space left between them, Mothers and Daughters, each generation living closely together as one.

Life was easy flowing then, immaterial and bright, each day kept within my rule, until Zeus the God Deceiver, that old woman thief, who the people named Sky Thunderer when they called him in their prayers, grew envious of my power and told Hades he could have my baby to be his woman. His woman! As if Persephone was no better than a mule. So Hades took her, creeping from the shadows of his Underworld when I wasn't looking, like the soul-stealing coward he's always been, and he dragged my baby to his kingdom, down into the Abyss where nothing except sadness ever grows, and she was lost to me.

I called for my daughter till my voice clamoured at the doors of heaven, but the flapping of his dark wings had stunned her. I searched for her footprints in all the hidden places, but his razor-sharp teeth had ripped into her flesh, his cold heart lying on her breast till everything good and wholesome in her was turned into winter.

Once Persephone was gone I had no joy left for feasting and flowers, no time for laughing with the moon, for combing out my hair or changing my dress. I let the floods run dry and stones took up the space where my heart had once beat, I never even washed, how could I help it; there was such a madness running through my head. So I cursed Zeus Child Snatcher and the Earth became a meaningless rock to me, worth nothing more than the dust on the soles of my feet.

PART ONE
DOROTHY – THE MOTHER

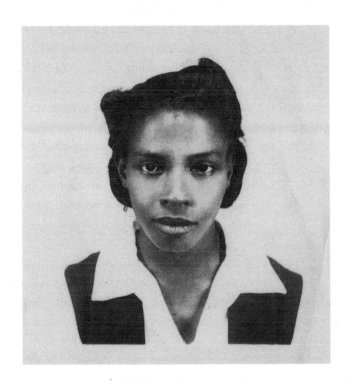

Brentwood, New York State, USA
May 1951

It's good the walls are white. In the morning, before they
turn on the electric, when the room is lit by the watery
sun that starts the day in this place, you can see the walls
are white. It's probably the only time you can tell the real
colour of anything around here.

This morning it's the young nurse who unlocks the door
and flicks the switch and now I hear it, the electric hum and
hiss of the yellow slither-slither that runs across the ceiling
of my head. The lights drench my eyes, seeping down my
body like a stain. Before I get a chance to shade my face the
nurse is there, standing by my bed.

'C'mon Dorothy,' she says, 'put that hand down; we don't
want any trouble today, do we?'

Huh! What she know about trouble, this young thing? She
shrugs her shoulders like I'm a stone in her shoe. I want to
catch her by the arms, hold her face up close to mine, but
instead I smile like sweetness.

'No, Ma'am,' I say and I'm glad to hear my voice sounding
soft and low. 'No trouble today. I have my hearing this morning, and trouble is the last thing I need.' They all love that
good nigger voice. Makes 'em feel safe. 'Please nurse, can I
have my comb?'

'Well,' she says, and now she's smiling. 'You're so much better aren't you dear; ever since you stopped getting all upset. Let me see you take your pills and we'll see what we can do.'

I swallow the tablets with the cup of pink medicine but for all that nurse-talk she doesn't see nothing worth looking at, and she 'do' even less. The sticky-sweet liquid sits cold in my belly.

They tell me I'm here because I'm sick, that they're doing all this for my own good, you know, 'cos I started screaming when they took my child from me. It took two men to hold me and a third to take my baby. They had to crack my knuckles open and I was kicking and cussing, but my little girl, she was screaming too, and that showed, they said, that I wasn't fit to be her mother.

The nurse walks back to her office when I show her my mouth's empty.

My feet are as cold as the floor they're resting on so I wrap the gown around me, but soon as I pull the nightdress it gapes wider at the back where the straps are torn away. I need to straighten my hair, get dressed-up for my hearing, but I haven't got my comb so I start jumping up and calling – please nurse, please, I say – but she stays in her office, writing white lies on empty paper and she doesn't look at me, even when I shake my head; can't she hear me screaming? So I suck at the air, take it down real slow, like I'm drinking in water through my teeth and I call again,

'Nurse,' I say, '*please* can I have my comb now? I have my hearing this morning.'

'Not this morning, honey,' she shouts back, 'no hearing, not today.'

8

Then my arms start flapping like they're washing hanging on a line.

'Nurse!' I shout and I'm begging for it now, talking till my tongue is running dry with babble-babble, and I'm feeling sort of heavy, so I walk back to my bed, but my face is like stone, 'cos the pills are working good, and I stand still without counting, just breathing out and in real . . . slow . . . but the next thing I know she's standing right beside me.

'Dorothy?' she says, as she taps me on the back. 'Dorothy, come on please, get up now. It's time to go.'

Behind her the attendants watch me closely without smiling so I know I must be silent and not ask too many questions.

'Where are we going?'

My voice is shaking so much I can hardly hear what I'm saying then there's all this crying and I just can't seem to stop it and it's messing up my face as I bend to find my slippers.

'I had a hearing set for ten-thirty,' I say, 'but it's too late to do my hair now.'

But thank you Lord, even though I know my lips are moving, nothing but a dribble comes out of my mouth. I swallow the salt-lick blub that's sitting at the back of my throat.

'Now don't you worry, honey,' the pink doll-nurse says, closing her glass eyes. 'There's nothing to worry about, no treatment today, just some men want to see you. Laurence and John will show you the way and I will see you later.'

I can't walk so straight 'cos I have to make each footstep go one by the other, then I feel their hands pushing on my shoulders as they move me through the door.

'This way Dorothy.'

Jacqueline Walker

The hall is long and dark and the floor is painted red. The windows are tall and set so high, right up by the ceiling, but that don't seem to help 'cos the sun can't see its way through the cold heart of this place. The attendant opens the door as I bite down on my lip – there – I can hear it now; the hissing humming-coming of the yellow slither-slither . . . and I'm swallowed by the darkness.

U.S. DEPARTMENT OF JUSTICE

Immigration and Naturalization Service

New York, N. Y.

– – – – – – – – X– – – –X

In The Matter Of : New York File No 0300–116510

Deportation Proceedings : Central Office File

Hearing Officer   : Charles D. McCarthy

Stenographer   : Abe Schwartz

Language   : English

Date   : May 22, 1951

Hearing Conducted at : **Pilgrim State Hospital,**

        W. Brentwood, LI, N.Y.

Against   : Dorothy Walker

       : Or Dorothy Brown

       : Or Dorothy Rebecca Brown

       : Or Dorothy Rebecca Walker Brown

Counsel or Representative : None

Present   : Dr Karen Mallins, Supervising

        Psychiatrist

Respondent   :

– – – – – – – – – – – – X

Pilgrim State

HEARING OFFICER TO PHYSICIAN:

Q Doctor, will you state your name and position?

A Karen Mallins, Supervising Psychiatrist.

Q Are you the supervising psychiatrist here at the Pilgrim State Hospital?

A That is right.

Q Do you have under your care and supervision at the present time a patient by the name of Dorothy Walker Brown?

A Yes, I do.

Q Can you tell us something of the history of Mrs Brown's condition?

A As the patient was born in Jamaica, British West Indies, little is known of her previous personal history except she was a very good student with extremely changeable moods. After marriage she showed little interest in her baby but was preoccupied with the desire to complete her Medical studies at Howard. She was first observed with definite mental symptoms on January 20, 1949 and was admitted to Belleview Hospital on January 30, 1949. She was transferred to Pilgrim State Hospital in the February. She was released on convalescent care into the custody of her husband on May 8, 1949 but failed to adjust and again became overactive and assaultive. The patient was returned to Pilgrim State Hospital on August 22, 1949 when she was found to be three months pregnant. She gave birth to a son here, at Pilgrim State Hospital, in

February 1950. He was immediately put into the care of the
New York Foundling Home. She remains in our care.

Q Dr Mallins, in your opinion, is Dorothy Walker Brown
   mentally competent to testify on her own behalf in this
   proceeding, the purpose of which is to determine whether
   or not she should be deported from this country?
A She has not been declared legally incompetent but she is,
   in my opinion, incompetent mentally, although she has
   fairly good contact and will be able to answer your
   questions.

Q Do you believe she is mentally competent to the extent
   that she would understand the nature and significance of
   deportation proceedings?
A Partially, yes.

Q What is the diagnosis of her ailment?
A She is a schizophrenic; she has dementia *praecox*, catatonic
   type with symptoms of mutism, confusion and erratic behaviour.

Q In your opinion, if deportation was ordered would she be
   able to travel without danger to her life and health?
A No, I think somebody should go with her.

   (At this stage of the proceedings the respondent was
   brought into the hearing room. As she is a mental
   patient and undoubtedly unable to comprehend the meaning
   of an oath she was not sworn.)

I lift my head. I can't see a bed or any straps today but the men look as if they're waiting for a lynching. Dr Mallins turns towards me and straightens her lips, her eyes staring out from her old lizard lids. Her coat is still clean so I must be the first. I am nothing, I am nothing. I must not scream.

```
HEARING OFFICER TO RESPONDENT:

Q  Do you speak and understand English?
A  Yes.


Q  What is your name?
A  Dorothy Walker Brown. Just a minute. Is this a hearing
   scheduled for ten-thirty a.m.? I was told I could get
   legal advice.


Q  That is true.
A  There isn't any here.
```

I put my hand to my head. My hair is sticking up natty and rough, and my face is unwashed. I have no brassiere or panties beneath my hospital gown but I know I must not scream.

```
Q  You have the right Mrs Brown, to be represented by counsel
   of your own choice at your expense. Do you desire such
   representation?
```

Mrs Brown, Mrs Brown! Like he's giving me a seat. Ha! That's it; that's how they did it, 'Calm down Mrs Brown,' when they tied me on the bed. 'Calm down Mrs Brown!' when they come

and took my baby till they're screaming, 'she's demented,'
and they catch me where I'm laying, swing me dangling by
my legs, with my arms strung up behind me.

A I have no lawyer, and, as a matter of fact, I have nothing to do with any courts when I have no lawyer. If my
   children go along with me I am perfectly happy to return
   to Jamaica.

Q Are you now a resident of the Pilgrim State Psychiatric
   Hospital in Brentwood, New York?
A Yes sir, I am.

When I got here I could see where I was, yes Lord, I could
see; but the shadows started coming so I'm kicking and
screaming as they tie me to the bed. Sometimes I was screaming so hard I wet myself, till they give me some pills, and I
keep real still, and I'm floating on the ceiling and feeling . . .
nothing. But they don't like that either, so they say they're
gonna fix me and they strap me on a table as they shove the
rubber in me so I don't bite through my tongue. 'Stand clear,'
they start shouting as they turn their backs to face me, eyes
crawling up the ceiling so the yellow slither-slither doesn't
climb into their heads.

Q Mrs Brown, I have here and I show you the warrant of
   arrest issued March 25, 1947 wherein it is charged that
   Dorothy Walker Brown, who entered this country at Miami,
   Florida by plane April 20, 1944, is in the United States
   unlawfully for the reason that you have remained in this
   country after having been admitted as a student and for

```
   a longer time than allowed you. Does this warrant
   describe you?
A  I have no doubt it does.


Q  Do you understand the charge?
A  Yes.


Q  Now I explained to you before your right to have counsel
   at this proceeding. Knowing you have such a right is it
   your intention to be represented here or not?
A  I have no representative here.
```

First I was told the hearing would be ten-thirty, then they
said it wasn't happening at all, but they can't hear the hissing
of the yellow slither-slither or the way that on the
ceiling . . .

```
Q  Mrs Brown, are you ready at this time to proceed with
   the hearing without representation?
A  I have nothing more to say, sir.
```

I must not scream, not move too much, not stand too still.
They give me the pills. The electric makes me normal. Their
eyes are crawling up the ceiling.

```
Q  Mr Stevens has, as recently as March this year, indicated
   he was your attorney in this proceeding. Does he still
   represent you?
A  I haven't seen Mr Stevens for a long time.


Q  I notice Mr Stevens is not present. Do you know why?
```

```
A  This hearing was supposed to start at ten-thirty and this
   is now ten to twelve.
```

```
Q  Yes Mrs Brown, but I have inquired at various offices here
   since ten-thirty and I have been told that nobody here has
   seen Mr Stevens. Do you have any explanation for that?
A  I don't know anything about that. Sir, I am in a mental
   hospital and I get my information through the doctor.
```

The man must be a damn fool! Just give me my babies, dear
God, save me.

```
Q  Do you wish to have your hearing this morning without
   representation or do you wish to be represented here?
```

What does he mean this little man, with his face like chalk
and his talk-talk-talk? That talk comes so slick from his tight
little mouth! What I wish? I wish to have my babies with me
. . . I *know* that my Redeemer liveth . . . Set me down upon
the rock, tie me now upon the rock, the rock of ages cleft for
me, let me hide myself in thee, in me, let the electric come,
let them run it through me head, let it slither, let it, let it . . .
I *will* comb my hair. I *will* not shout. No crying now. My
face can be the rock.

```
A  If there is any such representation I have already indi-
   cated . . . I have nothing more to say besides the few
   words I have just said which is, if I am being deported,
   I and my children on the same vessel, boat, plane or
   whatever it is, I will be well enough to go. And don't
   let any psychiatrist tell you I am not.
```

HEARING OFFICER TO PHYSICIAN:

Doctor, I think we may excuse Mrs Brown now.

BY RESPONDENT:

I want to go ahead with the hearing.

Q Mrs Brown, it is necessary for me to ask you these questions and I must ask that you answer them. Now, do you wish to be represented here, or do you not?

A I have already said all I intend to say at this hearing which is that I want to be with my children and don't let any psychiatrist or anybody else tell you I am not well enough to be deported as long as my children are along with me too.

HEARING OFFICER TO PHYSICIAN:

Q Doctor, you have heard the explanation I have given Mrs Brown concerning her right to representation. Do you wish to claim that right for her? Do you wish to arrange for her representation?

A I don't think we could. The hospital usually does not arrange for legal representation.

Q Is it satisfactory to you that this hearing be continued without representation?

A Yes.

Jacqueline Walker

```
HEARING OFFICER TO RESPONDENT:


Q  When and where were you born Mrs Brown?
A  I was born in Jamaica, British West Indies, Montego Bay,
   1915, March 17.
```

When I was a girl I woke to the touch of the sun, warm as butter, running down my face. That sun was so good it made me smile just to feel it; light so strong it parted the branches of the palm trees that grew outside my window; lights as sharp as splinters that ran across the surface of the water where the fisherman pitched their nets. Even at night the sky rained moonlight through the shutters of my room.

```
Q  Of what country are you subject?
A  I am a subject of Great Britain.
```

. . . but I was always more subject to my Dadda's bidding. I was his one girl-child, his special one. When they brought me to Pilgrim State the doctor asked me, 'Tell me Mrs Brown, how would you describe your relationship with your father?' So I made a face with my eyes popping from my head, doing what they expect from a coloured woman like me, then I whispered, as if I was speaking to a back-home friend, 'Him tie me breasts wid ropes so hard dey cut deep and deep till me bleed tru' me dress!' and I laughed, yes, I laughed, from the look on his face.

```
Q  How many times have you come to the United States?
A  Once.
```

```
Q  Are your parents alive?
A  My father is living.


Q  What is your father's name?
A  William James Ferguson-Walker.
```

My Daddy was a Headmaster, an educated, respectable man; he could speak lines from Virgil even while he was beating me, and his arm never wavered, not an inch, even when I was screaming. 'Spare the rod and spoil the child,' he'd tell Momma; she didn't have the strength to stop him spoiling me.

```
Q  Where was he born and what is his citizenship?
A  He was born in Jamaica, British West Indies and he is a
   British Subject.
```

As soon as I could I ran away, first from Dadda and then from the Island so he couldn't touch me again. The first time I left I wrote him a letter . . .

Dear Dadda,
  By the time you read this I shall be on my way. This news will no doubt be the occasion of great satisfaction to you, rendered still greater by the fact that I never intend to come back.

After that, I made a home with my grandmother in Kingston. I worked my way through college without Daddy's help. I was a natural, that's what my reports said, I was a natural scholar. 'Dorothy excels in the study of the Classical world, she has a talent for the Greek and Latin language,' but my real pleasure was always music. My voice was dark and strong. I got music from my mother, I loved her even more for it, but it was Dadda who made me a scholar; he beat learning into me as if he thought each stroke would bring me closer to redemption and Lord knows, I learnt those lessons well. When my teachers said I had a chance to win a scholarship to go to America, I jumped for it.

```
Q What is your race?
A I am of the Negro race.
```

When they took me to Pilgrim State I wrote to Dadda again, I told him I was expecting a child, that I'd been taken to a mental hospital. I begged him, please, Dadda, please, do what you can to help me. I kept the letter he sent me back.

> *Dear Dorothy,*
> *Your letter of November 28 came to hand yesterday. I must say, it certainly does not read as coming from an insane person. I am grieved at the plight you find yourself. And as though things were not bad enough you had to involve yourself in that way a second time!*
> *I hope it will be established that you are sound mentally and that your visa will hold so that you can get your profession.*
> *In the meantime don't give way. Keep as pleasant as you can and hope in the Lord.*

```
Q  What was you mother's maiden name?
A  Gladys McLeod.


Q  Of what country was she a citizen?
A  She was a British Subject.


Q  Where is she buried?
A  In Kingston, Jamaica, British West Indies.
```

Gladys was my grandmother's only child, so fair skinned she could easy pass for white, more of a girl than a woman when Dadda took her.

At first my Grandmother protested; what was a grey-haired, natty-headed teacher-man like him doing messing around with his students in the first place? Anyone could see he was too old for her child and even worse, look at his skin, black as a field-hand's back; how a daughter of hers could even bear to look at those African lips, let alone touch them! Still, it didn't matter what Grannie said – my Momma would have him. Nine months after they married the first of us children were born. People said that every growing thing Momma touched thrived, including us children; she had five in ten years. But sometimes life can take too much. When her last child died it only took one man to dig the hole and lay that baby to rest. Seemed like Momma couldn't hold on any longer, so she followed right behind her – dead within the week. They just opened that grave, put my Momma with her baby . . . made it easy to dig, I heard them say. I was eight years old, I couldn't understand; how could she follow baby and forget to take me?

BY HEARING OFFICER:

Let the record show that warrant of arrest identified by
the respondent is marked in evidence as EXHIBIT #1.

BY THE RESPONDENT:

I have no representation at this hearing and I am desirous
of being with my family. As a matter of fact, I had no
knowledge that there was going to be a hearing right now.
Before I came out of the ward the nurse merely told me some
men wanted to see me. She wouldn't tell me what it was. I
am not prepared. I did not have a chance to take anything.

HEARING OFFICER TO RESPONDENT:

Q Mrs Brown, you knew, did you not, that you were to have
  a hearing at ten-thirty?
A Yes, I was informed, but . . .

Q Are you trying to tell me now that you wish to get addi-
  tional documents to present at this hearing?
A Yes.

HEARING OFFICER TO RESPONDENT:

You may leave the Hearing with an attendant to get the
documents you wish to refer to.

   (Respondent leaves the room.)

Pilgrim State

The attendant doesn't smile but he nods his head. He takes me to the lockers and my hands start to shake. I pick up my handbag, push the papers inside and snap the clasp shut.

(Respondent returns with papers in her hand.)

Q I have the birth certificate of your daughter Pearl
   Brown. Do you have the certificate for your son?
A I will have a look for it here.

Q Mrs Brown do you have the certificate?
A I cannot find it.

Q Let us leave that for now. Are you ready to go ahead
   without representation?
A Yes.

Q When and where did you enter the United States Mrs
   Brown?
A I entered the United States at Miami, Florida on April
   29, 1944.

Q Was it your intention to remain permanently at the time
   of your admission to this country?
A No. I answered that question before.

Q Is your husband, Clifford Brown, able to help you?
A No, I have not seen him in quite some time.

That man, that man; dressed so fine! A cane-cutting, black-skinned beauty of a man. Each day with him was a hot sort of heaven, running under pressure and burning up with steam. No woman I knew could ever turn from his eyes, dark like melted chocolate, running down your body till they stuck to where the heat was. Lord, he had the biggest hands, and he knew just how to use them! That kind of man, they used to say, could talk the birds right out of the trees, and one of those birds lining up for talking-to was me. We looked so good when we walked down the street, people turned their heads just to see us, his chest plumped up 'cos it made him proud, he said, to be the one to have his arm round me.

After we married I stayed at Howard, continued with my Medical studies and Clifford kept his job in the factory. Weekends we honeymooned in the City. We never left our beds till late. We'd listen to Fats Domino one evening and Count Basie the next. We jived and jitterbugged and got home so full of life it seemed a danger to sleep in case we missed something extra. It seemed as if each day was made for us to do our loving, and then I got pregnant.

At first I thought well, if he loves me now, the baby will make him love me even better, but he started staying out at nights. When the loving wore out and no words were left, we fought as hard as we'd done the rest.

Q What are your children's names and when and where were
   they born?

Q Mrs Brown, do you wish to have the question repeated?
A No sir, I have two children; Pearl Diane Brown, born
   September 4, 1946 in Belleview Hospital New York.

Pilgrim State

When Pearl was born I got sick. I was crying every day, I couldn't move. If I lay down it seemed as if the bed had swallowed me, I couldn't speak, it was all I could do to eat. Then one night, Clifford started coming on to me with his old-time ways, loving me up, saying it was time we had a party and he would make the drinks. 'Hey darlin,' he said, 'drink this one right down for Daddy,' and he was smiling. But the drink tasted bitter and my head started swimming and I'm begging him to help me. He's standing so close I can feel his breath, but still he doesn't touch me, and then I'm falling, I'm falling, and he's standing there laughing till I'm tearing at his face, and the night is filled with sirens and they're taking me away.

Q Mrs Brown, can you tell us the name of your second child
  and state his date and place of birth.

Then Clifford started visiting me at weekends, but at least now there was no pretending; he says if I give him my savings he'll sign my freedom papers – I have no choice, so I pay him and they let me out. First night I was home he pushed himself inside me. Soon as he found I was expecting again he just picked up the phone, told the doctors I was sickening and they came back to fetch me. This time I was three months pregnant.

Q Mrs Brown, do I need to repeat the question?
A No, I have a son, Theodore Brown born the 1st of February, 1950 in Pilgrim State Hospital, Brentwood.

Jacqueline Walker

Getting bigger every day, waiting for that baby. The pain in my heart worse than the pain growing in my belly 'cos I knew they would take my baby from me. 'What does he look like?' I asked when he was born, but the nurse didn't answer, she just took my baby from me.

```
Q  Where are the children now?
A  To the best of my knowledge my son Teddy Brown, is in
   the New York Foundling Home under the charge of the
   social workers.
```

Even though my baby was gone my breasts didn't know it, they still swelled up the way they should. I was crying, so the nurses fixed me to the bed, the straps cutting welts across my belly. I can't move to call for help even though I'm hurting, even when the milk starts soaking through my nightdress and it's dripping through the sheets.

```
When I last had any information my daughter Pearl was
boarded out with a foster-family. My doctor tells me that
the social worker has been looking in at her.
```

```
Q  Why is it that neither of your children is with your
   husband?
A  My husband is a working man. He cannot take care of chil-
   dren. He needs a woman to take care of the children. I am
   that woman because I am the mother of those children.
```

```
Q  Now Mrs Brown, under the Immigration Act of 1917 an alien
   who is deportable from the United States may apply for
   relief from deportation if they can show they are of
```

good moral character or that such deportation may lead to
the serious detriment of a citizen of the United States.
Do you understand that?

A Yes.

Q Do you wish to apply for the privileges I have explained
to you?

A There is nothing at all I can say or do while I am in a
mental hospital. It is impossible. I am in a mental
hospital off and on since 1949. This is all impossible
for me.

I would like to say this for the record. I was in my
house at 270 Manhattan Avenue. About eight-thirty in the
morning of July 24, 1950 I was brought here. I was set
to work in the kitchen and I was a patient. I worked for
some time. Sir, I am missing my babies very much. I have
a five-month-old baby and a child. I collapsed several
times, and on November 29 I applied for the right of
habeas corpus. Well, it was postponed three times and I
was not told why but then I was told there would be a
hearing before Justice Byron Hill.

Q Excuse me Mrs Brown. Does this recital you are giving me
have any bearing on this immigration case?

A Yes.

Q What bearing?

A Well, I just want to show you that I know what I'm talking about. I have nothing more to say. I can't say nothing more. This is a court and I have nothing to do with
courts any more unless I have a lawyer. No, sir. I am

just a student who came to this country hoping to learn
something from this country to benefit my country. I made
a mistake, had two children, found myself running in and
out of mental hospitals. I have two children. I am a
mother. I am not a student any more. I am not a doctor
and won't ever be a doctor. I have two children and
that is the most important thing; to know what to fight
for in a case.

Q. Mrs Brown, do you have any friends or relatives in this
country who will take responsibility for you?
A No, I do not.

Q Do you have any money, Mrs Brown?
A No, I have just maybe eight dollars here in the property
office. That is all.

Q Mrs Brown, are you, or have you ever been, a member of
the Communist Party?
A No, sir.

Q Is there any further statement you wish to make before
the record of the hearing is closed?
A There is nothing at all whatever, nothing more that I can
say that I have not said already. Let me have my children. I am not going to leave them in any institution or
foster home.

BY HEARING OFFICER:

All right, Mrs Brown. You are excused then.

(Respondent leaves the hearing)

HEARING OFFICER TO PHYSICIAN:

Q You have testified that Mrs Brown is now suffering from
   dementia *praecox*, catatonic type. What is the prognosis
   in her case?

A Guarded.

Anchovy Town, Jamaica
April 1956

I listen for the train steaming up from the city and the shouts of the garden-boys when it arrives. I don't hear the cooks, or the maids, or the strong-armed laundry girls; they go home as soon as they can, but the boys have city money burning through their pockets and plenty of time to cool their heels so they strut and crow like roosters in the yard.

As twilight comes the women of my family pass by my window, gathering together at the end of the day to chew the cud and share the comfort of the old veranda. Soon their talk will soak through my head, over the buzz of the radiogram humming in my ear and the bark of the yard dog snapping at the gate. Lying on the bed by the cool white wall I hear it all, each day passes like water over stone, I wake or sleep, it makes no difference which.

I turn from the noise and fold my daughter in my arms. She comes each evening to sleep in my bed, a gift from the darkness, sweet as the smell of the jasmine flower that slips through the slats of my window.

Listen now to the creak of the wooden floorboards and the tip-tap padding of the women's bare heels as they tilt and sway on the old rocking chairs. The air is velvet thick

*tonight so they stretch themselves out long and lean. They
laugh and sigh and click their tongues, ruminating over
their own misfortunes, scratching and sniffing out other
folks' business; things not theirs to know or tell.*

'Well,' Iris sighs. 'Me and Dorot'y see each other quite regularly after she arrive in New York you know, the both of us
being such a long way from home and all. That's how it was.'

'So she miss home?' Enid asks. 'Me and Don never hear a
thing from her all these years she was gone.'

'Maybe deportation has taught Dorot'y a lesson.' Claudette
can't help but crow as she struts across the veranda, walking
around in a fine display of her own god-given righteousness.
'Her father always say she act like a barbarian. How she get
that little girl-child anyway?'

'Her name is Jackie,' Iris says.

Enid scrapes her chair across the floor as Claudette carries
on in her throaty craw.

'Ah, yes. Jackie, that's it. She's a high colour, yellow gal so
her father must be white. Dorothy would have met him when
she come out of hospital. How long was she in that place
Miss Iris?'

'Now, let me recall,' Iris pauses a while before she's drawn.
She doesn't much care for Claudette and her high-handed
ways. 'When I last see her she would have spent almost one
and a half years at Pilgrim State. It must have been spring
of 1950 when I first visit her. What a journey! Out of the
city; I have to get a train after the subway but it take me
all the way. That place is bigger than this town you know,
thousands and thousands of people living there so it have
everything it could need – a farm and shops . . . it even

have a railway station all to itself. But Lord, it make me shiver first time I see it; cold you know, like it never get the sun.'

'But tell me something now,' Enid says. 'With all their money, how come America have so many mad people in one place?'

'From what I've seen they're all mad!' Claudette exclaims. 'When they're not shooting and hollering at each other they're dancing and singing in the most inappropriate manner.' She flaps her large, washerwoman's hands.

'Lord help us, Claudette,' Iris laughs. 'How would you know what happen there? The nearest you come to New York City is the last time you went to a film show; when was it tell?'

'Still never mind, the whole place is a madhouse from what I see; cars and people rushing everywhere.'

'But how Dorot'y look when you see her?' Enid rocks her chair and her voice sinks low. 'I hear they tie her up in a room by herself and leave her.'

'That an' worse. It was late when I got there, I already eat something on the train. When they bring her to me, she walk like an old woman, all broke down with her eyes half open like a zombie. She come an' reach her hand to me before I even see who it is. Made me jump from my skin. "Dorot'y?" I said, "is it you?", an' she tell me what happen. Jesus Lord, what a thing to hear! Clifford have his girlfriend put something in her drink, make her act crazy so they take her away and leave the elder daughter with him.'

'So, she was mad then,' Claudette sniffs.

'Hmm! Well, it's true,' Iris clears her throat. 'She cry and look sort of wild but she never seem mad to me, no indeed.

It's a torture what they do to her! You know, they never even let her see the boy when he was born. They just take him straight'way and put him in a home.'

Straight'way they took him, pulled him from my belly before I even have a chance to stretch out a hand and feel him. I hear him shout as they cut at the cord. I try to sit up. I shout, 'Give me my baby!' and now I'm screaming, crotch spread wide, my back arched high as my legs try to pull from the grip of the straps, held in those stirrups like an upturned crab. The doctor never even speaks a word to me, he just tells the nurses to bring sedation 'quickly please' while I lay on the bed and howl like a dog, praying to the Lord for some sweet salvation and, oh, then I see him, swinging like a rabbit by his heels, his fists boxing shadows till they wrap him and take him away from me.

'Lord knows, anyone would feel mad in such a situation. That poor girl she lost the first child already, and all the time Clifford was making sure they would keep her locked up in that hospital!' Iris sighs and scratches her head. 'And you know, even when they let her out it's in his care, he have the last say and she was no better than his slave, soon as he say so, they take her back.'

My breasts grew fat as ripe plums splitting in the heat, aching till the milk ran down to my belly, weeping for that child, bleeding for that child, tied on the bed as I dripped on the floor . . . 'Iris,' I said. 'How can it be; how can they take my own baby from me?'

'It was a long time before she manage to get herself out of that place, and still the authorities trying to deport her, and of course Clifford is helping them as much as he can you see, so him an' Dorot'y carry it on and on, fighting like cocks in the yard, going to court an' every damn foolishness you can think of!' Iris thumps her heels on the floor.

From Pilgrim State to Penn Station I covered the scaled-up skin of my knees with my last-year dress. Sitting on the train with no stockings on my legs. Washerwomen's shoes worn down at the heels. Hiding the shame of my uncovered head. Shutting my mouth on my hospital breath. Didn't lift my face as the train pulled away. Couldn't raise my eyes till the dried-up fields and the shadows of the pylons were out of sight, not until the firefly lights of the city were dancing on my face, bright as diamonds in the sunsetting high of a Manhattan evening. I skimmed the ground when I stepped from that Pilgrim train, carried along by the beauty of it all, till my head was spinning and singing with the street-spangled rhythms of that city.

'My Lord, you should have seen her when she first come to me, such a state of excitement, and then she collapse like some little broke-down thing; I just take her in my arms, and put her to bed, and she sleep like a baby right t'rough to the next day.'

Soon as I could I tried to have custody of Pearl returned to me. I told the judge, 'I am the mother. She should be with me.' But the judge barely lifted his head, he just shuffled the pages of the hospital report; 'schizophrenic dementia', reading it over and over till he's looking at me like

I'm a contagion. 'Custody,' he says, 'custody decided in favour of the father, Clifford Nathaniel Brown.' That man cut the heart from me; no noose in his hand, no flick of the switch, but as he spoke I dropped to the floor.

'One thing about 'Dorot'y,' Iris says. 'She's a good mother. She love those children better than she love herself. You know the night before she go to meet Teddy for the first time she was so agitated she could not even lay down to sleep, she went walking all through the night.'

By dawn the streets were empty, the weekend city hardly stirring beneath its blanket of cloud. Already the sidewalks were powdered with snow, feet crunching down on the frozen ground and a sticky frost etching glassy flowers at the corners of the windows. The wind cut its way through the alleys, slicing down the streets, stabbing at my nose as the snow started falling, heavy this time, flakes big as feathers so they danced in the breeze, blowing in my mouth as I stepped from the subway. The sign said 'New York Foundling Home, Sisters of Mercy of New York, 68th Street'.

Before I was more then a step in the door she was coming at me, one hand at her veil and the other one straightening the pleats of her skirt as if I'd caught her unprepared. Her white bonnet seemed jaunty somehow, tipped to one side like a sailor's cap, and I couldn't help staring at a plume of auburn hair that had fallen from the corner of her veil.

'It's such a cold day, isn't it?' She rubbed her hands. 'I'm Sister Monica. How can I help you?'

'I'm here to see my son, Teddy Brown. I am expected.'
I gave her the letter from the social worker.
'Thank you. Would you wait here please?' She pointed
to a line of empty chairs and I sat down, singing a prayer
through my half-closed lips.

> *Rock of ages cleft for me*
> *Let me hide myself in thee.*

Let me hide myself ... How will it be, him and me? I
wiped the New York winter from my hands, trying not
to shake as I watched Sister Monica walking through
the door.

'Mrs Brown,' she held the baby up so I could see him
and the blood came rushing to my head. 'This is your
son, Teddy.' She was speaking slowly now, as if her
tongue was practising the words. 'Mrs Brown?' she said,
but I couldn't answer, I just looked at my child; he was
waving his fists for me.

'So after that,' Iris continues, 'she stayed with me till she
got her own place. And let me tell you; she work every hour
God send so she can have that baby with her.'

I have one meeting after another. I have to prove I am
fit to be his mother; 'An' who else would be better?' I
ask the social woman. Hmm! So I make sure my apart-
ment is warm and his cot is ready and they check me
out; one damn fool question after the next: 'For how
long were you kept in solitary confinement? What do
you remember of the electric shock therapy?' Made me

want to shout, 'Try it sometime sweetheart, see how
you recall it!' But no, I had learnt my lessons well enough
and I stayed quiet, till I pass all their tests and at last
they say yes, I can have my baby back with me.

'But how she look?' Enid asks. 'You know, after she come
out of Pilgrim State Hospital?'

'Well,' Iris speaks slowly now. 'She was a changed person,
that is true. She was good with me, though perhaps not so
trusting as before, but you can't blame her for that. Once she
found her own place and left me I didn't hear much from her,
not till she call me years after that, right before they were
about to deport her.'

File A-7762256 New York   Jan 31, 1956

Re: DOROTHY REBECCA WALKER BROWN aka DOROTHY REBECCA FERGUSON
BROWN et al in APPEAL AGAINST DEPORTATION PROCEEDINGS

Decision of the Special Inquiry Officer

DISCUSSION: This record relates to a forty-year-old female,
a native of the British West Indies and subject of Great
Britain whose only entry into the United States occurred at
the port of Miami, Florida by plane on April 20, 1944 at
which time she was admitted as a student.

The respondent was married to Clifford Nathaniel Brown on
September 29, 1945. Her husband is also the subject of
immigration proceedings. She has been separated from him
since 1951. There is presently pending a divorce suit with
cross complaints of adultery.

The respondent has three children; Pearl born September
4, 1946 and Teddy born February 1, 1950 whom she states are
the issue of her husband and Jackie, born April 10, 1954
who was not fathered by her husband.

The respondent was an inmate of the Pilgrim State
Hospital, a mental institution, from February 7, 1949 to May
8, 1949, and from August 22, 1949 to December 17, 1951 when
she was placed on convalescent status. She testified, quite
reluctantly, that after her final release from the hospital
she met a married man. She said he was nice to her, got
her a job and promised to marry her as soon as he got a
divorce. As a result of their relationship she had a child
born in April 1954 or thereabouts.

We have carefully examined the entire record that
relates to these proceedings and it is our conclusion that
the record establishes that the respondent has not been of
good character. It is ordered that the appeal is hereby
dismissed and that Mrs Brown should be deported with
immediate effect.

'When she call and tell me they are set to deport her . . .
well, my heart drop to my belly, but what can I do? She have
no chance for another appeal, see how it look. But still she
was hoping they would deport Clifford as well and that, I'm
sure, is the only reason she get on the plane at all. She lose
everything you see, and which one of us would not seem mad
after that?'

'But who,' asks Claudette, 'is Jackie's father? It's not Clifford, that's for true, even if her last name is Brown.'

'I can't say too much there. Dorot'y would never speak a
word of it to me, but let me tell you, whoever it is, he have

some money; she borned that child in a private hospital and who do you think would be paying for that?'

'Who?' they chorus.

'Must be the father –'

'Ah . . .' and they let out their breath.

'But you know, I can't make her talk at all,' Enid says, and her voice is all whispers, as if she's caught the edge of my own shut-up silence. 'Not now, Lord bless her. She just sits in her room since the day she come back. Sometime she cry and makes a disturbance. Next minute she all silence, an' speak not a word. Most days the only person she will see is Jackie, not even the boy get a look in.'

'All this is well and good enough but tell me,' Claudette shifts her chair and it grates on the floor. 'What are we to do with her? She arrive with hardly one suitcase for the three of them and not more than fifty dollars in her hand. She was lucky that at least one of her brothers could take her in, and even more fortunate that he should marry with someone of your good nature Enid, especially with you having so many children of your own to look after, and you let her come at such short notice. Of course, we all doing what we can to help Dorot'y but it can't go on like this, we all must know that. Chah! That one – she's always been trouble. Her own father said it; nothing good enough for Madam Barbarian!'

And she laughs, happy for once to have such an easy place for her bile to rise up and leach.

The sound from the radio suddenly swells, drowning her words in a familiar croon.

I turn to the window. The sickle-edged moon is at the cleft of the mountain.

'Dorot'y, it's Enid,' I hear a knock on the door. 'Come now, darling,' she says. 'It's time for this to stop . . .' Enid strokes my face. 'Since you arrive back home you shut yourself up.' Enid recalls our dance-hall days, her fingers tracing tracks across my cheeks, running down the lines where the years have touched us both. 'You have to get up some time, think of the children you have; you can't keep on grieving for the one that is gone.'

I am gone; I am flotsam washed up on this shore, slipping like silk through the shrouds of my own recollections. What am I to do? Her glassy eyes watch me. I'm drifting in a land-locked sea . . .

'Dorot'y, please talk to me . . .'

And at last, the darkness closes over me.

The child stirs.
  'Mommy?' she calls.

What am I to do? They will say I am sick.

'Mommy?'
Her sweet berry breath brushes at my cheek as she curls herself back towards the curve of my breast.
  'Please Mommy, talk.'
She raises a hand, drops it so it falls on my mouth, falling like a leaf as she calls my name, her fingers reaching up to find the parting of my lips.
  'I love you,' she murmurs.
  I watch her sleeping till the night grows old and pale, watch

her sleeping as the stars sink back into the dawn, then I rise from my bed, creeping from the shadows of the house. My Lord, the world smells sweet this morning, dripping with goodness, like a new sort of Eden. The sun has only just lifted the hem of the horizon, stretching honeyed fingers from the hills behind me across to the far-off sea. As I raise my head to catch a better sight of it, those arrow-headed birds sweep away the last piece of mist. I turn to the house and return to my daughter.

'I am here Jackie,' I whisper, 'I have come back and I promise I will not leave you again.'

Anchovy Town, Jamaica

June 1956

These days I feel better. These days I get up with the morning and after the house chores are complete I spend the rest of my time, as much as can be spared, sitting on the veranda, just Enid and me. Today the children are playing in the yard. This will be the last time I plead to those government people, so I hold the pen carefully as I write the letter.

US Attorney Office
Washington DC
8 June 1956
USA

Dear Sir,
I am requesting your permission to apply for read-mission to the United States. I was deported with two of my three American-born children, Teddy and Jackie, on 23 April, 1956. This has been a consider-able hardship for us all as we are rendered absolutely destitute by this action. As far as I know there are

two main reasons put forward for my deportation:

1) That I suffer from a mental disturbance. This is absolutely untrue as I never had any trouble that way until my estranged husband and his family managed to have me committed to Pilgrim State Hospital. I was released after three months, put back through the parole system on two occasions and finally released in 1951. Since that date I have had no trouble whatsoever. I am fully capable of working and managing my own affairs.

2) That I had failed to show good moral character. I presented a number of testimonials from reliable witnesses. The regrettable fact that I had two children whose parentage was denied by my husband does not necessarily indicate a bad moral character since my husband has been adjudged the father by the courts and on the birth certificates.

I would also like to point out that my husband, Clifford Nathaniel Brown, has remained in the USA and I am getting no support from him for the children. If I gain re-entry I will be willing to do any sort of job, even domestic work, for their support.

In the meanwhile my husband has retained custody of my eldest daughter Pearl who, from latest reports, is being looked after by a woman called Dearwood at Jefferson Avenue, Brooklyn. I was awarded visiting rights once a week and now, in this situation, I don't know if I will ever see her again.

My American-born children will also suffer increasingly if I don't get back to America as jobs are scarce here, the cost of living high and the living conditions terrible.

I hope you will give close consideration to the above facts and give me another chance at making a livelihood for myself and the children.
    Yours respectfully
    Dorothy W. Brown

'I'm glad to see you are keeping yourself occupied Dorot'y.' Enid smiles towards the papers stacked on the table.

She's a fine looking, wholesome sort of woman, heavy boned but with delicate nostrils and well sculpted features so her face has a child-like look, even though she's more than reached the later years of life.

'You have some news?' she asks.

'Well, not really; just the same from the authorities and I still haven't heard a thing from Pearl.'

Enid pulls a stringy bundle from a bag and moves the vase of plastic flowers out of the sun.

'The Lord will protect her,' she mumbles as she fixes her glasses firmly on her nose and unwinds a hook from the ball of white yarn, looping the string between her thumb and forefinger. Her hands are always full of some kind of business.

'Dorot'y,' Enid says. 'Me and Don have been doing some thinking.'

Enid raises her head, shoves the spectacles back in place at the bridge of her nose before she re-winds the yarn around her fingers.

'You and Don thinking?' I say, knowing of course that everything that follows will have come straight from the tight-lipped mouth of my pick-and-choose brother.

'Yes,' Enid says, poking a finger up at her spectacles. 'Me and Don.'

I feel a glow spreading across my skin as I try and conceal my unreasonable irritation at the too-big glasses sliding down her nose, at the smell of plastic flowers growing old on the table, at the doilys that smother every possible surface, the paint-by-numbers pictures of English gardens which cover the walls and, before Enid has time to tell me one thing more, even the antimacassars and the cushion cases I'm sitting on become the source of my increasing agitation.

'Dorot'y, we think that it is time that you accepted your situation so you can start to arrange things for your long-term future, you know, what you and the children are going to do.'

What we are going to do, Lord! Maybe, I'm thinking, maybe we could give Enid some assistance in fulfilling what must be her lifelong mission to cover every last piece of God's blessed empty space with some bit of fru-fru nonsense.

'I would have you here as long as you like, but Don – you know how he is.'

Yes, I know my brother's ways, more like our father than anyone I know, but still, I realise I'm relieved at what I hear because it's true; it's time for us to go.

'Thank you Enid,' I say. 'I know we can't go on living on your charity. You have been so good to me and the children, I will not forget it.'

A doctor bird swoops in front of the veranda, his scalloped tail trailing on the ground. He scratches the earth and tilts his head, one eye on me, as he lifts his tail and leaps back into the air.

'But still, it will take some time. I have to get work and

find a place to stay. Only thing that makes sense is to go back to Kingston –'

'Dorot'y,' Enid pats my hand as she speaks. 'I will be glad to look after the children for you till you find your feet, you don't have to worry about that.'

And I'm thinking, what a heart this woman has, what a truly generous nature; and at once I feel ashamed of my previous uncalled-for irritation.

'They will be just fine here,' Enid smiles. 'And soon as you want, you can come and get them. I will let you have a little money, enough to help you on your way till you find some work; and you don't have to worry about paying it back, it's from my own savings, so I am the one that can see to it.' Enid drops the half-finished doily on her lap and puts a hand on my arm. 'And you know Dorot'y, you are always welcome for a visit, whenever you want to come back.'

Anchovy Town, Jamaica
August 1956

My belly feels like a nest for butterflies today so I have to use the toilet and wash my hands for a second time before I leave for the station. Lord help me, I must not cry or I won't be able to take one step from my children. I put a quick, lipstick smile on my face before I kiss them, but it feels like the love of Judas I'm planting on Teddy's lips. I tell him not to fret, that it won't be too long before we'll be together again. He's trying so hard to be a good, brave boy. I see him squinting back the tears so he won't bawl. It tugs at my heart when I see him put his arm around his sister, tugs at my heart and makes me proud just the same.

'Don't worry,' Teddy says. 'I will look after Jackie till you come back,' and he crushes my knees with his kisses, 'I love you, Mommy.'

I brush a hand across the nap of his head. Teddy takes off his glasses and wipes his cheeks. Next I turn to Jackie and I'm dreading this now. First she's quiet, standing by her brother, a thumb in her mouth, then she grabs at my hand and pulls at my skirt, digging her nails into my skin.

'Mommy!'

I knew she wouldn't let me go easy, but Enid is there and

ready, holding her back as I stoop and pull her arms from around me. I'm trying so hard not to hurt my little girl, but still, I do it; tearing her away, pulling at her fingers, even though she's screaming with, oh, such eyes and it's 'Please, Mom-mee, please' as I open the gate. I want to turn back, wipe away her tears, tell her not to worry, but Lord knows I have to keep walking. Now she's running; she must have got free. I know she can't get past the gate but even so, I have to listen to her choking, I have to hear her. I won't turn my face in case I see her – I can't see her, I have to keep walking, I have to listen to her, know she's climbing on the fence, begging me, shrieking like her heart's being ripped from her body. Jesus! I never thought . . . I never thought.

Even when I get to the station I can hear her screams. I can hardly step my feet onto the train. Soon as I sit I turn my face so it looks like I'm staring through the window, but I'm crying and I barely see a thing, just the screams stay with me, just the screams; separating her from me.

Kingston, Jamaica
September 1956

I could have got work cleaning or washing clothes, but the colour of my skin, too dark so they tell me, meant I was incapable of waiting on tables or serving in the better class shops of the town.

When I first came to this place I prowled like a cat. I missed my babies so much I couldn't sleep; not enough air for my soul to breathe, not enough space to even set down a chair, just a bed and a paraffin stove that festered in the corner. When I shut my eyes there was only the darkness. No scent of jasmine coming through my window, just the heat of the city rising from the floorboards and the bed resting silent and smooth beneath the window. Then suddenly my thoughts rose up and I began to retrace the steps that had brought me here to cry at the moon. I became angry at my own shortcomings, ranting at the injustice of my situation until I learned something new; how to live small like the person I'd become, a poor woman in the poorest part of town. And soon as I did that, I got offered a job as an assistant in a pharmacy, not the best work, but at least I could start counting not waiting, counting the pounds till I had enough money to bring my children home with me.

*   *   *

49

They are tired but still they run; scuttling underneath the breadfruit tree that stands in the lane and sends its branches through the breeze like the threads of a well-worked embroidery.

They are tired but still they run – running through the yard, running as I open the door to the house and right away they're jumping on the bed, squealing and laughing as they bounce up and down like a pair of jack-rabbits, and even though I tell them to hush and be quiet I can't help but laugh and join in the fun, rolling on the bed and screaming just as loud when they tickle and make wet kisses on me.

'Hush now!' A shout comes through the wall. 'Some people is asleep!'

'It's all right,' I whisper, through the fingers on my lips, 'It's just Miss Constance but we must be quiet, no more noise, come to bed. Quickly now.'

We put on our nightclothes and lay together, their heads fitting snug inside the crook of my arms, one in each, and I'm filled with such love that it feels like my heart is humming with joy.

Next morning my babies are up with the sun and the place is full of their gladness, the bedclothes jumping with their laughter and tricks till they bounce from the bed and race through the door, but it's early yet, and the yard is still quiet. A haze of pink-morning drifts into the shack as the day begins then it's cock-crow chickens chasing hens round the houses, scratching and pecking as they high-step their way round the tubs and the women who rise early enough to go to the stand-pipe before they have to leave for work.

'Morning Dorot'y,' Sunshine shouts and waves her hand,

stretching the threadbare edge of her gown across the sides of her mountainous hips. 'Y'all right?'

I nod and smile. Sunshine – interested in everything she sees – screws up her short-sighted eyes towards the children as they scamper to the side of the porch.

'Is your pick'ney?' she calls.

'They are.'

She can't see a hand in front of her face.

'Fine looking, like their mother, eh?' We laugh.

By now the sun is warming up. I wipe a hand across my brow as Miss Constance walks past with a child perched low on her bony hip.

'Morning Miss Constance, I'm sorry for waking you and Delroy, the children were so excited.'

'Miss Dorot'y,' Miss Constance's plaits bob up and down as she speaks, the ragged tails of hair escaping from the edge of her dirty bandanna. 'Don't you mind about me, it was Delroy make me say hush-up last night and he has all day to sleep! How was your journey?'

I pat the head of her dirty-nosed child, I can't tell which one this is, they all look the same, hanging like a fringe at the hem of her skirts.

'Constance! Where's me breadfruit?'

Delroy calls across the yard. Constance has no more malice than a jackass in the field, mind you, she has no more sense either, that's for sure. She waits for my answer, staring at me with her slow-brown eyes.

'Fine, Constance,' I say. 'But you have to mind me now, I must get the children breakfast before I'm late for work,' and I turn back to the house.

'Jackie,' I call. 'Come now. Fetch the comb and put your head down.'

Her hair is loose at the front but the middle just knots up whatever I do. I rub the Vaseline into her head as she wriggles against my legs.

'I told you, hold still!'

Jackie puckers her mouth like she's sucking on lemons. Her shoulders rise up as I draw out the comb. When I finish with the combing I tie each plait with a ribbon and quick as a cricket she's out to the yard, so I sit and finish my own careful dressing, pressing the fuzz from my natty morning hair with the help of the hot iron comb. When the straightening is finished I use the tongs to roll up the edges, sculpting my hair into work-time order. I will wear my good green dress today, yes; that dress will go well with the leather bag, then I can carry the white gloves sort of casual in my hand.

Most days I'm out to work early and back so late the truth is, I barely see the children at all. Miss Glad watches out for them using what she has left of her one seeing eye. She's old, all worn out from too much laundry work, sitting on her haunches till her knees swelled up, but she's kind all the same and gets by, just about, on what her own children send her from their dollar and pound pay cheques that she changes at the bank.

Today I have plans, so I come from work a little early. Soon as I turn the corner I see Jackie. I scoop her into my arms and walk to the shack.

'Have you been a good girl?' I ask as I sit and take her on my lap.

'Yes, Mommy.'

Her nails are black from digging in the dirt. On her face a stain makes a rim around her mouth.

'Jackie, what's that on your face?' And now I see it, the dirt crusting up around the corners of her lips. 'You have to stop eating that dirt!' So then she hangs her head, 'Oh, child,' I take my fingers, wet them with spit and rub the dark stuff away. 'Promise Mommy you will not eat the dirt any more? It will make you sick.' She looks back at me with these hang-dog eyes. 'Good girl,' I stroke her head. 'Now tell me, how is Miss Glad today? Did you do what she told you?'

'Yes,' Jackie curls like a cat at my waist. 'Present,' she says.

She holds out her hand and gives me her treasure; smooth, brown stone of a lychee fruit.

'Thank you.'

I kiss her face and hold the seed closer to my eyes so she knows how much I like it.

'Sing dicky birds.'

I start the way I always do, my hands spread out so she can see all the fingers before I bunch them into fists at the back.

Two likkle dicky bird sittin' on de wall,

I use the same sing-song voice Jackie hears from the market women downtown. I flick a finger as I call out each name.

One name Peter de udda one Paul,

Jackie laughs, falling on the bed and kicking up her legs.

Fly away Peter, fly away Paul,

and my fists swoop behind my back and disappear again.

Come back Peter, come back Paul.

Now I make a face, my eyebrows raised with my eyes open wide so I look like a clown. This gives Jackie such cause for hilarity that she's almost choking, her breath coming out in little gasps between the gusts of laughter. Suddenly I'm reminded of that girl I heard screaming at the gate and I wonder at the way such a simple thing can make her happy and forget what has happened.

'Come now, we're going out.'

I've saved enough and we can walk all the way. I call for Teddy, I put a thick shine of lipstick on the pout of my lips and as I stare in the mirror I have to smile at myself – I look so good with my skirt nipped into my still-small waist; yes . . .

The sky is hot and dark as pitch, no moon tonight, just a sticky heat that makes my dress hold my body tight as skin. I make sure I keep a good grip on the children as we go down the half-lit, all dirty Kingston streets, crowded as carnival, as we meet the heaving traffic of people, as we enter the tight-edged slick of the night and the cheap-talc sweat of the people.

Mek it hot when you put it in de pan

We pass the quiet shops and the gaudy all-night stalls stacked high with fruit and fish. Young men, lean as lizards, lounge against noisy counters where calypso songs play back-to-back. The boys tilt their hips to the music, shirts flap-flapping on their bare brown chests as they stand with their groins thrust out against the street, eyes so full of lewdness that their thoughts slop over me and every other woman they see.

> Fry me plantain in your hot hot oil
> Keep it burnin' till you come up to de boil

And me ... Well, I swing my hips and lick my parched lips and I'm breathing through my mouth and I feel sort of full, like a good ripe peach, as we all walk through those uptown streets.

Though the roads seem filled to bursting already, more people are coming, spilling from an open-walled shed of a place – the worldwide home of the *Zion International Church of the Redemption*. They steam as they sing, sweat rubbed glossy as oil on their faces, hands clapping time with the one-soul syncopation of their cheap tambourines.

'And I say to you,' the pastor leaping to the platform shouts at the crowd like he's whipping his dog. 'Withhold not correction from the child, for if you shall beat him with the rod he shall not die.'

'Yes, Lord!' A woman jumps from her seat.

'Thou shalt beat him with the rod,'

'Alleluia!' she cries again.

'. . . and shalt deliver his soul from Hell!' yells the preacher.

'Praise Him!' She raises her arms and at once she is joined by the whole damn-fool flock of these ignorant jackasses, arms raised towards a dark sort of heaven with the blood-lust glinting in their eyes. Lord have mercy! I turn my back and pull the children towards me as I walk towards the honest haranguing of the hawkers and hustlers propping up the counters of the all-night music bars.

By time we arrive at the open-air picture house, the place is already packed with people. Even though the roof is open to the sweet night air, the walls are running with sweat, and then the sign goes up, 'Elvis Presley in *Jailhouse Rock*', and I'm back, back in their whitewashed dream of America; white faces and shiny shoes.

Soon as the beat starts the place erupts, heat venting out through the aisles because everybody's up, tight-hipped dancing all around me, bodies closed in, the darkness behind and Elvis at the front on the movie screen with a voice that sinks a hunger inside me and eyes that make me think of ice-water melting in the sun.

Teddy jumps from his seat and he begins to boogie, tap-dance jiving, but I can hardly see him, there's just the flash of his teeth in the flicker from the screen and the beat of his heels on the floor. His steps are so good that a crowd starts to gather, clapping and shouting as he swirls and drops to 'Jailhouse Rock'.

Now Elvis straddles the screen, his hips buck and thrust and we match his moves. The grind of the music heats our bodies to a frenzy so I don't care that the air hangs heavy with our smell, and that the only thing waiting for me tonight is an old tin shack because at least, for now, I feel sassy as I am, the sap rising strong still, thinking of my jive days, thinking of my love days, thinking of clean streets and shiny shoes.

PART TWO
JACKIE – THE DAUGHTER

Kingston, Jamaica
March 1957

Some people call these things acts of God and if you think He really is a joker, you can see their point of view.

There was barely any warning, just a sudden thickening of the air and an ungodly silence that settled on the city as the sun began to rise behind the Blue Mountains.

At the first reluctant tremors Dorothy jumped to her feet, the thin nightdress wrapped around her legs and her hair sticking up like those piccaninny dolls they sold cheap in the shops downtown.

'Jackie, come!'

Dorothy pulled at Teddy's arm, dragging him from the bed, and through the door.

The scene in the yard was like an old-time movie, all speeded-up action and bug-eyed confusion as people swarmed like ants from their nests. Dorothy spun round, her arms waving wildly as she screamed.

'Get out!'

But Jackie didn't move, she lay where she'd been sleeping, her dark eyes glistening as the earth shrugged to life and the shack began to sway beneath her. And it seemed to the child that in that moment the light bulb had become a phosphorescent firefly that jumped against its flex, transforming the dreary patchwork of the room with a kaleidoscopic brilliance that possessed her imagination and took her shining, like an angel, up towards the heavens.

Dorothy screamed again, 'Jackie!' And though she heard her mother's frantic screams, Jackie could not leave this exquisite motion, a sway that seemed both strange and familiar, like the time she rode the circus elephant and felt his haunches rise and fall. She remembered the thrill that had pulsed through her body that night, sitting on his back, slipping down the saddle as he lifted his foot, her heart racing on till his next giant step took her up so high her fingers had grazed the starry ceiling of the night. She had opened her mouth and her mother, thinking she would cry, had yelled, 'Stay still now!' so she had stayed where she was, and let the great beast take her where he wanted, and they'd swayed together, dancing there, under the moon, till she felt no more fear, just a thrill that curled a heat inside her belly.

A roar sounded up from the earth, a yawning, primeval call that seemed to go on for an age, rushing towards them like a steam train. Dorothy ran back to the house and caught hold of Jackie. This time she ran like a Fury, out through the yard, up towards the ridge. She leapt over the fence, speeding past the shacks and the telegraph poles, covering the child's head as she raced below the cat's cradle of power lines that bobbed and swayed to the new rhythms the earth was drumming beneath her. Dorothy grabbed the child, reeling like a drunkard, as she sped towards the clearing. They only just managed to reach the track when the ground began to helter-skelter and all they could do was stand with the others, rock from side to side, twist or fall, tip-toe balancing on the quivering earth as their bodies gyrated, swaying obscenely, mouths gaping open as the fear bubbled up like water in their throats; then the floor gave way.

'Hold me now!' Dorothy shouted.

Jackie heard her mother's fear as the ground began to rip, pulled apart by the force of the earth which twisted and coiled beneath them. The air sparked electric currents as the dancing telegraph poles stretched too far, snapped with a hiss, falling back till at last they tore free of their anchorage. Dorothy screamed. Jackie clutched her mother, gripping her nightdress as they fell down together, onto the hot, dry dirt. Suddenly the awful bellowing ceased and the ground was still. The earth was scarred up by the ridge but a breeze was stirring from the hills and already, somewhere in the distance, there were bells and sirens screaming. Dorothy looked across the track. The shacks seemed little different, just as shabby as before, still leaning one against the other in their usual ramshackle way. Dorothy felt the fragility of her own poor existence curling like a snail's shell on a concrete slab as a silvery line of tears ran down her cheeks and over the curve of her lips. She stroked the children's heads.

'Don't cry, Mommy.'

Jackie leaned towards her mother, but Dorothy had turned, pulling away from the child, and there it was again, that slither in her head, flicking the switch that would take her there, now, to that cold white space, hands on her shoulders, hair sticking up and a face unwashed. Huh! You see, I have no panties . . . I am lost, lost in the garden, dear Lord, take this cup from me. I *will* comb my hair. I *will* not shout.

She would not have the children see her like this, lying in the dirt in her threadbare clothes, trembling with desire for that terrible abyss. Dorothy closed her eyes and pressed a fist into her belly. She could not breathe. It felt as if a rope had been pulled from her stomach to her throat, everything tight, her chest fit to burst with the skin of her cheeks stretched across her face and the child just tugging, talking on and on, when all she could do was feel her heart thud-thudding, counting out the days to the end of her existence. Jackie reached behind her mother's head, frantically pulling the fuzzy down of hair which grew at the base of her neck until Dorothy's breath came again, flowing at last with a great sigh as the air moved through her chest – now in, now out.

Dorothy lifted the child from her lap and stood, facing the sliver of shade that was forming at the bottom of the track.

'Mommy, where you going?' Jackie cried.

'C'mon now. We'll go to the shade.'

It was going to be a long wait before they could go home and the sun was burning with the unrelenting heat that scorched the shantytown in the driest season. She picked up the child clinging to her skirts and took the other one by his hand, stepping around the huddles of people, as she moved towards the pocket of shade. At last a listless wind was moving between the houses, covering their faces with the faint red dust of the desiccated earth that settled in the gulleys between the shacks. Dorothy was parched, her throat thick and coarse. Soon they'd need water but the line of weary people at the standpipe was already stretching out some way, and she couldn't carry Jackie much further, the child seemed heavier than usual – and this unforgiving heat! She would sit in the shade and rest, slip away as soon as they were sleeping; it would be so much easier – not just for her but for the children as well. She'd move real slow, ease their weight from her lap, let their heads fall gently before she stood; they'd never even know she'd gone.

Soon the sun was at its highest but she couldn't leave it much longer. She eased the children's heads onto the ground. Thank goodness, she thought, they barely moved. Dorothy stood, picking up an empty can as she made her way towards the standpipe and the waiting queue of people and at last her tears could run free, cooling on her face, falling like raindrops on the flowers of her dress.

The hymn spread like wildfire across the shanty, first one, then a great host of voices swelled the choir, the song rolling like a wave from the shacks, out past the ridge towards the mountains until it echoed in the foothills of the forest.

When upon life's billows you are tempest tossed,
When you are discouraged, thinking all is lost,
Count your many blessings, name them one by one,
And it will surprise you what the Lord hath done.

Dorothy looked up. It was Constance stumbling towards them.

'You all right, Miss Dorothy? Ah real glad fe see you.'

Constance was barely dressed, the same old bandanna stuck on her head but her nightdress torn and stained at the edges.

'Yes, Miss Constance, I'm all right. How about you?'

'I can't see Delroy. You see him?'

'No, but if I do, I will tell him you're looking.'

Though if there was any luck in this world, Dorothy thought, the quake would have opened up its mouth and swallowed that man whole.

The ground had not moved for some time. Dorothy decided it was safe enough to return to the shack. Trails of weary people were already finding their way back along the broken tracks. She looked into the sky. Even the moon seemed heavy that night, rising from the ridge of the mountains as if it was reluctant to show itself. Dorothy walked across the empty yard, stepping over the furrows the twisting earth had ploughed into the path. Except for a few lights here and there the town was dark but the sky was clear and Dorothy got all the light she needed from the pendulous moon that arched its way above her. She was aching to her bones, each step slower than the last, as if she was walking through water. Dorothy climbed the steps and pushed the door.

'Come on,' she turned towards the children. 'It's safe now.'

As she opened the door the moonlight rushed ahead, running on the floor in a flash of quicksilver. She looked back into the hot, black night. The moon was still rising, casting a halo around the dark outline of the children. She kissed their heads. Apart from the singing, the town was strangely quiet, folks moving round with a delicacy which seemed to Dorothy awkward and out of place, speaking in tones they mostly kept for funeral days. Dorothy stared into her house. It seemed they had been lucky; hardly anything was changed, hardly anything in fact was even out of place.

'Thank goodness,' she muttered, lifting the lamp and shaking it. 'There's enough oil for the night.'

She placed the light on top of the chest, filled the kettle and lit the stove. The children sat on the bed as they drank the sweet mint tea Dorothy had boiled on the paraffin stove.

The power was down all over the Island, but that made little difference to Dorothy's normal evening routine, and while a passing stranger might have raised an alarm at the somewhat haphazard sloping of the roof, the shack had always looked precarious, as if the only thing stopping it tumbling right over was some uncertainty as to which way it should fall, so by eight o'clock that evening they were already eating their usual dinner of bun and cheese. Jackie finished the tea and licked the crumbs from her fingers.

The lamplight cast shadows across the walls, softening the lines of their poverty, erasing the clutter of clothes and possessions that languished in the corners of the room. Jackie yawned, rubbed her belly and stretched, reaching for the slate and the thin grey stylus that lay on the floor.

'Sweet Jesus!' Dorothy sighed, closing her eyes as she lay on the bed.

'Mommy,' Jackie pulled at her arm. 'Look what I did.' Jackie held up the slate.

In the middle of the slate was a house in a field. Four windows and a large door opened onto a path that ran beside a gabled fence. At the top of the picture an oval sun sent beamed lines of light through a cloudless sky, while in the foreground two stick-like, bulb-headed figures dropped heavy flowered garlands from their opened out fingers. The exuberant joy of the child's drawing filled Dorothy with misery. She looked around their one-roomed house; more of a lean-to than a house except, as she would sometimes say, all it ever leaned against was another old, rickety shack. There were gaps large enough to let in daylight, or moonshine, at the top where the walls were unevenly attached to the roof. Sometimes when the wind was blowing from the north the rain ran in rivulets down the inside of the ceiling, etching dirty watermarks across the shabby green walls. When she'd first moved in she'd tried to make the best of the place. A curling sheet of newspaper proclaimed 'Supreme Court rules Montgomery's segregation laws are unconstitutional'. It was pinned next to an older, crudely coloured picture of the Virgin Mary, her pale, improbable moon face pressed up against a profile of Billie Holiday whose half-open, half-burning eyes and lips gave the impression of a woman caught someway between ecstasy and song. Dorothy closed her eyes. The light on those fading wide lips made her recall another time she'd sat in a low lamplight, his face close to hers, with the hot, sweet musk of the dancers rising in her nostrils as they shimmied on the floor. She opened her eyes. The Virgin's once white dress was streaked from neck to toes with a flowing, yellow stain. There would be no happy endings for them here in this place, of that she was sure, like everything else they would soon be submerged by the never ending struggle to keep alive; fighting off the rats, fighting with the weather or the rent man, trying to find the money for just enough food and knowing all the time that whatever she did her children would end up like all the other no hope pick'neys who grew up, hard and fast, in the shanty part of town.

'C'mon now, lay down.'

Dorothy straightened the covers as the children rushed

behind her, falling against each other, jumping from the wooden chest onto the bed. And why, she thought, could they never be still, always knocking things over like a pair of untrained mules even inside the house.

Dorothy sat at the end of the mattress as the children pulled the sheets over their heads. Teddy was asleep soon as his head met the pillow but Jackie's eyes were following her every move and Dorothy felt it now, almost like a pain, her love for that child, it tugged at her heart like the weft in her soul.

'Strange,' Dorothy whispered. Abraham was only tested one time, and even then, Dorothy thought, God had spared him at the end. Maybe He felt differently about girl children, or maybe, she chewed her lip, maybe He just happened to be looking the other way when her time had come. Ah, well. This daughter, she was sure, this one was hers to keep; a sign just as clear as the burning bush of the renewed promise of His eternal love.

Dorothy was too tired for any more thinking. She blew out the light, got into bed, pulled her daughter towards her and closed her eyes.

'Is it good Mommy? You like the house I draw?'

'Yes, darling. I like it very much.'

'It's me an' Teddy at home.'

Jackie smiled, nuzzling closer to her mother, but Dorothy was already sleeping, her breathing heavy and low. Jackie lay as quiet as she could, the pulse of her mother's heart beating soft against her face. She turned towards the shutters as the geckoes chased their tails across the ceiling and then she heard it again, the shanty's own song, hanging like a dewdrop in the heat.

Count your blessings, name them one by one,
And it will surprise you what the Lord hath done.

This time Jackie followed each word, carefully counting
her blessings, just like the old song had told her to, her
thoughts brim full of as many happy endings as she could
think of till she drifted to a space, somewhere between wake-
fulness and sleep, where she saw herself standing by the slate
house she had drawn, its lines filled out now by the substance
of her dreams. Someone was calling. She looked towards the
house. On a wide veranda her mother was standing, her face
unmoving, though her lips mouthed a silent appeal. Jackie
lifted her arms. White flowers spilled from her hands and as
she followed their fall, the shoots of a liana bush began creeping towards her, its dark tendrils seeking out her body, snaking
around her ankles, till their stalks were so high they looped
over her legs, crawling up towards her thighs as they pressed
her body to the earth. She managed to lift a foot before the
living plant pulled her back again, scratching her legs as she
woke with a jolt.

'Mommy, Mommy!' Jackie screamed, leaping from the
sheets onto the pillow.

'What happen?' Dorothy jerked awake, startled eyes
blinking through the darkness of the room. 'Stop it! Be
still!'

She grabbed the child's arm.

'Mommy, I feel something move on me feet.'

Jackie brushed at her body with wild, waving hands.

'You just dreaming. Hush up and lie still before we have
every person complaining at you and me.'

But Jackie would not be quiet.

'No, Mommy. No!'

'What happen?' Teddy yawned.

'Just be quiet. I have to see to something.'

Dorothy got up from the bed. It was always the same with this child she thought, scared every night, jumping up at every damn thing. She made her way round the bed to the lamp and struck a match. The brief flare lit up the room for an instance, revealing the startled faces of the children. Dorothy carried the hurricane lamp back towards the children.

'Get off the bed. C'mon. Mind away.'

The children clambered onto the floor as Dorothy pulled the covers from the bed. The flickering light cast a shimmer on the shadows, enlarging each fold of the worn-out spread into a wide plateau of undulating slopes and valleys. Dorothy lifted the lamp and pulled the pillows to the floor. The sheets were stained and crumpled, but there was nothing on them that a good shaking couldn't smooth.

'There's nothing there,' Dorothy said, with an exasperated sigh. 'Lay back down, honey. Please.'

'No, Mommy!' Jackie wept, her voice choking now, taking little gasps between each word, 'You-have-to-do-it-properly!' She pointed to the corner.

Dorothy lifted the lamp again, pulling the sheet taut and this time, as she raised the light, she caught sight of something else, a shadow moving, its blurred outline made more solid by the stretch of paler sheets. Jackie yelped as she saw it.

'There it is Mommy, there!'

It lay paralysed, trembling; a scaly tail bent upwards and back. It looked like the crabs they found on the beach, but its long tail and claws, which grew from its head, gave the creature a strange and grotesque appearance.

'What is it?' Jackie asked.

'Don't touch the scorpion! Leave it or it will sting you.'

The scorpion lay motionless on the sheet, but something else was moving on its body. Jackie peered into the darkness. Clinging to the scorpion's back were two smaller figures, perfect copies of their mother. Even in the lamplight Jackie could see the quiver of their tiny tails.

'Watch where it is; mind out!' Dorothy shouted. 'The earthquake must have disturbed it. Keep your eyes on it. I'll be back.'

The children jumped to the side of the room, their eyes still fixed to the bed.

'Mommy,' Jackie pleaded. 'It has babies on its back.'

There was a flash of metal as the scorpion darted out, first one way and then another. With one movement Dorothy lunged across the bed, snapping the insect in two with a sharp click of the shears. Jackie's stomach heaved as she looked down to see the insect not dead but still walking, each piece of the insect carrying a baby on its back, almost as if it was unconcerned by its own awful dismemberment.

'Nasty!' Teddy grimaced covering his face with his hands.

Dorothy opened the chest, took out a bottle and opened it. Jackie knew what it was – her mother's best rum, clear as water and strong enough to cure the fever or any such pain. Dorothy poured the rum carefully over each section of the insect's body. The tail part curled up tighter than before as the infants let go of their mother's back. Helpless now, the babies struggled for a moment, their upturned legs still attempting some escape as they lay in the shallow pool of rum. The head part of the scorpion-mother walked for a while until, as if it had only just noticed its new lopsided habit, it stumbled and came to a halt.

Dorothy lifted the lamp and took a spoon from the drawer, scooping up the pieces and carrying them back towards the chest. She wrapped them roughly in a sheet of old newspaper and threw them into a corner of the room. Tomorrow she would tip them out with the rest of the rubbish. For now, they could stay exactly where they were.

'That's it, back to bed.'

Dorothy blew out the lamp. Jackie lay down. The patch of alcohol was cool at her feet and she squirmed, lifting her legs so she wouldn't feel the sudden cold dampness of the sheet.

'Girl, be still!' Dorothy hissed, her voice slicing through the silence with an edge that made Jackie whimper.

The sun was rising again behind the Blue Mountains. Dorothy could already see the first hints of daylight creeping through the gaps at the ceiling.

'Goodnight, darling. Go to sleep.'

Dorothy spoke softly now, regretting the previous harshness of her tone. True, the girl needed to be stronger, just like everyone said, but she was hardly more than a baby, still not quite three years old and a child should not be forced like some out-of-season flower, she knew that too well. Anyway, she thought, there's no person living been born perfect, you learn as you go, everyone has their own burden to bear, carrying their weakness along with their strength. And she remembered her own garden of temptations, a place where white flowers grew their own sweet fragrance of oblivion.

Dorothy stroked her daughter's cheek. No, the child would learn well enough in time.

Kingston, Jamaica

January 1958

Must have seen it coming, she thought, that old rooster, the way he squawked!

Great-grandmother sucked the air through her teeth as she folded her dressing gown across her chest.

'Lord!' she laughed, slapping the carcass on the table, 'I had to be quick with you.'

She looked at the bird. A sticky red line was seeping from his beak. Great-grandmother carried her plucking chair out to the yard.

'Good thing . . .' she muttered. 'It's all in the planning. No need for any fuss.'

This was Great-grandmother's favourite part of the day –

the world all hushed and the sun sitting pale in the new day sky. She retraced her steps towards the kitchen, picking up her favourite knife and two bowls, one for the feathers and the other for the guts and she smiled – he'd make a good meal, she was sure; strip off the feathers and chop off his head.

Great-grandmother liked to have everything set just right, everything placed in good order before she started. She grabbed the rooster by his claws holding him close to her face so his head was level with her eyes. Funny thing was, she thought, they always seemed to know when their time had come – even when she wrung the head nearly clean off their necks, even when they stopped twitching, their eyes still had that look. She let the rooster drop against her hips as she walked back to the yard. Oh well, she shrugged, chop off the head and singe the skin, open him up, save the guts for the juice and however he was looking, he'd make a good meal.

Jackie sat up and rubbed her eyes.

What had woken her so early? She could feel her mother, still fast asleep, just beside her. It must be that old rooster kicking up again Jackie thought; after all, he'd been acting strange all day.

It was too early, the light was only just peeping through the shutters. She'd had such fun having Mommy to herself all yesterday after Teddy had gone, until she'd had to put on those nasty Sunday shoes and walk all the way to her Great-grandmother's house, wasting all the day listening to the old women talking and talking and never even playing. Now it was the morning Jackie really wanted to go out and play, but she knew she had to be quiet and not get up too early, Great-grandmother didn't like her walking around before she should, but soon the sun would be climbing on the rooftops and it would be too hot to play in the yard. Never mind, Jackie closed her eyes, she'd wait for Mommy, wait till it was time.

The rooster bowed, dipping his head and posing for a moment with his head erect, chest stuck out so everyone could see his brilliant red comb. He was giving his first parade. He hopped two steps and stopped again, tilting his head till a pert grey hen with a fine curve to her tail-end caught his attention and whoosh, he was off, chasing and strutting down the yard.

Jackie pushed out her chest, hopping and scratching at the ground with her bare-toed feet. A new young cockerel! She was impressed. He looked so fine, so pleased with himself, crowing and swaggering all around the place. She was sure she could learn to strut like him, lunging at the floor and crowing like a bugle, so that's what she did with each hop-and-step, stopping every now and then to flesh out her chest and jerk her head up and down.

She looked at the veranda and wondered how many days she would have to count before Mommy would take them back home. The cockerel crowed again. Jackie spun round just in time to see him running back to his pen. She raced towards him. He was so beautiful with his sharp yellow feet and his dark glossy feathers, and then she stopped; but where was her friend, she wondered, the fat old rooster? He never ran away, but this one – ah, well. The young cockerel glanced back for a moment and pecked at his feathers.

'Puk, puk, puk.' Jackie clucked and flapped her arms.

The cockerel scratched the ground, stretching up tall so his deep-throated crow could ring across the yard. The silken feathers of his neck caught the blaze of the sun as he flapped his wings. Jackie covered her ears, threw back her head and squawked as loud as she could. The cockerel lunged towards the child. Jackie shrieked with laughter and jumped out of his way. The chickens, the chickens! They were the best things to play with at Great-grandmother's house and this new cockerel was the best of the best; he looked so funny, all puffed up and sort of silly at the same time.

'Jackie, leave the chickens alone before they hurt you. Come here for dinner, now.'

She stood on one leg and hop-scotched to the house.

'Puk, puk,' Jackie said, scratching and pecking as she squawked up the steps of the veranda, 'Puk, puk . . .'

'Hello, darling,' Dorothy said.

'Puk puk, puk. Not darling; chicken, chicken!'

Jackie waddled her backside in a show of such self-importance that Dorothy couldn't help but laugh.

'Oh, sorry, Missy Hen. Why don't you come on up and roost over here by me?'

Dorothy gathered the child onto her lap.

'You should let Jackie sit on her own seat for a change,' Great-grandmother looked towards the empty chair.

'No,' Dorothy flinched. 'It's fine; she's fine. She can be on my lap.' The old woman could still make her feel like a child.

Great-grandmother cleared her throat.

'Of course – she's your daughter.'

Dorothy stared at her plate but her mind was resting on the buzz of a fly as it circled the table. The air was thick with heat. It seemed like an age before Claudette brought the food but when she finally appeared it looked as if the waiting had been more than worth it; dishes piled high with mashed-up yam, thick yellow plantain, mountains of steaming, green callaloo, fat dumplings squatting in their own sweet gravy, and all of it smelling so good.

Jackie's mouth began to water. She sat up straight as she could, more than ready to start eating, but soon as the food was on the table Claudette disappeared again into the kitchen.

'Here it is now,' Claudette called as she came back through the door. 'Dorothy, you say grace,' Claudette held the last dish in the air, 'then we can get eating . . .' Claudette placed the plate carefully on the table. 'No need to hurry; there's plenty for everyone,' she said with a flourish. 'Grannie's fried chicken!'

She covered the chewed-up bones with a cloth. One thing was certain; Dorothy brushed a fly from her face, Grannie made the best fried chicken of anyone she knew.

She had told Jackie that she could leave the table but the child would not leave her, she was still clinging to her skirts; *and* she hadn't touched her meal – she'd just started weeping as soon as she'd seen the meat.

Dorothy stood, cradling her daughter so her head lay in that place where it could easily rest beneath her chin. She walked to the veranda. The old woman was already sleeping in her chair. Good, Dorothy thought, no need for talking, just sit for a while, Jackie sitting with her, her warm baby breath running down her skin while the slow-buzzing flies danced circles round her head or rested on the walls or the tables.

'Come.'

Dorothy pulled the child towards her, lifting her legs so

she could sleep with her arms wrapped around, rocking in the chair as their clothes sucked up their sweat. Jackie curled her hands, nuzzling her face between the cushions of her mother's breasts, and it seemed to Dorothy as if the child was inside her, still joined by the cord, and she stroked the curve of the child's back as if it was the swelling of her own mother-belly. The old woman opened her eyes.

'Put her to sleep,' Great-grandmother whispered. 'It must be nearly time now.'

'No, not just yet,' Dorothy hesitated. 'She won't sleep, not yet.'

But the truth was the old man was right, it was late already, the sky was burning ochres and reds as the sun dipped below the line of the coconut trees. And even though she could be fierce, she had a way with chickens, kept them so well, knew exactly how to handle them from the time they were eggs till they were on her table.

'All right then,' Great-grandmother thumped her bare feet onto the floor. 'But it don't do no good to always let the girl have her own way; all that fussing – getting from the table before she's even finished . . . Waste is a sin as bad as the next.'

A sin! Dorothy licked her lips. This day's work was a sin by itself, and the thought of that sin had set a coldness running through her heart. She let her eyes close and saw, as if in a dream, Abraham with a daughter and the knife glinting in his upheld fist. She opened her eyes. But there was no choice now, she had to see it through. The sun had stoked a fire in the sky that evening, all that was left were the embers of the day.

'Come, darling.' Dorothy kissed the child. 'Let me take you inside. You can have a sleep.'

Dorothy carried Jackie into the house, laid her on the bed and closed the shutters. Soon, she thought, soon. She undressed the child, pulled off her own dress and hung it carefully on the back of the chair.

'I'll lie next to you. You're so tired, aren't you baby.'

Dorothy watched as Jackie's eyes drooped, as her cheeks softened, as her breath slowed and steadied, as her head fell back at last against her arm and the pillow.

'I love you.' Dorothy kissed the fragile skin of her temples. The child turned.

Hush little baby, don't say a word,

But Jackie was already sleeping, sinking and dreaming-in the words of her mother's song.

Momma's gonna buy you a mocking bird . . .

By the time Jackie woke from that seamless sleep the world had returned to its first-light stillness, that time when the earth is so hushed and unmoving that the smallest movement feels like an intrusion on the day. First thing she noticed was the side of the bed looking all smooth as if no one had ever slept there. Then there was the smell of her mother's face-powder hanging in the air.

Jackie jumped from the bed, padding past the empty chair and standing on tip-toes to reach for the door handle.

'Mommy?' She shivered, her head peeking outside the crack of the door.

In the half-light of dawn the walls seemed to melt away, moving back towards the shadows where she'd always known they'd come from. Jackie clenched her fists, feeling it tight now, something inside her, while all she could hear was the thump, thump beating of her heart. Where was Mommy? Fear quickened in her guts, moving to her throat till she swallowed it down. She stepped into the hall. Hush now, Jackie thought, no noise! But it was too late, the shadows had heard already and they rustled around her, stretching out their feelers from the night-shaded spaces where her dreams came out to play.

'Oh, no,' Jackie whispered through her closed-up fingers. She was sorry, so sorry; she hadn't meant to wake them. All she wanted was Mommy, her mom-mee, but all there was were the shadows laughing and calling, waiting for her there, pretending they'd be silent if she passed them in the hallway. Now what could she see? Mr Evil was pricking pins into her eyes. Jackie bit her lip as she opened another door; but there were so many doors, more than she remembered, with the endless kitchen cupboards and a bathroom with a toilet sitting right there close beside it and why was it always *her* doing the finding? She whimpered as she turned another handle in the nasty creaking darkness where the whispers of silence had come sneaking out to greet her — and her voice came out much louder than she'd meant it. I'll find that naughty mommy, Jackie thought stomping her feet, and then I'll be cross and I'll say, 'Where were you, Mommy?' and then she'll be sorry.

Jackie swallowed the tears as she reached for the handle of the last door.

This room seemed deep as a cavern. Jackie turned slowly, but even though the sun was at the shutters, all she could see were the shadows stretching out towards her — and suddenly there it was, something else stirring in the darkness. She spun around.

'Come child.' A voice called to her through the dimness. Jackie saw a skeletal hand reaching out as if to touch her and she froze, her eyes seeking out the mouth of the voice she had heard – yes, it was someone she remembered, but it wasn't her Mommy, then she saw, even in the half-light, the old woman's eyes.

Great-grandmother was sitting in the bed, her nightdress pulled open at the chest where the creased-up skin hung in folds at the base of her neck. Jackie couldn't help but shy away, the sight of her great-grandmother's body, all that flesh coming out from the cover of the bedclothes, made the child recall a turtle she'd once seen pulled from its shell. Jackie walked towards the bed, her sweaty feet making little ripping noises on the floor as they lifted up and back from the cool pink tiles.

The ripening glow of the morning had deepened the furrows on her great-grandmother's face. Jackie thought she must be the oldest talking-thing there'd ever been, aged beyond the point of caring, but there was nothing frail in her eyes, nothing weak in the beak-like arch of her nose.

'Great-grandma,' Jackie said, walking closer to the bed, 'where is Mommy?'

'She gone.'

For a moment it seemed to the child that Great-grandmother must have misheard her so she asked again.

'I told you girl,' Great-grandmother's voice had grown insistent. 'She gone.'

Jackie did not move but then she was falling, falling and screaming, screaming as her legs folded neatly beneath her.

'No!' she shrieked, 'I *want* my mom-*mee*!'

'Get up child,' Grannie yelled back. 'Get up, and hear what I tell you.'

But Jackie was not listening. She knew it! It was real! It was real! Her screams rang out like hammers on the ceiling as her tears boiled up, hot behind her eyes, streaming down her face as she choked on her breath. Jackie leapt to her feet and ran through the door, racing down the hallway, running and screaming while the doors kept slamming and Great-grandmother was shouting, 'Stop it! Stop it!' Jackie shrieked at the darkness, filled with such a fury that fear did not stop her, doors couldn't hold her – not with the fire burning hot in her head, not with the fire burning up in her soul. Jackie's nose slimed rivers down her chin and she didn't even care, let it drip, let it drip, let the dirty snot-slime drip glue everywhere, let it crust up her face, Mommy was gone. And then she fell, curled up, as if into a shell, and rocked herself to silence on the floor.

Great-grandmother stood at the doorway. Soon Claudette would come back from her night shift and she could help her get the girl fixed up and ready for the day.

'Lord, what a noise,' Great-grandmother sighed. The child would stop the ruckus soon. 'All that mess on the floor.'

Great-grandmother smoothed down her hair. Well, she hoped the girl wouldn't end up like her mother. Mind, she thought, her skin is good, a good, high colour where Dorothy's was dark like her father's; more than a drop of the African in *his* veins . . .

Great-grandmother tied the waistband of her dressing gown firmly around her chest.

'Always kicking up a fuss that girl,' she clicked her tongue.

'Blood will show.' The child trembled on the floor. 'Don't cry, girl. Be good and don't cry. Mommy will come back soon.'

Great-grandmother went to a jar and picked out a bun, the one she'd been told was the child's favourite. She'd been saving it for a special time and surely, this must be it. She held out a hand, sat in the chair and sang the song of the two dicky birds, but Jackie didn't laugh, she didn't even smile, because she knew that 'soon' was a lie that grown-ups told.

After all the crying and running they left Jackie alone till night-time came. When at last they put her to bed all she could remember was the smell of her mother's hair, fresh as a new-cut coconut a finger's-touch away, and all she could think of was the ache in her belly and the sadness that was waiting for her in the big empty sheets. She pulled the covers over her head, wrapping them tight so the shadows couldn't see her, but there was no fooling them – no fooling them at all – they just shrugged and sighed, they had time to spare, snapping at her footsteps at each darkening corner, waiting for the night when they could come out and play, so Jackie learnt how to sleep like this – her body lying rigid with the sheets wrapped all around her so she looked so small and white that they hardly ever saw her.

Great-grandmother closed the door on her way to the kitchen. When the child had stopped crying, she'd forgotten now how long that had taken; when the child had stopped crying it hadn't taken too much time to bring her round to good, useful habits.

Great-grandmother walked to the kitchen, opened the shutters, put the grease in the pan; after all, it was plain for everyone to see how the girl was thriving. She took hold of the knife and peeled the pink shell covers from the ackee fruit, carefully picking the flesh from the seeds. But of course, Great-grandmother smiled, the child was bound to be all right; how else could it be in such a God-fearing household with clean clothes and proper food inside her belly? Ha!

Great-grandmother walked down the hallway, opening the door to call the child to breakfast and there she was, Lord save us, laying in the bed, wrapped so tight in the sheets you'd think she'd already been laid out cold and ready for her grave.

'Come child,' she called. 'Get up now.'

And she dropped the white dress onto the chair and left the door open so the girl would know it was time to get up and eat.

Kingston, Jamaica
March 1959

J ackie ran to the gate.

She lifted her skirt and rubbed her legs. The blow had left a perfect set of pink finger marks. She licked a hand and wiped it across her skin. Soon, yes, soon, he would come. Jackie climbed onto the gate and pulled herself up, closing her eyes and squeezing out the light so everything turned red.

On Sundays the aunties came to Great-grandmother's house in batches; first the ones fresh from church, sombre as crows in their blue-black dresses.

'One, two . . .'

Jackie leant across the gate so she could count them on her fingers.

'. . . three . . .'

Then came the ones who smelled like old flowers.

'. . . four, five . . .'

And last of all, like always, there she was, Auntie Sissy. Jackie jumped down and pushed a fist into her belly.

'. . . six,' she whispered.

Aunt Sissy glanced at the child, nodded and squeezed herself carefully between the fencing and the opened gate.

'A-h-ummm,' Jackie coughed.

Aunt Sissy had a face like a lemon, rough and yellow, with little red bumps that seemed to flower on her skin before they ripened into spots with creamy heads. Uggh! Teddy had to live with Aunt Sissy, him being too dark, as Great-grandmother had told her, to stay in the house with the rest of them. But where was Teddy, where was he now?

There he was. Jackie waved her hands, grinning so wide that her smile seemed to reach right across the fencing. Yes, there he was; the best Superboy to her Lois Lane! She laughed when she saw him because he always did it that way – coming through the gate, sort of bouncing as he ran, with his grown-up shoes and glasses.

'Good afternoon,' Sissy shouted.

Great-grandmother acknowledged Sissy's arrival with the slightest tilt of her head. 'And to you Miss Sissy.'

'Can't complain,' Sissy clutched the handrail as she heaved herself up the veranda steps, 'long as I have breath in my body I can't complain.'

Sissy went on to tell them about the veins big as tapeworms that throbbed in her legs, the bunions like eggs that grew from her feet, the constriction which held her bowels to ransom and the quiet forbearance she showed in spite of it all.

'Miss Sissy,' Claudette called, rising from her chair. 'It's good to see you. How are —'

'And you Miss Claudette.' As she spoke Sissy's tongue slipped into the gap between her front teeth so each sentence was accompanied by a hiss, as if she was a balloon letting out wind. 'And this heat.' She went on, the fastenings of her dress gaping wide at her chest as she fell into the chair. 'Lord, let me take me weight from me feet,' Sissy gasped, her mouth grabbing at the air as she prised her one-size-under shoes from her puffed up feet, 'You have to pardon me, but you see, they swell up so bad, Lord,' Sissy took a handkerchief from her handbag and dabbed at her brow.

'Will you have something to drink Miss Sissy? I made some fresh lemonade and by now it should be cool . . .'

'Well thank you, Claudette, I'm sure, but I won't, thank you. I have such a pain in me belly.' Great grandmother raised an eyebrow. 'Just iced water will do.' Sissy snorted like a horse and settled back into the chair. 'It's a miracle, me doctor say to me, "Miss Sissy," him say, "it's a miracle just to see you still standing on God's earth".'

'And we all more than grateful for that I'm sure, but seeing as you sitting down just now —'

'And me need to so, I tell you. Lord Jesus knows I must be a martyr; that boy.' Sissy shook her head. 'That boy is such a handful. He have bad habits.'

Jackie glanced at her brother.

'Come,' he whispered. 'Before they see.' Teddy took them to her favourite place, underneath the table where the cloth hung down like a tent. 'You all right?' He wrapped an arm around his sister.

'Yes.'

'You hungry?'

Jackie was always hungry on Sundays.

'Yes.'

'Here you are.'

Teddy took a furred-up lump of coconut-ice from his pocket. He could see the remains of the pink handprint still glowing livid on his sister's leg. Jackie pulled down her skirt, grabbed the sticky lump and shoved it in her mouth as Teddy took a pack of cards from his other pocket.

'I made a letter for Mommy,' Jackie said. 'Do you want to see it?'

Teddy nodded his head. Jackie had hidden the note inside her panties.

'It says:

Dear Mommy, I love you veree much. When I cum to see you necks time I would lik a new Daddy and a red bike. Luv Jackie

I wrote it by myself.'

'It needs correcting,' her brother said, 'and anyway, how are you going to send it?' Jackie hadn't thought about that, so she was relieved when Teddy asked, 'Do you want to play cards now?'

'All right then.'

He shuffled the cards, dividing them carefully, giving half to his sister. This time, she thought, I mustn't cry, even when I lose, even when his hands turn the cards so fast that my eyes can't even follow them.

'Snap!'

They played the game with silent moves, stifling their laughter as best as they could while the aunties chattered on like a crowd of hungry John-Crows fighting for a meal.

'Lord, but you bringing up the child so well, and she such a good, quiet girl.'

Jackie examined her fingers.

'Yes, you know,' another joined in. 'It's such a joy to see her since her mother left her with you, Miss Katie; she getting such good habits. God-willing you can keep her here with you. Everyone can see how well the child is doing.'

'Well, Dorothy has found good work in Canada but she say life is hard.'

The aunties clicked their tongues, 'Uh-huh.'

'She want to go to England,' Great-grandmother continued. 'Soon as she can, she say she wants to bring the children to be with her and then she will take them all to England. I tell her how they doing just fine here, but she say the children need a good education. I tell her, leave them here, I tell her and you know,' Great-grandmother lowered her voice, 'now she has got herself into that same difficulty, maybe she will leave them with me, I don't know but I hope it can be so. I always telling her —'

'Lord help us, you always telling her but you never tell me?' Sissy wiped her face. 'The same difficulty! Again, for true? Surely to God, not again. What is wrong with that woman, she can't keep her legs from falling open?'

A shrill ring chiming from the hall cut a sudden swathe of silence through their righteous indignation. The aunties sprang to attention, as if some long remembered bell had called them to a sit up in school-time order.

'Claudette,' Great-grandmother called, 'Get it please.'

'Oh Lord!' Claudette jumped like a startled bird, 'Who is it now?' She flapped her arms wildly and rushed to the telephone squawking as she grabbed the phone. 'Yes, thank you.' She nodded her head, 'We will accept it. Hello?' Claudette placed the receiver closer to her ear. 'Oh yes, Dorothy. They here, they fine; they doing just fine. And you?'

Even from their hiding place the children heard their mother's name so they were already scrambling out as Aunt Claudette called them.

'Quickly now,' Claudette said, 'I can't seem to hear too well what she saying so don't take too long. You first, Teddy.'

Teddy took the phone. 'Yes, Mommy.'

He was nodding too, pursing his lips as he stared through the window.

Jackie tried to imagine what could be happening inside the telephone to make her brother listen with such a look on his face. He said 'yes' just like Claudette and what did it mean – 'Mommy on the phone'? Jackie looked around. She couldn't see Mommy on anything. Soon it would be her turn but, never mind, it didn't seem too hard to say 'yes' and nod while you were saying it; to say 'yes' some more and only sometimes 'no' but not very often until at the end you had to say 'goodbye'.

Teddy passed the arm of the telephone to his sister. It was heavy and slippery in her small, damp fingers. She closed her eyes.

'Hello, darling. Are you there?'

And there it was, in her head, the voice beneath her eyelids.

'Jackie? Can you hear me? Are you there?'

Jackie opened her eyes and stared through the window; heard but couldn't see, waves on the sea.

'Where are you?' Jackie asked. Her eyes filled with water. 'Are you at the beach Mommy?'

'No darling, not at the beach. I'm a long way away.'

Whoosh, whoosh . . . Jackie's mouth quivered as she heard her mother laugh, but there it was again, that rushing-hushing rolling of waves and ocean-sea.

'I'm in a place called Canada. How are you?'

Could she listen and not cry? Be still and still listen? Her mouth twisted as she chewed on her lip.

'Are you being a good girl?' Jackie shut her eyes. 'I love you so much; so very, very much. How are you my darling, are you all right?'

She was in the waves, the waves in the sea, and though Jackie wanted to say 'no' that she was not right, not all right at all; that Great-grandmother always beat her for spoiling her dress, and what about the chickens, and why, oh why was Teddy too dark, and many more questions, and a lot more crying, she knew it was naughty to make such a fuss, so instead she just said 'yes' or 'no' because all she really wanted was to fall down and cry.

'Mommy,' Jackie choked. 'Where are you?'

'I told you, sweetheart,' and now the words came slow. 'I'm in a place called Canada and it's so cold today that there's snow on the ground. Do you know what snow is?'

'Mommy, when are you coming back?'

'Soon, baby,' Dorothy said. 'Soon.'

Kingston Airport, Jamaica
April 1959

Her feet didn't touch the floor but if she stretched from the seat as far as she could, she could just about manage to look through the window and down to the sea. She was in her best, her Sunday-best dress, the one with the yellow waistband. Auntie had combed her hair this morning, straightened it, plaited it close to her head, plastered it down neatly with Vaseline and finished off with the ribbons she had chosen for herself. She didn't like the dress. The lace scratched her neck and the label they had pinned through the collar dug into her skin. It said 'Jackie Brown' followed by a whole lot of numbers written in black ink. She could read it for herself. She didn't know why they'd put that label on her, she knew where she was going.

Jackie's stomach heaved as the plane loped upwards, nudging its nose above the cotton-wool clouds. Funny, she thought, how could it be? She knew how a paper plane could fly, pushed by her hand till it fell to the ground, but this thing was so heavy with all the people in it. She looked back through the window and watched the propellers turning.

'Listen,' Teddy whispered, 'the plane stop now.' He tilted his head, an ear towards the floor. 'Oh God, we're gonna fall.' He sniffed. 'Can you smell the smoke?' Teddy started to sway. 'Look how the plane go.' Now he was shaking. 'First your feet burn . . . Oh God! I feel it, feel it hot now.' Teddy lifted his legs from the floor. 'Ouch! We burning!'

Jackie looked down. Yes, she could feel it, the heat rising up and yes, a smell that made her nose wrinkle and the blood start to run from her fingers.

'Then the sharks will come to eat you and you'll never see Mommy again.' Teddy couldn't help smiling at his remarkable self, 'Ha!'

He threw back his head and now Jackie could see, things were exactly the way her brother had described them, the flames at her feet, the heat licking at her skin till it bubbled and peeled, the flesh underneath it trembling and stinking, that same awful smell as when Great-grandmother burned the feathers from the chicken. She knew it, she knew it! The shadows, the sharks, the burning in the sea!

'What's the problem sweetheart?'

Teddy gazed through the window as the hostess-lady stooped down beside them.

'I want my mom-mee!'

'We'll be there soon,' the hostess whispered to Jackie. 'Not scared are you? Just look,' the lady nodded down the aisle, 'there's nothing to be scared of; I'm not scared, and look at all these people, they're not frightened are they?'

But all the words Jackie tried to say to be an answer seemed to come out of her mouth like a whimper.

'Aw, come on, honey.' The hostess gave Jackie her handkerchief. 'Wipe away those tears and we'll make it all better; we have something very special for girls that are good. You dry your face and I'll go and get it.'

Jackie wiped her eyes and covered her mouth with the handkerchief.

'Here you are,' Jackie smelled flowers as the hostess-lady bent over her again and she breathed them in, 'just for girls who are good; my special sweets, but you know, first of all you have to stop crying or else they won't work.'

It was a mountain of candy, more than she had ever seen before, heaped on a silver plate like the one they used at church on Sundays.

It was true what the hostess had said, Jackie thought, they must be magic – she was starting to feel better already. There was every colour candy she could think of, reds and yellows bright as the ribbons for her hair, purples and greens and all of them sparkling like the sequins on her mother's best dress – but no blues . . . Her mouth fell open. But where were the blues and which one to choose? She picked two red sweets, unwrapped one and put it in her mouth. The sweet, pink liquor flooded into her mouth and she closed her eyes as that rainbow feeling slid down her throat.

*   *   *

By the time she woke it was dark and the lights of the city were rushing up towards them. Jackie turned, sank back into her seat and stretched out her legs. Teddy's face wasn't brown any more, a grey pallor had settled on the skin around his eyes and a slick line of spit was dribbling down his chin from where he'd thrown up in a bag. Uggh.

Jackie smoothed her skirt around her knees. It must be nearly time because the voice on the radio said the plane was coming in to land and Mommy would be there, in that land-that-was-coming.

'We are now descending on our final approach. Would passengers please return to their seat, fasten their seatbelts and make sure all luggage has been put away,' said the radio voice.

The hostess-lady said, 'Have you got your straps on?' and then, 'Oh, good girl. You know I have to go and sit over there, but there's nothing to be scared of, not now you have the magic candy, and soon, when we've landed, we'll take you to your mommy.'

She smiled so prettily, that nice hostess-lady, but then there was still more waiting, and the bumping when they landed at the airport, and the waiting some more, till the lady took their hands and they went down stairs that moved without walking to the even bigger space with the high-up ceiling and the plump red chairs set out neatly on the floor.

Jackie couldn't see outside. The night had sealed the windows tight as a shutter and the white strip lighting inside the hall bleached the life out of everything it touched. Jackie had never seen so many people all together and she wondered, where did they come from? All these people, marching without stopping, just like ants when you dug them from their holes. Her eyes reached up, searching through the crowds, but with all these people, how could she ever hope to find her mommy? She couldn't see further than the knees of them, not past the trousers and the skirts of them, the walking so fast and the coats on them. Jackie covered her ears till the lady pulled her forward. Jackie yawned and put a thumb into her mouth. Where was Mommy? She closed her eyes.

'Would Mrs Dorothy Brown please come . . .' the radio said. Jackie jumped.

'Yes Mommy now!' She squeezed a hand into a fist and thumped it hard onto her leg.

'. . . to the Pan American Airways desk.'

Then Jackie played the game where you close your eyes and imagine you can tell when something will happen by saying 'now' and opening your eyes. She said it a lot of times, 'Please Mommy *now*!' but *still* she wasn't there . . . Maybe, Jackie thought, maybe Mommy had forgotten, but that made her throat all dry, so she decided instead to swallow to where the sweets were swimming in her belly, but then nothing went down, so she gulped again, clutching at the hand that was holding onto hers and then she saw – yes, there she was – her mom-mee! Her mom-mee! Yes, she'd been good! She jumped in the air, and now they'd be together, for ever and ever – no more smacking and chickens on Sundays; the chickens, the chickens, running without heads on . . . Jackie leapt up and down. No more screaming in the yard and the rainbow could stay shining inside her belly forever. Jackie squealed and pulled herself free.

'Mommy!'

She ran like she was flying, her arms stretched out as she saw her mother turn towards her with a smile.

'Darling!'

Jackie threw her arms around her mother's legs and Dorothy bent, stooping on her haunches, first pulling closer, then holding her away, cupping her hands around her daughter's face so she could look deep into her eyes. The child seemed older, different to the way she had left her. Dorothy winced, as if someone had picked a scab from her skin.

'Where's Teddy?' Dorothy stood and wiped a hand across her face.

Jackie pointed to the counter. Teddy was sitting on the floor, his face more mauve now than grey.

'Him eat till him sick.'

Dorothy looked down at her daughter.

'Mommy, Mommy!' Jackie tugged her mother's skirts, 'Him sick, Teddy sick.'

'Huh!' Dorothy pulled the child's hand roughly from her hem, 'Stop pulling at me child! And when did you learn to speak like, like a country girl?' Dorothy turned towards the doors.

Didn't need a touch but it sent her reeling, scorching the rainbow . . .

'Come on,' Dorothy called. 'We must go quickly. There's so much to do before we get on the boat.'

. . . waves in the darkness, her mother in that sea and the blood rushing now to the surface of her skin . . .

'Jackie, hold my hand. Quickly I said.'

There he was again, Jackie thought, she hadn't known that Mr Evil could come on the plane all this way. Jackie wiped her eyes, catching her mother's hand as they went through the doorway. When Jackie looked up she could see no stars. The city had drenched the skies with its own orange light, washing out the silky darkness of the night in a haze of bright neon but, oh, there it was, the same moon she'd seen at her Great-grandmother's house, but looking heavy now, swollen and round, hanging in the sky like her own mother's belly.

Southampton, England
April 1959

It seemed as if they had been travelling forever, first on the plane from the Island and then days on the boat. Jackie rubbed her eyes. No, this was real, the fog lapping up against the side of the boat, blowing in waves so it looked like the air had turned into water; it looked like a dream but it was real.

The men fastened the rope from the ship to the ground, lifting the stairway and fixing it down and that was it, just like that, they were joined to the land. Jackie shivered and shoved her hands into her pockets. The cold had seeped through every seam and buttonhole of her cotton dress even before they stepped from the ship. This place; no blues or green, just every shade of grey she'd ever seen, and then some more besides. Jackie wiped her face and looked at her fingers. The dampness shimmered on her hand and in the mustard glow of the street lights it seemed to the child as if her skin had taken on the same silver-greyness of everything else around her. She looked up. There was her mother. She could barely see her, the fog had painted dark circles on her face where her eyes had once been, and every now and then great plumes of boiling steam gushed from her mouth and nose so she looked like a dragon from the story books.

'Stay close to me. Hold my hand.'

What a journey, Dorothy thought, as she stepped over the gutter. The children's faces seemed pale in the gloom. Where was the station? The baby kicked. She stroked her belly. The crossing had been nothing but a trial, a trial; all three of them cramped up in such a small space with her four months' swelling and being sick every day. Lord! She looked at the suitcases piled up on the ground and felt all her hopes rising up again. This was it then; a home at last for her and the children, a new home in the old country, a new-starting mother in the old motherland. She smiled and pursed her lips, picking up the battered suitcases that were marked with her name. The handles bit into her fingers. She hoped she wouldn't have to carry them too far, not too far, she hoped, before they got to the station.

Dorothy narrowed her eyes and peered through the darkness. The street lamps dropped shallow pools of light around their stems but the rest . . . Something about this place; was it the fog? Well no, she'd expected that, but perhaps, perhaps it was the solidness of the place that made it seem so strangely unfamiliar. She shook her head. Somehow she'd thought she'd know this England, this green and pleasant, God-save-the-Queen land of hopes and glory, but still, it seemed strange. A man cried out '*Hee-ven-ing pa-purr!*', repeating his call and she followed that voice, dipping her feet in the rhythm of his words, each line shining in her head as the words came back to her, those *Children's Treasury – Poems for All* succulent verses that she knew so well, rolling her tongue on the James of it all, the Wordsworth, Tennyson and Shakespeare of it all, but however she tried she just couldn't see the hosting of daffodils as a possibility, not in these satanic streets, not in these smoke-blackened mills, no clouds of yellow-gold to dissolve the flesh in, no. This place was flesh, flesh on the bone, not just the words but the flesh and white bones of it all.

'Mind your backs!'

A man hurried past pushing cases on a trolley, his nose running slime down the curve of his lip. His neck was white as turkey skin at the gap where it showed between his collar and kerchief. He stopped for a moment and coughed, spewing up a glob of mucus which he spat into the gutter. Dorothy followed him along the street.

And everything here seemed full of water; it ran from the rooftops, filling each dip and crevice so the roads ran wet and black as rivers.

'Good Lord,' Dorothy sighed as she breathed the fog deep into her chest. The night sweated out a dampness that settled on every piece of clothing. She coughed again. Jackie squeezed the soft fabric of her mother's dress.

'Come now, Jackie, keep hold of my skirt and Teddy – you take her other hand.'

And then they ran, jumping over gutters and onto the pavement. Dorothy glanced up. The sign said 'Southampton'. But where now she wondered? All these people rushing past her and the cases getting heavy, and all those trains at all those platforms throwing out steam at their wheels and funnels as if they were ready for a full steam-and-go, but how was she supposed to know who to stop and what to ask for?

'Excuse me, sir,' Dorothy said. This man had a kind face. He took the cigarette from his mouth. 'Where can I buy a ticket?'

The man's eyes glanced at the suitcases and on towards the children before eventually he smiled.

'Over there, by the kiosk, love.'

He pointed a finger to the side of the wall.

'Love'; Dorothy couldn't help but smile back at him. Imagine! She'd always thought of English men as so proper, so reserved – to think that already, and even with the children; well, she raised a hand and smoothed her hair.

'Thank you.'

She picked up the cases, swinging her hips as she followed his directions towards a line of people.

Jackie shivered. All she wanted to do now was sleep. The cold made her feel so tired, the effort of it all, making sure her clothes stayed snug around her body, and minding all the time where her feet stepped in case they got wet, and however much she tried she couldn't help shivering. The line of people inched slowly forwards. At last Dorothy was standing at the head of the queue.

'Thank you, sir,' Dorothy said. 'I need three tickets to London for me and my children.'

And tired as she was, there was a thrill in her voice. Tickets for London; she had said it, Dorothy Brown come all this way to say it. Tickets for London. Bringing the children, just like she'd said – never giving up, working every hour to bring them here – to this England.

'Quick,' she said, 'hold on to me. We must run before we miss it.'

Jackie ran alongside her mother, passing through the crowds of people who walked without looking, stared without smiling, with their shoes tap-tapping like a heartbeat on the ground.

At last Dorothy opened the door of the train. She heaved the battered suitcases up into a basket and slumped into the seat, glad to be sitting in something near warmth, at least for a while. Soon the chug-chugging rhythms of the train sent the children rocking to sleep, but Dorothy couldn't rest, she turned to the window and caught the reflection of her own face, staring through the darkness with these little scared eyes, seeking out a future that she knew must be there in a place she couldn't yet see.

Dorothy reached into her pocket and found the crumpled piece of paper with the phone number on it. Yes, thank the Lord it was still there. She passed her finger over the note, turning an ear to listen for the sound of the paper rustling in her pocket as she sent wishes out into the night. Please God, she prayed, let someone answer when I phone that number, let them give me a bed, if only for a night or two.

Teddy opened his eyes, turned over and went back to sleep. Good, Dorothy thought, the longer the children sleep the better. She stuffed a hand back into her pocket searching to make sure that the piece of paper was still there, and then she rested her head on the seat and watched as the street lights pierced holes through the darkness, watched as the yards came closer and closer, running beside them till it seemed as if the train was speeding on the walls, running so close you could see inside the houses, built like cards piled one against the other.

A streak of hunger pulled at her stomach. There was some fruitcake and a lump of cheese she'd wrapped in tissue and carried all day in her handbag but no, not yet; that was all the food there was to last them till morning.

The train slowed.

'Jackie,' Dorothy called, 'Jackie and Teddy wake up. I think we're there.'

First thing, Dorothy thought, find a telephone and work out how to do the numbers. A place for the night would give them a chance to rest, maybe if she was lucky, they could stay there longer and she would have time to get the children warmer clothes and she could begin looking for a more permanent place for them to live.

'Come on kids, quickly,' she beckoned towards them.

Although her eyelids were heavy with sleep, Dorothy put a smile on her face. This was not the time to falter, she told herself, not in front of the children; any hesitation on her part could only make things more difficult. She lifted the suitcases onto the platform and held an arm out for the children as they stepped from the train, rubbed their eyes and leant against the heat of her body. Dorothy opened her handbag. Her hands were busy searching for the tickets but her mind had already left the drab half-light of the station platform. She was making plans for herself and the children, even for the little one who was sleeping now, thank goodness, inside her. Dorothy paused. Ever since she'd left New York she had kept one dream going; the one that had her finding a place where she could make a good home for herself and her family, surely England must be it, the place where her children could go to proper schools, where there were free hospitals and government housing and soon, after the baby was born and she was back on her feet, soon she'd get a job and earn enough money so she could start searching for Pearl again. Dorothy gripped the handles and picked up the cases.

Brixton, London
May 1959

'Can't you lot read?'

Oh yes, she could read – every damn word of their ignorant, misspelt, mealy-mouthed signs; it was just taking her some time to really get the full picture. Dorothy led the children to the end of the street.

'You stay here and keep out of sight.' Dorothy stood the children behind the corner. There'd be a better chance of getting a place if they weren't seen, at least not straight away, she was sure of it. 'And don't shift an inch, not till I come and get you, you hear me?' And after all, she thought, there was no need for them to see it happening.

Dorothy could only walk slowly now, her belly seemed to weigh-up the cost of every movement. Sweet England, she shook her head, only three days left – four days since they'd landed, so that gave her just three days to find somewhere else for them to live. She thought about her favourite reading, the part of the psalm where the Lord says to leave your father's country; ha! Recalling those words in this place made the Bible seem like stories for children, but she had to admit it was those kind of stories that had kept her going, searching for some kind of promised-land shores. She rested for a moment. Problem was, she thought, keeping hold of that dream was starting to feel more like a burden, dragging her down like an empty old suitcase. Dorothy let the air whistle out between her teeth. Maybe she needed to let it go, just for a while. She straightened the curve of her back. Lord! And the three of them sharing a bed wasn't helping. She put a hand on her belly; well, it was the three and a half of them in actual fact and the half-one getting bigger every day. She smiled as her eyes found their way to the near-up horizon where the junction met the shops and the row of shabby houses and yes, she could see them, there they were – two little brown heads bobbing out from the corner where she'd left them, hidden from view. She turned, searching back along the lace-curtained terraces for the next grimy card.

> Room to Rent
> No coloureds, No . . .

Can't understand it, her brows closed together, there it is again; the Irish in the middle; just the dogs and the coloureds seemed to change position.

'Oh Lord,' she muttered. 'What a world is this!'

Dorothy clicked her tongue, but there was no time to think about all that just now, she had enough to chew on as it was; no space for thinking, time wasn't waiting, babies weren't for waiting. She lifted her head. Do You think, she prayed, do You think You could stop whatever You're doing for moment and share this load with me? And it might be that Dorothy's prayers were answered because she managed to make a smile out of nothing in particular and she spread it on her face, sending it back towards her children as she walked up the steps. That smile stayed on her face even after she heard the growling because she froze until her hands began to shake and the fear of those dogs crawled up inside her throat.

'No girl,' she whispered. 'Don't you mind at all,' she pressed her lips – after all, she thought, if they love their dogs, who knows where all their loving might stop?

The door opened.

'Yes.'

Always a face, never much more, just a head cleaving out from a hallway or sometimes a knee pressed up against the door, just to make sure, of what, she didn't know.

'Yes?'

The voice scraped the air like metal as the breath hissed out, curling from the lips.

'Excuse me,' Dorothy said, 'I'm sorry to disturb you but I saw the card in the window, the one for the room, and I was wondering –'

'You what!'

The once white, lipstick-talking face was glowing purples and reds.

'Can't you lot never read?' it screamed.

And there it was again, always the same; the door slam-shutting right up against her face, but now there was spitting and the dogs joining in, leaping and howling at the smell of her skin as the card fell from the window.

'Bleeding wogs!'

Jackie always covered her eyes, she didn't need to see to feel what was happening; Mommy stepping up with her head held high, a hand at her hair till the knocking and the crash-bang-slamming. That was the bit she kept from her head, at least till her fingers had stopped going cold, at least till her heart could become like a stone and the shame had grown big enough to pump the heat back around her body.

Tap-tap, she hears her mother's feet, smells her own fear as the nasty banging-slamming sound brushes on her skin. Now where's Mommy? Jackie put a thumb into her mouth, wishing so much that her mother wouldn't do it, all that knocking and all that asking because then, maybe then, they could go somewhere else, hide in a hole, cover their faces and then people wouldn't hurt her mommy any more.

Jackie's belly was floating like a jellyfish twisting to the surface so she had to stroke her nose and suck harder on her thumb. But even with the stroking and the sucking her stomach still churned, and what with the rising in her stomach and the nowhere to run, all she could do was stand where she'd been told to and watch her lovely mommy walking back down the road with the nasty slamming-banging goo dripping from her face.

'All right,' Dorothy's nails were biting pink crescent moons into her skin. 'C'mon, don't take it like that. It'll be all right.' Dorothy took hold of Jackie's hand, 'Hey, best girl; are you so cold?' She stroked the child's cheek, it seemed flushed. Dorothy hoped the child was not getting sick. 'We're bound to find somewhere soon. Let's get something to eat.'

She couldn't take them back to the house, not just yet. They weren't allowed into their rooms before five o'clock. Dorothy looked into the sky, seeking out the clouds. The day would stay dry, thank goodness. Maybe, Dorothy thought, maybe they'd strike lucky when they started looking again.

Brixton, London
May 1959

Although the room was at the top of a large Victorian house, it didn't seem to matter what hour of the day it was, it always seemed dark. Perhaps, in the early life of the house, the walls had glowed with colour and daylight had streamed through the windows, but by the time Dorothy and the children had taken up residency, every surface and wall had taken on a uniform tone of sepia.

The room had a slanted ceiling, a small draughty window that looked towards the railway track, a sink with a cold-water tap, a double bed, a small wardrobe, a set of drawers and a fold-down table that was pushed against the wall.

Dorothy opened her eyes and shut off the alarm. It was half past seven. She sat up, hanging her legs from the side of the bed as thoughts of the day formed a list in her head and the pressure from her bladder sent her rushing downstairs. Thank God, she thought, the sickness was passing. She climbed back up the stairs, opened the door and there they were, her children, still sleeping in the bed and this next one doing somersaults inside her belly. Dorothy pulled the curtain and looked through the window, past the railway track and the road and the distant rooftops till her eyes drifted over to the last row of chimneys set above the houses like jagged teeth. The whole house rattled like a milk crate each time a train ran along the track and no matter what she did the place seemed cold, but right now this room was the answer to Dorothy's dreams. She remembered how she'd stood knocking at the front door that day, expecting the worse, but praying, as always, for the best. When the door had finally opened she'd flinched, trying so hard not to beg for a room that she had drawn blood from her lips.

'My name is Bliss,' the woman had said. 'Mrs Bliss. Looks like you got your hands full, eh?' The woman had smiled, raising an eyebrow at the children and the suitcases. 'Yes, the room is still free but I don't know that it's suitable really; it's meant for one person you see, and I don't usually take families.'

'But,' Dorothy pleaded, 'we just need something for a while. Anything will do, just to give us a start. The children are really well behaved and I'll make sure they're quiet.'

Mrs Bliss had agreed.

'Can't say it's much for you and the kiddies,' Mrs Bliss said as she showed Dorothy the accommodation. 'But if it can help you out,' she switched on the light, 'you're welcome to have it till you can find something better.'

Dorothy had wanted to kiss that woman, but she'd thought better of it, she'd noticed that English people didn't like being touched too much, so she had thanked Mrs Bliss and given her the cash deposit instead because, whatever the room was like, it would be the start of their new lives in England.

Now, this morning, standing there looking through the window, Dorothy could hardly believe they'd been in England for two whole weeks. Already she had got them a place to stay and soon, after the baby was born, she'd get off of Social Security, she'd move them to an apartment, or perhaps even a house, so the children would learn to expect better things.

'Wake up kids,' Dorothy called, turning from the window, 'morning time and school today.' She opened the cupboard. A loaf of bread. Dorothy peeled the greasy paper from the butter and sniffed; yes, it still smelled good. 'C'mon I said!'

Jackie sat up, rubbed her eyes and squeezed a hand between her legs.

'Go to the toilet now, before you wet yourself,' Dorothy called. 'Teddy take your sister.'

She spread the butter chunk-thick across the bread. If she was going to find somewhere else for them to live she'd have to do it fast, before she got so big that even wearing a coat or carrying a shopping bag in front of her belly wouldn't hide the bump. Dorothy reached for the jam. The truth was, this room was really too small for them, only just enough space to walk around the bed, but at least they had somewhere for now and the children could start school.

Jackie ran through the door and jumped on the bed. She could find her own way to the toilet, even with her eyes closed, just by the smell. At night Mommy let them use the wee-wee pot, but not in the mornings because mostly, by then, Mommy had thrown up already and emptied it away.

A train clanked past the backyard wall. Jackie had put her clothes on the chair the night before so they'd be ready for her first day at school, pants folded neatly on top of the dress, just like Great-grandmother had shown her and – *shriek* – the kettle hissed, whistling up the morning so then they'd all be ready.

Jackie pulled her dress over her head, whirling and bending like the best ballerina so she could reach across the table, grab the sweetened milk, gulp at the tin that had 'Carnation' on it and wipe the dribbles from her mouth before her mother could see. The milk felt so good on her dry-morning throat that she had to hop around, snatching at the bread and jumping straight back so she could tear at the crusts and drop them down between the mattress and the table. Then she jumped, standing there waiting for Mommy, always slow her mommy, getting slower all the time, and Jackie just waiting, wanting to be there already at the C-A-T cat, M-A-T mat, school where she would know how to do it, the running in the yard and the reading and the writing and the speeding like a train till her breath gave out and she'd drop down, look up and laugh at the sky.

Dorothy and the children walked along the road and crossed by the park gates. Jackie tried to see if she could follow the white-balloon clouds as they raced across the sky. The breeze tugged at their clothes, lifting skirts over legs, throwing handfuls of paper and petals into the air where they swirled and fell into the sunshine-littered streets. Jackie skipped along the edge of the kerb. The gutters were choked. For weeks the trees had been holding on to their blossoms but now the wind was rocking the branches, shaking flowers like rattles so the petals were torn from their stems and thrown across the pavements till the gutters disappeared in ankle-deep drifts of the falling spring.

Dorothy wrapped the scarf around her face.

'Lift me, Mommy,' Jackie pulled her mother's hand. '*Please*, Mommy, *do* it.'

Dorothy heaved Jackie by an arm so she could jump like

she was flying over the pavements, past the houses, till they got to the shop at the corner where they sold only sweets. Jackie slowed for a moment, dragging at her mother's hand as she gazed through the window – look at all the sweeties! Jackie liked money. Mommy had money and said if she was good and didn't cry at school, she would give her a penny in four shiny farthings. She squeezed Mommy's hand. Sixpence pieces were silver with flowers. Jackie jumped across the next line of paving. Shillings had the crowns of the queen on their tails. Pennies had the lady in the helmet on them and the half crown felt heavy as treasure but the farthing, oh the farthing! Before she could carry on thinking about money her mother had yanked her hand so she'd know to be careful to walk around the dog mess. Before Jackie had a chance to complain they were standing by a step with a stone-edged gate which had 'Girls' carved in fancy letters around the archway.

'Now remember,' Dorothy leant towards the children. They were ready for school, Dorothy knew it, but her heart still sank at the thought of leaving them there by themselves. 'Remember,' she paused, 'I know you're always good, but anyway . . .' There didn't seem much else to say. 'I'll take you in this time and I'll pick you up right here at the end of school.'

Dorothy clasped the children's hands as they walked through the empty schoolyard towards an open door.

'Can I help you?' a voice asked.

The question came from a thin, pale-mouthed woman, the words snapped off at their endings, in that curt, English way, but her smile was friendly enough.

'Yes, thank you. I'm Mrs Brown. I spoke with Mr Jenkins on Friday. He told me I could bring the children this morning.'

'Oh yes. You can leave them with me.' Dorothy let go of the children's fingers. 'Don't worry Mrs Brown, I'll make sure they're well looked after.'

Jackie turned, following the back of Dorothy's head with her pinprick eyes. Her mother had always seemed like a mountain, so tall that Jackie had to tilt her head just to see her face when they stood next to each other. Now she saw how small her mother looked, how small her mother really was as she walked across the empty schoolyard.

The classroom was bright, with large, airy windows, copper-glazed tiles which reached a third of the way up the walls and wooden desks arranged in rows so the teacher could easily walk between them. By the time Mr Jenkins brought Jackie into the class, the rest of the children were already at their desks, bright button faces turned expectantly towards the front.

'Good morning Mrs Murray,' Mr Jenkins said. 'I have a new pupil for you. Her name is Jackie Brown and she has come a long way to join us today, all the way from an island called Jamaica.'

Jackie could feel her cheeks burning red. Mrs Murray smiled.

'How nice,' Mrs Murray said. 'We will all have to make sure that we look after Jackie very well, won't we children.'

'Yes Miss-is Mur-ray,' the class chorused, almost together.

'Thank you Mrs Murray,' Mr Jenkins smiled, 'I'll leave her with you then.'

And it was true, as Jackie looked at all those faces staring up at her, suddenly she felt as if she'd been left quite alone. Jackie pushed the tears back down to where no one could see.

'All right, Jackie,' Mrs Murray put a hand on her shoulder, 'let's find you a seat.'

Mrs Murray showed Jackie to an empty desk, the one that faced its back against the wall. 'Now Jackie, you just sit there, I'll come back in a moment when I've settled the rest of the class and we can have a look at some books.'

Jackie tried her best to keep still but it was all so new, so different from the school she'd left on the Island, and she couldn't help thinking, even though the teacher was talking and she should have been paying attention, about the way her desk had an ink well dropped into a hole in the top corner and a cupboard inside it when she lifted up the lid. Jackie's eyes moved across the room towards the walls. The ceiling was high but Jackie could make out little scabs of paint that had curled from the surface. Halfway up the wall a row of windows faced the empty playground while, if she turned the other way, Jackie could see another set of windows that looked onto a corridor. At home; well, at Great-grandmother's house, the teacher was always standing at the front pointing to the C-A-T cat, M-A-T mat, writing on the board which you copied on your slate. Here, in this place, there was paper and they put it in the bin, even when it wasn't used on both of its sides and the walls were covered – pictures and paintings, numbers and sums and letters and words . . . They even had plants in the classroom, Jackie didn't know why, and there were cupboards filled with books, and a set of chairs around a table with cushions.

'All right children,' Mrs Murray said. 'First you are going to finish off the tracing you were doing yesterday while I listen to some reading. Get your rough books out.'

Jackie hoped that Mrs Murray would come to her first so

she could read all the pages and then Mommy would say she'd been good.

'Jackie,' Mrs. Murray walked towards the back of the class, 'I'd like to hear you read first today please.'

Yes! Jackie couldn't help smiling, because she knew all her letters, and she could read books really well so she knew she'd get the farthings. Then Mrs Murray said, 'Right, let's see what you can do. We can start here.'

Mrs Murray put the book on her lap so Jackie could see the pages, but it didn't make sense, the words didn't go with the pictures, because there they were, a girl and a boy, playing in a yard but the words were saying – 'Janet and John play in the garden. Father is at work'. But what did that mean? What was a garden and oh dear, how long would the Father be gone? Jackie rubbed her eyes and stared at Mrs Murray.

'I don't know what it means,' Jackie said as she felt the back of her eyes swell up with tears.

'Don't worry my dear, it's my job to teach you to read, we can start you off with something else. How about drawing some letters?' Mrs Murray smiled, 'You can trace them if you like.'

But Jackie didn't like tracing at all, because it was boring. She wanted to be back with the words and the books so she could find out the meaning of 'garden' and see whether the Father was ever really coming back, but next it was playtime and the bell rang so she smiled and said, 'thank you' and followed the other children out towards the yard.

The sun was shining on the skipping-jumping girls, smiling and shining on the sing-song day with all its clapping and laughing as the boys chased and tumbled on the ground without minding it was dirty. Yes, Jackie smiled, at last she would be playing, playing with the balls as they bounced against the wall, playing with the skipping, skipping with the ropes that were swinging, and the hop-scotch singing, and the singing with the skipping. Jackie waited for a space so she could jump between the ropes.

> On the mountain stands a lady
> Who she is I do not know,
> All she wants is gold and silver
> All she wants is silver and gold.

'Hello,' Jackie smiled at the girl with the nice yellow hair. 'Can I have a turn?' she said. The girl spun quickly; a pretty pirouette, staring at Jackie for a moment and sniffing the air.

'You smell wog!' the pretty girl screeched. 'Don't you *ever* dare talk to me again.'

And this one was Jackie's, her own slam-bang shutting tight inside her head and it hurt so bad she thought her blood would get too cold and maybe then she'd end up dead, except the same thing happened the next day and the next, and her heart kept on beating and her blood stayed warm. And soon, when the fear burnt the tears from her face, no one could see her crying any more, and everyone thought she was happy, but just in case anyone might see, Jackie learnt to lift a hand and stroke the parting of her hair, and she always tried to smile, especially when she saw her lovely mommy, because then she'd get her farthings, shiny and shiny, and there's four of those in a penny.

Jackie loved going to school. Every day she read the books – as many as she could. *Janet and John Go Through the Garden Gate.* Jackie liked to spend her days finding different ways to smile. *Janet and John: Books One, Two* and *Three, Learn to Read.* The books smelled nice. 'Mother bakes cakes. Janet and John play till Father comes home'. *Be Brave Little Noddy. Noddy Goes to School* but *Mr Meddle Muddles. Don't Be Silly Mr Twizzle.* Naughty little Gollies should never live in Toy Town, they should live with other Gollies in Golly Town. 'Wogs go home!' The Golliwogs are rude. *Cheer Up Little Noddy*, it's the Gollies who steal, taking Noddy's car; poor old Noddy. Oh dear, *The Golliwog Grumbled.*

Jackie looked at the paper. You see, Jackie thought, that proves it; emptiness *is* a white thing – the light shining up from the empty piece of paper so she had to shade her face but only, yes only, when there was nothing on it. Once Jackie had learned about white she realised that colour wasn't just for looking at, every colour had a meaning and a feeling, if only she could hear it, if only she could find what it was when she listened to the thoughts in her head.

For a long time yellow had been her favorite colour; that warm banana feeling that was shiny as summer when she went run-running with nothing but happiness humming in her head.

Some colours had got hard to find. Once she'd had all the colours at her fingers and feet, running through the shallows of the Island's sea when she'd loved that earth, sucking it dry till the dribble ran sweet like blood between her teeth. But in England, where she lived now, they covered up their spaces and the sun seemed shy, hiding its face behind clouds and fog almost every day so she had learnt to wait, watching for the times when the sky was blue, then she could go and jump in the park, stand by the window, or follow the sun as it fell towards the ground, washing its face in the blush of the almost night-time.

Brixton, London
17 July 1959

All things bright and beautiful
All creatures great and small

It was Friday. Jackie had been going to her new school for ten weeks and two days and she wasn't sure how many hours. Jackie liked the singing best at morning school, but even the praying was good enough; to close her eyes and sit in the darkness and think how He'd made her and everything else.

All things white and wonderful
The Lord God made them all

Even though she sang the hymn as loud as she could, Jackie knew some of it was wrong; all things were not white and wonderful, but she had learnt to say words exactly the way she heard them in this new place so people wouldn't laugh at her so much any more.

When the class came back from assembly Mrs Murray was already there, standing at the front of the classroom.

'Now sit down children,' she said, 'and don't touch anything till I tell you.'

Mrs Murray wrote the date on the blackboard, *Friday, 17 July, 1959*, her arm flowing down and up as she followed the lines the letters made so she looked like she was dancing or waving her arms – she did that every day. Jackie loved the way Mrs Murray curled the bottom of the '*F*' when she wrote on the board on Fridays.

Mrs Murray clapped her hands.

'Thank you children . . .' She perched on the edge of the desk. 'Quiet please.' She stroked the neat pleats of her skirt and folded her arms. 'Now, today is Friday and that means . . .' the children smiled, 'it's painting time.'

Although it was the smallest size, Jackie's apron covered her body from her neck to long past her knees, trailing on the floor like a gown from the dressing-up box. Each table had been set with a careful arrangement of palettes and paper, mugs for paints and water, a large and small brush and a pencil.

'Oh dear,' Mrs Murray shook her head. 'I can see there are still some children fidgeting at the back even though I've told everyone to be still, no mouths or fingers moving please, then we can start the day.' Mrs Murray's hawk eyes swept across the silenced rows of desks. 'Now, I want you to look at the person sitting next to you; that's it, look at your partner's face very carefully.'

Jackie didn't see the point of looking at an empty chair, so she rolled the ball of her forefinger over the cupid letters which had been gouged from the surface of her desk.

'I want you to put up a hand and tell me all the things that you can see on their face and I will write the words on the board,' Mrs Murray continued.

Jackie's fingers pierced the love-heart letters with her nails as the rest of the class called out their list.

'A nose.'

'Eyes.'

'Freckles.'

'Well done,' Mrs. Murray smiled. 'That was a lot of things! Now I want you to keep thinking of all those things you've seen on your partner's face because this morning you are going to paint a picture of yourself and I want you to remember exactly what you should draw. Now, first of all children, draw the outline of your face, do it nice and big; fill the paper, that's it – and when you're ready . . . Oh dear,' Mrs. Murray pursed her lips. 'I'm afraid I can hear someone talking instead of listening . . . That's better; now, when you're ready you can start putting in all the things from the board which should be on a face.'

Jackie looked down. The jam-tart paints shimmered up from the pots.

'And if you finish your painting today, you can take it home this afternoon to show your Mummies and Daddies.'

Jackie picked up the pencil and there it was again – the white of the paper, empty and empty with the light shining up but she could change that . . . She drew the shape of her face, the chin nicely pointed with the forehead wider at the top, like an egg. The eyes – her eyes, were the shape of two fishes, sharp at each end with short black lashes and then she drew the nose, never easy, so she pencilled in a set of nostrils instead. Next she drew the ears, setting them neatly at the side of the head, but she'd saved the best for last – her lips; a perfect kiss when she closed them together and sweet as a mango when she smiled, that's what Mommy always said.

First thing to paint was the skin. Jackie looked at the bowls;

a juicy yellow next to the red, a velvet blue beside the black. Mrs Murray had told the class they could mix and make new colours. Yellow and red made orange, blue and yellow for green. Nothing changed the black except for white, but the white, well, the slightest bit of colour changed whiteness.

Jackie took a brush, put a glob of white paint into the mixing dish, added a touch of red and stirred. Then she spread the paint across the empty outline of the face and, when it was dry enough, she coloured the cheeks in a darker hue, a hint of something more russet than the rest. At last she was almost finished, just some brown for the hair and the eyes, yellow for the ribbons and it was ready to take home and show Mommy.

In the afternoon Mrs Murray said they could have a story if they did their writing practice really well. Jackie rested her head in the cup of her hand, following the dots with her pencil to fill in the spaces that would make up the letters but she was drowsy and her eyes were heavy with sleep. She longed for the bell, but the clock on the wall seemed weary, edging its hands past the minutes so slowly that Jackie felt sure it must have forgotten how to count the moments so she counted them for herself, first in her head, and then on her fingers.

Outside, through the windows, Jackie could see the sky was a clear and perfect blue. Summer had filled the day to bursting and it was pouring in through the glass, pushing its way through the opened curtains, flooding the desks and the shadows that pooled in wells by the corners of the book-shelves. How she longed to be outside. Every now and then a bluebottle fly or a bee, made drunk with the heat, crashed against a glass pane, and once Jackie saw a butterfly come through an opening and her thoughts had drifted towards the reds and browns of its fluttering wings until the creature had turned, wheeling its way back towards the empty playground and the sun.

At last the bell rang. Jackie always tried to be the first to the cloakroom so she hurried now, grabbing her coat and rushing out towards the doorway, keeping her eyes to the floor and her thoughts from the girls who'd cut her, if they could, with their eyes. Jackie pushed past the flood of noisy children till at last she reached the playground and she could raise her head and send a smile beaming out towards her mother.

'Mommy, Mommy!' Jackie waved her arms as she reached the gate. 'I've done a picture for you Mommy!'

Jackie tugged at her mother's hem, but Mommy was busy, too tired to listen to what she was saying again, what with the baby still growing inside her and all the other things that seemed to fill her mother's head.

'Have you seen Teddy?' Mommy asked.

'He was in the cloakroom.'

Mommy clasped her fingers.

Mommy's belly was getting so big now, Jackie thought, so big that she even needed help to put her shoes on in the morning. Sometimes, when they walked down the street, Jackie would pretend she wasn't really with her mother because she hated the way people stared at the bump.

Jackie jumped hop-scotch steps around her mother, shifting her weight from foot to foot.

'Boo!' Teddy shoved his sister, 'Ha!' he yelled.

Jackie lurched and fell back against Teddy.

'All right,' Mommy called, 'no fighting.'

But the children were already running through the gate,

down along the pavement, laughing as they bounced, whooping as they watched for who would be the first to fall onto a crack. Teddy spun, twisting on one leg as he landed with a flourish. Jackie lifted her arms as she searched for a slab but her brother was flying already, suspended in the air – a bird, a plane . . .

'C'mon Supergirl,' Teddy called, looking back towards her through his Clark Kent glasses. 'I'll help you Jackie – mind out for the humans!'

The children left walking to the Earthlings as they soared above the flatlands of the High Street then they circled and dived, leaping from the kerb where the black and white crossings cut canyons through the streams of screaming traffic and they could, for a moment, swoop between the cars. Dorothy took the key from her pocket.

'Can I play outside, Mommy?' Jackie asked.

'All right,' Dorothy said, 'but keep your shoes on – you hear me?'

Mommy always did that, Jackie thought, she always told her the same thing every time. Dorothy shut the door as Jackie ran back to the street.

Although it was only four o'clock the pavement was already lined with children – girls standing or sitting in knots of twos and threes, making up stories of Mommies and Daddies as they rocked battered prams and dolls to sleep. Jackie crouched by the gate, sniffing at the film of sweat that was cooling on her legs. She shoved her fingers into the deep, dry cracks where the hedge had pushed its roots into the earth.

'Right,' said the girl with the short brown hair. 'You be the mummy and this is the baby and now she has to go to bed because she's too sick.'

Jackie yawned, rubbing a careless hand on the rough, pimpled skin that covered her knees.

'All right then. I'll be the nurse so I have to give the baby her injection.' The other girl made her finger into the point of a needle.

The ants had built a nest at the corner of the slab by the hedge. Jackie lifted a stone, following the line of insects as they swarmed from the concrete back towards the mouth of the nest. She picked a leaf from the privet hedge and dropped it carefully into the path of the ants.

'. . . And then we can put her to bed.' The girls exchanged a satisfied nod.

Over her shoulder, past the hedge, Jackie could see where Teddy had escaped and her eyes trailed eagerly after him.

'Can I play?' Jackie called to her brother.

'No!' Teddy glanced back. 'You play with the girls.'

'Who's "it"?' Jackie shouted, ignoring the answer so her brother would think she hadn't heard him. But Teddy didn't wait for his sister. Jackie sprang up, racing to the bottom of the street until she saw Teddy clambering through the broken fence that opened onto the bombsite clearing at the corner. Before the war that clearing had been a line of brick houses, a mirror of the children's own smoke-grimed homes, set within a terrace of streets which led to the rail track that took workers to the city. Now all that was left of those houses was the footprint of their brickwork, a set of stained mattresses, a dilapidated cooker and here and there, a few empty beer bottles.

Jackie scanned the horizon. The game had started and the 'it' boy was racing, dashing from his hide, down towards a slope where a clutch of children had already found shelter by a clump of bedraggled stripling trees. A few lone stragglers had taken their chances in the open, but everyone was watching the it-boy running and then all the children ran, everyone shouting, 'He's coming! He's coming!' and 'Mind!' as they scattered from their hides like rabbits out of nets. Suddenly a boy called out, 'He's touched!' Jackie turned. Teddy had stopped half crouching, where he had been tagged, then, as Jackie watched, it seemed as if her brother's body unfolded. Teddy was the it-boy now so he could take his time, lift his head, send his gaze speeding like an arrow past the slope towards the other children while his feet edged inches closer to the bushes. Teddy froze for a moment, stretched again, turning his head this way and that as if he was sniffing the air until at last he seemed to pull back, tight as a bow, as his shirt-tails flapped in the wind – then he sprinted. Jackie trailed behind, her pulse keeping time with her brother's footfall and her face shining bright from the sun that burned reds and golds into her skin as they ran all together – now this boy, that boy – always running as the sun slipped down against the roof-topped horizon.

'Jackie, Teddy,' Dorothy was calling from the fence. 'Come now.'

Jackie stopped, her chest heaving as she wiped a hand across her brow. The breeze stroked her face, cooling her arms and soothing her body to a tingle but still the chase pounded in her ears.

Oh no, Jackie thought, it must be too early to go inside. She looked up – and there was the sun – she could still see it hanging in the sky. Jackie wanted to say, just a bit more Mommy, could she stay out and play for a little bit more? Could Mommy stretch out her arms and make this time go on forever . . .

'I said it's time to come and I don't want to hear any argumentation,' Dorothy repeated.

Jackie sighed, following her mother down the street and through the door.

'Hush,' Dorothy whispered. 'Don't make a commotion.'

But it was too late, Mrs Bliss was already at her door, a dark silhouette cut out of the gloom of the dingy hallway.

'Hello darlin's,' Mrs Bliss said. 'How you settling in up there then?'

Jackie clutched her mother's legs.

'Fine, thank you.' Dorothy used her best English accent.

'Blimey, you look tired. When are you due?'

'September; not too long now.'

'Why don't you let the kiddies come in for a while? They can watch some telly and I'll give them their tea.'

Dorothy hesitated. She wasn't sure that the children would drink English tea.

'Go on,' Mrs Bliss smiled, 'they'll be fine with me and you can have a rest. Looks like you need it.'

Dorothy turned to the children.

'Please, Mommy,' Teddy said, 'can we?'

'Are you sure?' Dorothy asked Mrs Bliss.

'Course I'm sure. Wouldn't have asked if I wasn't would I?'

Dorothy hesitated for a moment and then nodded, 'Yes, thank you, like you said, I can do with the rest. Just send them back when you've had enough.'

Mrs Bliss patted the curled-up ends of her crisply permed hair. 'Don't you worry, I'll let you have them back.' And she laughed, her wide red lips breaking open with a sound that made Jackie think she was coughing but her face was kind, all creased up so it looked like it was moving even when it wasn't.

'C'mon kiddies.' Mrs Bliss pushed the door.

It was a large, cluttered room, lulled from the darkness by the evening light which made its way through the lace curtains. There was a small, plastic-topped table that stood at one end of the room near the door and a carpet that went all the way to the walls, even underneath the chairs. Jackie liked the way the swirls of greens and oranges stretched right across the floor. Everything seemed clean and was placed in good order, magazines and photographs, flowered vases with fluted arms on the mantle and a set of ashtrays made of glass, one with Brighton written on it, but the room smelled as if the air never changed, even though the windows had been left wide open.

'Harry, these are the children from the upstairs room.' Mrs Bliss turned towards the man slumped on the sofa. 'He can't always hear what you're saying,' she told the children. 'You have to raise your voice sometimes.'

'Say hello to the children, Harry,' Mrs Bliss' voice sounded as if she was the teacher calling the class back to lessons from the playground. 'It's Jackie and Teddy who've moved into the room upstairs. They've come to watch the telly.'

Harry Bliss was swathed in blankets from his waist to his slipper covered feet. One hand stayed under the coverlet but the other rested like a claw on top of the blanket. Mr Bliss stared at the children. Parts of his face seemed taut and shiny where blotches of rose pink scars had stretched the skin like plastic from his forehead down towards one ear where the lobe was missing. Mr Bliss smiled.

'Hello young'uns.' Mr Bliss' face hung as if a weight was

pulling his chin towards the floor but although he talked slowly, his eyes remained lively, darting from one child to the other, even as his words came slurring out from the side of his mouth.

'Come on then,' he tapped the cushion, 'come and sit down next to me and Mrs B will put on the telly and get us a drink, won't she?' he said, winking at Mrs Bliss. 'Some biscuits are in order I think.'

'Righty-ho; tea for two, and what about you children? Would you like some squash?' Mrs Bliss asked.

'Yes, thank you,' Teddy said.

Jackie nodded but she hoped it wouldn't happen, all that squashing, at least, not until she knew them better, because she really didn't like the way people in the streets in England rubbed their hands into her hair and touched her to see if she was real; squashing sounded like it would be more of the same, but if her brother said 'yes' then she'd better do the same.

'All right. I'll switch on the TV,' Mrs Bliss leant across, turned a knob and walked towards the kitchen, 'I'll be back in a mo'.'

'Come on I said,' Mr Bliss patted the cushion again and gave the children a half smile. Teddy sat down. 'No need to be shy you know,' Mr Bliss smiled a set of crooked lips at Jackie. 'I won't bite,' and he laughed. 'I haven't got enough teeth left for biting children any more!'

Mr Bliss had always liked children. He'd bought the big house before the war, when he'd first got married, intending to fill its rooms with all the kiddies he could make, but those dreams had disappeared, along with his ear, in the explosion that had numbed the part of his brain that connected his thoughts with the right side of his body. So instead of children,

Mr Bliss had decided to fill his home with whoever came knocking, as long as they were decent and could pay the rent.

The television hummed and flickered.

'Blimey,' Mr Bliss laughed, pointing at Jackie. 'That girl looks like she's been hit by lightning. Haven't you seen a telly before?'

It was like a dream, Jackie thought, or more like magic – the way the telly was small and looked like a cupboard. Mrs Bliss brought the drinks in on a tray, arranged the mats and put the glasses and cups on the table.

'Sit down darlin'; we can't see through your head you know.'

Mr Bliss took a packet from his pocket, pulled a cigarette from it, tapped it once and twice on the tip and wedged it into the corner of his drooping lips.

First there was music, a shaft of light, and the top of a woolly head. As the camera moved forward Jackie could see the man had a hat of pretend hair, dark and curly, something like hers, but shorter. Jackie gasped as he turned and she saw the face with its wide, white lips and shiny black skin. At first Jackie wondered if he was a dead thing, but then his eyes flipped open and the mouth stretched across the black face, the lips raw and naked as a flap of ripped-off skin.

Way down upon the Suwanee river

His chest pumped, his voice choked, but the lips were still grinning while his gloved hands clenched the rim of his hat as if it was a rope.

Suwanee, how I love you,
How I love you

Now the stage was fully lit Jackie could see there were even more Gollies, each one so much like his brother that she could hardly tell the difference one from the other, except for a stripe, or a spangle, or whether he was strutting or popping up and down. The Gollies swaggered downstage towards a paddleboat steamer where a line of dancing women high kicked their way from the deck to the stage. Now the first line voice was swamped by the chorus, washed aside by the medley of banjo songs which followed, each tune so well laced into the next that Jackie had to guess where one stopped and another began. One Golly-man, with a stars and stripes jacket, sat on the side by himself, but when the others saw him they leaped to meet him, rolling their pool hall eyes back towards the dancing ladies.

> De Camptown races sing dis song
> Dooh dah, dooh dah . . .

Arabesque, arabesque, the dancers do-c-doed until the music slowed to a funeral beat.

> Way down upon de Suwanee ribber,
> Far, far away,
> Dere's wha my heart is turning ebber,
> Dere's wha de old folks stay

They dabbed dry eyes with their spotted black and white handkerchiefs.

> Oh Susanna don't you cry for me,
> 'Cos I come from Alabama
> With a banjo on my knee

And then the dancers kicked their legs even higher, stretching arms and fingers towards heaven till they sank down onto their knees and the music came to an end.

It should have made Jackie happy to watch all that dancing and singing, but she felt as if she'd been stripped. Jackie pulled her skirt over her knees.

'What is it called?' Jackie asked.

'The Black and White Minstrels. It's my favorite,' said Mr Bliss, 'I think they're fantastic. They've got their own show starting tomorrow. You can come and watch them again if you'd like.'

Jackie looked at the screen.

'So where are you from then?' Mr Bliss asked. A dribble fell from his lips and ran down the cleft of his chin as he took another noisy gulp of tea.

'We come from Jamaica,' Teddy answered.

A nest of hair had made a home in the space inside Mr Bliss' sliced-off ear.

'I bet it's hot there.'

'Yes.'

Jackie looked at her fingers.

'Do you miss it then?'

She pursed her lips.

'Jamaica I mean, do you miss it?'

'We like being with Mommy,' Teddy replied.

'Oh yes, lad, course you do,' Mr Bliss put his cup down. 'So what language do you speak in Jamaica?'

Jackie wished Mr Bliss would stop talking.

'We just talk English,' Teddy answered.

'Well, *you* may think it's English, but it sounds pretty funny to me,' Mr Bliss laughed.

Jackie thought, well, he sounds pretty silly to me, asking stupid questions and leaving strange bits off the endings of his words. But he did seem kind, and there was the telly, and they seemed to have forgotten what they'd said about the squashing.

'Is everyone coloured there?' Mr Bliss asked.

'Where?'

'In Jamaica.'

'Almost everyone,' Teddy said.

'So how come your sister is much lighter than you or your mum; is she a half-caste then?'

Jackie flinched and her eyes went back to the white tips of her fingers. So it was true, she thought, a half; even Mr Bliss could see there was part of her missing.

'Stop asking so many questions, Harry,' Mrs Bliss said. 'Leave 'em alone and let us watch the telly without all your talking. It's Dixon next.'

'I was only interested,' Mr Bliss turned back to the television. 'Just wanted to know.'

Jackie walked up the staircase, opened the door and sat by the table waiting for her mother to fetch her something to eat.

'Mommy,' Jackie said. 'Mrs Bliss has a television and Mr Bliss has only half an ear on one side and you have to shout at him sometimes so he can hear you.'

But Jackie could see her mother was not listening, she was staring right through her as if she wasn't really there. Maybe, Jackie thought, maybe Mommy would be more interested if she talked about the Gollies and their black faces.

136

'And on the telly, there were some Gollies and they looked just like they do in the books . . .'

But Mommy still wasn't listening.

'And I did some writing at school,' Jackie tried again. 'It was really hard because we had to write about our mommies and daddies and I said . . .'

Now Mommy listened, but she wasn't smiling.

'Jackie, haven't I told you enough times? When will you learn to hold your tongue?'

Jackie could see there were tears in Mommy's eyes, she wasn't sure what she had done, but she knew it must be bad. She pinched her leg. Why could she never just be quiet and do what Mommy said?

'I'm sorry Mommy, don't cry, I won't do it any more.' Jackie promised herself to remember that if she asked too many questions it was naughty, and that if she talked too much to other people so that Mommy couldn't cope, like Great-Grannie said, that was naughty as well, because if she did talk too much maybe Mommy would have to leave her again and it would be her own fault because she was always being so naughty. Jackie climbed from the chair, put her arms around her mother's neck and searched for something else to say.

'I made this for you Mommy.'

'Oh; let me see.'

Jackie fetched the rolled up paper and put it on the table.

'Thank you.' Dorothy stared at the painting, 'I like it very much, but what about the colour?'

Perhaps it was the ribbons Jackie thought; perhaps red next time would look better.

'Jackie,' Dorothy said. 'What do you think of the colours you've used?'

'Don't you like the yellow?'

'Oh yes, it's very pretty, the brown with the yellow, but what about the face, the colour of the face?'

But Jackie was sure the face was exactly the way it should be, just like everybody else had painted, except hers, she knew, was the best.

'Are the cheeks too red?' Jackie asked.

'Give me you arm.' Dorothy placed the child's hand against the face of the picture. 'What colour is the face you painted?'

'Pink.'

'And what colour is your skin?'

What colour? Jackie looked again. *She* was a colour!

'That's why we're called coloured, sweetheart. Our skins are made of every shade of brown you can think of, some so light you can barely see it, others so black they almost look as if their skin is blue.'

Colour seemed simple when Mommy talked about it like that, but then even more questions came into Jackie's head like how come they call English people white when really they're pink and even, yes, she'd seen it, even sometimes a little bit blue? And why did white people say she was a half-caste thing when she was so much darker than they were anyway? It must be like the paint, something like that – if all things were white and wonderful the way it said in the morning song then you'd start with some white then you'd add the bits of colour . . .

'Some people have brown eyes and some have blue, that's all. It don't really mean anything,' Dorothy said.

But Jackie knew better, colours had meaning; meanings and feelings. She was a half-caste coloured girl, so the white girls pinched their noses because of her smell. *She* couldn't smell it because – because *she* was a wog who'd come on the banana boat from Golly Town and now she was nearly five and a half years old and Toy Town had the books with the pictures in them but still . . . The more she thought about it, the less it made sense; if she was only a half thing, then where was all the rest?

'What can I do if it's all wrong then?' Jackie asked.

'Just change it, add a bit of colour, it won't take long. Anyway it's bedtime. Go and use the toilet and remember, be quiet this time.'

When the children came back Dorothy was already in her nightdress and she'd pulled the pot towards the end of the bed so it would be easy when they needed to pee-pee in the night. Dorothy switched on the light as the children brushed their teeth, wiped their hands and faces and jumped into bed, pulling the covers over their heads.

'Hush now, I told you,' Dorothy said.

Underneath the blankets the world was glowing. Jackie yawned and sucked her thumb.

'Teddy,' Jackie whispered, 'where do the Gollies live?'

'What do you mean, what Gollies?'

'The ones on the telly who dance and sing.'

'They're people, stupid,' Teddy yawned. 'White people. They put black paint on their faces, but underneath the paint they're white.'

Teddy turned to the wall, rocking his head from side to side. Soon he'd be asleep. Jackie pushed her face up between the rose and yellow hints of the sheets and the scratchy blankets and then – *whoompf* – the bed sank down and Mommy was with them, and they were all together at last with her mother so heavy and breathing really hard till she turned on her side, swung her arm towards the table, and turned off the light. Jackie squeezed her toes, rubbing her feet against the mattress before she curled up tight as a C-A-T cat on the M-A-T mat. Jackie was glad that everything that hurt could be tucked into the space inside her head where it could so easily be forgotten. There was no more talking after that and she knew she'd be safe. When she was in assembly and singing about heaven and the brightness of the beauty this is what she thought of – to dig in the earth, to run so fast that her feet tipped her shadow, or to lay like this, soft and loved at the sweet, dark ending of her day.

Brixton, London
17 July 1959

Dorothy walked downstairs and opened the door. She was glad it was Friday; tomorrow the children would get up by themselves and she could stay in bed for at least another hour.

The air was warm already, heavy with the scent of the cats and the sweet privet hedges that sheltered at the fencing by the gate. She put the coat around her shoulders and pulled the front door shut. Today, she decided, today she'd get the bus there and do the shopping on the way back.

The morning sky had stretched a seamless blue horizon from the rooftops behind her to as far as her eyes could see. She shrugged, lifting the collar of her coat so it stood against her neck as she walked along the pathway, past the weeds and the dustbins that squatted by the side of the pavement.

Even though it was a lovely morning Dorothy had wanted to stay in bed – it was the first time for so long that the children had let her sleep through a whole night but she was still weary, her heart cold like meat and the sunlight seemed to make no difference to the comfort of her hands or feet.

Dorothy paused as she got to the corner, wrapped the scarf around her head, pushing the buttons of the coat through their fixings as she headed towards the crossing. Her footsteps echoed down the street, bouncing back towards her from the fencing. She squeezed her fingers into a ball. It had taken till summer to stop blaming the climate for how she was feeling. At first she'd tried stuffing strips of paper into the cracks by the windows, then she'd saved on food so she could feed the gas meter and keep the heater on the setting marked 'high'. Then she realised that this cold had nothing to do with draughts or dampness in the air, after all, she'd gone through worse in New York; no, this frost had another meaning. Truth was she was all by herself in this country and she was lonely; it was her soul that was chilled. After that, Dorothy had given up stuffing paper around the skirting, putting on extra layers beneath her dress and she'd gone out searching for company, trying to get a taste of something familiar, but there was no Harlem in this place, or none she could find; the few coloureds she'd met seemed more like children, barely old enough to tie their own laces and none had been further than backyard places, not until they'd got onto the boat while she . . . So Dorothy tried searching through her own recollections, maybe, she thought, if she found some more suitable memory, something rich and warm, it would keep her going till she made new friends. But her memories seemed altered somehow, as if they'd been worn thin; some things remaining, but all of them changing and she had no history in this place to wrap herself up in. She'd have to learn to get used to this kind of cold.

Dorothy dropped her eyes to the pavement, following the trails of green where grass and dandelion seeds had escaped from front gardens and embedded themselves in the cracks between the concrete. It was then, as she turned into the High Street, that she heard him

When first I saw the love light in your eyes
I dreamed the world held joy for me

The old soldier was standing at the corner, his voice reaching out towards the people who were rushing at the day. He seemed clean, Dorothy thought, almost presentable, though his clothes were shabby and his boney shoulders hung from his too big collar like the rest of his threadbare suit. Dorothy glanced at his feet. He had one leg missing. His trousers were shiny at the knee and his one shoe was scuffed and held together by a neat loop of string.

I love you as I loved you
When you were sweet

The soldier tapped his medals as his voice came to the end of the chorus. Dorothy searched for her purse, took a penny from her bag and put it in his tin. The sound of the old soldier's rough lament followed Dorothy like the flow of a gravelled river till it formed an oasis in the wasteland that had begun to form in her mind.

'Thank you, love.'

The soldier put the penny in his pocket and squeezed the stump that had once been his leg. Dorothy turned, following the shoals of grey people that moved towards the bus stop and the train station but then she halted, thinking of this man, this beautiful, broken-up man who was singing his heart with no one listening – and all she'd given him was a meagre penny-portion. She turned, walking against the stream of people, till she found herself standing again in front of the old man.

She sang,

> River Jordan is deep and wide,

For the briefest moment Dorothy's voice floated above the noise of the High Road before it wavered and was swallowed, at last, between the stamping of the passing feet and the clamour of the traffic. The old man looked up. Even though he'd barely moved, Dorothy could see he'd heard, so she raised her voice and continued,

> Milk and honey on the other side,
> Hallelujah . . .

The old man winked and raised a hand to his cap; an impish salute. Dorothy smiled all the way back to the bus stop.

This morning she had asked Mrs Bliss to draw a map to help her find her way to the hospital. Dorothy took Mrs Bliss' directions from her handbag, along with the appointment card, and rolling the papers carefully in her hand so she could quickly open them out and show the address to the bus conductor when he came for her fare. If he was friendly he'd remember to tell her when to get off the bus. After the doctor, they'd arranged for her to meet with a social worker-woman to make arrangements for the children and the baby that was coming, so soon now, so soon.

Even though she was standing fourth in line with a bag half full and a back that was already aching from the way people's eyes were staring holes into her belly. Dorothy's feet were still tapping time to the old man's music. Yesterday this waiting for the bus would have made her feel as if she was standing on the edge of despair, but with all that early morning singing still sending milk and honey moments pumping through her head, the day had turned her sights towards a new horizon, a new way of looking at the life she had chosen. So now when she thought of the life that was growing inside her, when she thought of all the life that was going on around her, underneath her feet, beneath the concrete, even under the stone faces of the people on the bus, she couldn't help humming and smiling to herself, and the best thing was, the thing that capped the rest, was when a stranger, old enough to be her father, hair so white you could take it for snow, rose while she was standing, no seats on the bus, and said, as he lifted his hat, 'Madam, excuse me, would you like a seat?'

Dorothy unbuttoned her coat and took the weight off her feet.

The doctor had told her everything was as it should be, that it was looking as if the baby would arrive on time for the first week in September. Dorothy hadn't really minded the poking and shoving, but she wasn't too sure how she was feeling about the meeting with the social worker. Dorothy knocked at the door.

'Come in.'

She pulled the handle and saw her – there she was, the social worker-woman writing at a desk

'Good morning,' Dorothy said. 'I'm Mrs Brown.'

'Oh yes,' the social worker's pale eyes flicked towards Dorothy, 'I was expecting you earlier but never mind. I'm Miss Jones,' she held out a hand. It was damp on Dorothy's skin. 'Would you sit down please, I won't be a moment.'

Miss Jones didn't wait for Dorothy's answer as she pointed to the chair.

Dorothy sat, the curve of her back set straight against the chair as a flush of irritation began to rise at the sight of the woman's head dropped in front of her as if she wasn't even there. Miss Jones grabbed a file.

Dorothy's eyes ran across the baby pink, home-knitted sweater and the head bent over, hair like Shirley Temple, except that her frizz was set like concrete around her sagging red face. In another situation this might have been enough to raise more than a smile but now – this woman had decisions to make about her and her children, and that, she knew, was no smiling matter.

'I have some information on file already but I'm afraid we do need more details, Mrs Brown, before we can decide exactly if and how we can help you.' Miss Jones scratched her head. 'Let's see. Yes, today's date is Friday, 17 July.' She glanced up from her desk. 'If you could start by telling me something more about your situation.' Miss Jones coughed, waited for a moment and coughed again. 'All right then; why don't we start at the beginning?' Miss Jones made her face stretch to something that might, in other circumstances, be mistaken for a smile. 'Mrs Brown, you told my colleague last week that you had been studying in America for some years?'

'That's right; I won a scholarship in Jamaica to study Medicine at Howard University in Washington D.C. I was intending to become a physician.'

'And did you complete your training?'

'No, I became pregnant and a separation from my husband left me . . . destitute.'

'And what are you living on at the moment?'

'I had a small amount of savings when I arrived but I am now dependant on Social Security. I intend to look for work as soon as the baby is born and old enough to leave in day care.'

'Oh yes, of course, after the baby,' Miss Jones decided it was time to practice her smile again. 'When are you due?'

'The doctor this morning said the first week in September.'

'And do you have any relatives or friends in this country who can help you during the confinement?'

'No, I do not.'

'Is there anyone who can look after the children while you are in hospital?'

'No.'

'Where is the father of the children?'

'As I said, we are separated. He lives in the United States.'

'And you came from Jamaica – when?'

'No, not from Jamaica, I came from Canada. I was in Montreal for about a year until I had earned enough to pay the passage to England for myself and the children.'

'Thank you for clearing up that confusion; it says here that you're in temporary accommodation at the moment – the three of you sharing . . . one room with the use of an outside toilet?'

'Yes, that's correct, but we're moving next week, something more suitable; two rooms on the ground floor, so we'll be there by the time the baby is born. What I need, what I'm hoping for is help with the children for when the baby is born and maybe some practical support for a while after that.'

Miss Jones raised an eyebrow.

'I'll run through the options . . .'

*　　*　　*

That afternoon Miss Jones wrote her report with some care. It was important, after all, Miss Jones knew, that she got it right; there was nothing else on record about this family and she had a feeling that the Social Services would be seeing them again; and this one had delusions – a medical student! They come to this country, they must think we're fools, spinning any piece of nonsense just to try and get better treatment she supposed. Miss Jones began her report:

```
Mrs Brown appears to be an intelligent woman but seems to
be somewhat detached from the reality of her situation. Mrs
Brown is seven months pregnant having come to the UK in
April of this year. She has very little money, no friends
or family, and appears to feel suspicious of authority
figures. It is clear that when Mrs Brown goes into
hospital that the Authority will need to make arrangements
for the children. I suggest that we look at planning for a
six-week stay for the children at the Hollies Children's
Home in Sidcup, Kent.
```

It was an end of a time. Dorothy put a hand on her belly as the baby curled and kicked inside her. Yes, an end of a time she thought. The children ran ahead, speeding down the road, the hoods of their coats buttoned up with the rest left loose to make capes that hung from their necks.

Dorothy hadn't seen the news till she'd gone to get the children their candy from the store; it was then she'd read the paper. 'Billie Holiday, famed jazz singer, age 44, died yesterday in the New York Metropolitan Hospital.' Same age as me; Dorothy's eyes wandered to where Jackie and Teddy were hiding by the dustbins, exactly the same age, except for a few weeks. Dorothy knew she was supposed to pretend she hadn't seen the children. It wasn't hard, she was distracted, she couldn't get the thought of Billie singing and living, choking and dying out of her head. Lord, give her mercy, but there it was, just like that. Maybe Billie was dancing with the angels right now.

Dorothy waddled up the path.

'Mommy,' Jackie asked. 'Can I stay out and play?'

Dorothy nodded; she was relieved the children seemed to be making friends. She'd been worried at first about how they'd cope, what with all the changes they'd had recently, especially at school. Perhaps it would be better to leave it for a while before telling them the arrangements that had been made to look after them once the baby came. Jackie in particular had been having such nightmares, though she seemed more settled now, always smiling and full of stories of who she had played with when Dorothy met her after school.

Jackie sat on the steps, pulling off her shoes. She must still think she's still some pick'ney in the yard, Dorothy smiled.

'Mind you keep your shoes on, you hear? And stay with Teddy.' Trouble was, Dorothy thought, when the child wore bare feet here, it just cut up her feet.

Dorothy opened the door and walked up the staircase. She unlocked the room, pushed the door, let the bag fall to the floor and threw her coat onto the bed. She knew she'd better put a shilling in the meter otherwise the electric would cut out halfway through the evening. Dorothy took the last shilling from her purse, shoved it into the slot and turned the butterfly key. Enough electricity to last at least through the evening and tomorrow her money should come in the post – they'd promised. Dorothy picked up the shopping bag and carried it to the cupboard by the sink, unpacked the food and rested for a moment by the window, squinting past the nets and the railway track, over the rooftops till at last her eyes settled on the distant, floating pinprick of an aeroplane tacking its way across the sky. She fastened her thoughts on that plane, stretching her dreams across the Atlantic towards her eldest daughter. Dorothy sighed, however far way she was, Pearl was always there inside her, didn't matter what anyone said or how long it would take, she would never give up trying to find her. She stroked the brittle lace of the net curtain between her thumb and forefinger and pulled the newspaper from her handbag.

```
The immediate cause of death was congestion of the lungs
complicated by heart failure.
```

Dorothy walked to the bed and kicked off her shoes. All that beauty of Billie's — she remembered it; and to think of that voice of hers fighting for air!

```
Miss Holiday had been under arrest in her hospital bed
since June 12 for possession of illegal narcotics. She
arrived in New York with her mother in 1928. For a while
they eked out a precarious living, mostly from her mother's
employment as a housemaid. But when the depression struck,
her mother was unable to find work. Miss Holiday tried to
make money scrubbing floors ...
```

A train raced away along the track outside the window. Dorothy sat on the bed and rolled onto her back, her eyes fixed on the sticky paper she'd stuck to the ceiling that morning. Most of the flies were dead already, but two or three still struggled to get free, jerking their legs every now and then against the glue that would hold them fixed until the end. Dorothy's eyes rested there, but her mind was someplace else.

The night she'd got pregnant with Jackie they'd seen Billie sitting at a table at the Savoy Ballroom. What a place! Soon as you were on the sidewalk you felt as if you'd arrived somewhere special just from the way the sound of the music always seemed to be waiting to welcome you in. It had been the perfect place for her and Jack to meet – the best dance hall in Harlem, whites and coloureds mixing together and the lindy-hopping, jive dancing music that they played had always managed to set them singing through the night and into the next day whatever else had been going on. Maybe they'd drunk too much because she was feeling like a beauty, so when he said how she looked like a goddess she'd raised her head and laughed in agreement, deciding to believe him, after all, there'd been such power in her arms, in her legs when they'd danced that night. Or perhaps she'd do better to blame what happened on the closeness of another New York summer night, the way its heating-up magic always seemed to make her want to strip down to her soul. Or maybe it was just the sound of all that loving and living that was coming from the dance floor that made her forget the days, the way the sunlight would show on their skin, because she knew they both wanted it, wanted that baby, however bad that was with Jack's kids still sleeping and his wife tapping her heels as she waited for their father. The truth was, at that moment, all Dorothy had thought of was how much she loved him, and all she could feel was the heat of him rising and her body so tight that it burst at his touch, gaping so wide as his fingers stroked her body that she just didn't care, and he didn't care, and anywhere he loved her felt good and right until they fragranced the night, dripping such loving from their lips that the taste of it burnt kisses on their tongues. And afterwards they were so happy they still didn't sleep, even though the morning was knocking at the windows and it really was time for him to leave.

Jack sang to her as they lay on the bed. She stroked his back and he kissed her feet. She laughed even more and watched the smoke from his cigarette curl towards the ceiling, but that was then . . . Dorothy smiled, sat up and walked to the sink to pour herself a refill of water. That baby had come in April – a little girl and, true to his word, Jack had made sure she'd got the right attention – he had paid for more than everything she'd needed. In exchange he'd asked her, and it didn't seem to matter so she had promised, not to tell anyone about him, not even the child, not until she was old enough to understand how complicated things had been. She'd called that baby Jackie after him; she was her secret, precious thing.

Dorothy opened her eyes. The meeting with the social worker was laying heavy on her mind, all those questions; and the thought of the coming hours of labour she'd soon have to go through to finish off making the new baby weren't helping, it was all too much. She was too tired to cook tonight. Anyway, the children would be happy with jam on their bread and cocoa to drink – they got their dinner and milk free from school everyday. Dorothy put on her shoes and went down the stairs, back out to the street. Two girls were sitting at the kerb, one had a face like a grimy elf, with wisps of fine blonde hair trailing over her face. The other was dark eyed with stains of something leftover caked around her mouth and nose.

'Have you seen Teddy and Jackie?'

'They're down there,' the grubby child pointed to the end of the road where part of the fencing had been kicked through. 'At the bombsite. Have you got a baby in your tummy?'

Dorothy looked at the pair of urchins and laughed. They looked so earnest clutching their half-naked dollies to their dresses.

'Funny you should say that because it's true; how did you know? Maybe you'd like to help me once the baby's born. I see you've been practising.'

The girls stared at her belly, nodded and put their heads together.

Dorothy decided she'd take the walk to the bombsite real slow, make it last as long as she could. The sun had already turned towards the coming evening. The sky to the west had turned to gold where it was dropping away at the horizon. Dorothy wondered what Jack was doing today, this evening, this moment, and even though it was getting hard to recall his face, his voice, there were times, when Jackie was laughing or screaming, when she remembered the way he'd looked that day they were sitting in his car and she'd told him they didn't have much time left. The child had reached up and pulled the pearls from her neck, bursting the string so the little white balls had landed like a storm of hailstones in their laps.

Dorothy came to the end of the street, walking towards the lengthening end-of-day shadows that were crawling along the pavement from the wooden fencing. She stepped over the partition, bending her head, just about managing to squeeze her belly through the gap – and there he was, her son, chasing around as if his life depended on it and Jackie trailing after him like she always did. Dorothy shaded her eyes from the slant of the evening sun as she followed the chase. How they can lose themselves, there's nothing more important for those children right now than the moment they're in.

'Jackie, Teddy – it's time to come home,' Dorothy shouted.

Teddy stopped at once but Jackie was already opening her mouth to speak.

'I said come now, and I don't want any argumentation.'

Dorothy put her hand on the child's head. A heat of blood was rising through her scalp. She'd promised Jack to take care of their child and she'd do what she could, but she was scared for Jackie, it was so hard to grow up anywhere as a little coloured girl. And after all, she thought, things must seem so strange to her, what with everything that had happened, what with everything that was still going to happen to her.

Jackie stumbled through the door.

'Hush! Don't make a commotion I said.'

But it was too late – Mrs Bliss had opened the door. Lord, Dorothy thought, please let me have no trouble, let the day end in peace, but all Mrs Bliss seemed to want was some company, to say hello, and ask if she could have the children for the evening. Sometimes Dorothy wondered if Mrs Bliss was lonely, spending so much time in the house with that poor husband of hers.

'Are you sure?' Dorothy asked.

But it seemed Mrs Bliss was sure. Dorothy hoped the children wouldn't go blabbing their business to the landlady, she'd warned them against talking to strangers often enough but it didn't seem to make much difference. Thank goodness Teddy had enough sense for a body twice his age, but Jackie . . . In

the end she'd left the children downstairs and had gone back
to the room so she could lay down again, turn on the radio
and let its babble take her back . . . another time, another place
– the first time she'd met Jack, holding hands as the crowd
crushed them together, standing with their people, the coloured
and the white, no difference between. They had marched to
City Hall trying to save those poor coloured men who were
heading for a government lynching the next morning for what
the papers said was the rape of a white woman – huh!

'Negroes lynched, Nazis freed, where is our democracy?'

That's what they'd chanted, but it had made no difference
– that same day the courts had freed some old SS guards but
they'd gone and hung those poor coloured boys, strung them
up anyway, and it seemed to Dorothy a healing thing to let
Jack's white hands in, so they'd gone back to her place and
played Billie's 'Strange Fruit'.

But the flesh between them was always there . . .

Dorothy jumped. The children were already at the door,
running around and making too much noise while she was
still wiping the sleep from her face and trying to find the
strength to climb off the bed and get food on the table.

Brixton, London

20 July 1959

M ommy had told her she could change the colour.
Jackie splashed the black paint on the back of her
hand, rubbed it so it dried to an even stain and
put the brush on the table. She lifted the pot to her nose and
breathed in. Yes, there it was. At last she could smell that
place on the Island from long, long ago where the earth had
boiled and bubbled, she remembered one day it had even
shaken at her touch, everything stirring and life rising up
from the darkness – she had seen it. Jackie was standing in
the classroom but her feet were gripping onto sometime else,
to a moment, a day she could still remember, when she'd
stepped on that place where the earth was like chocolate
squeezing through her toes, when she'd stepped on that place
where the earth had pressed her heart-beating feet to its soul
with its kisses when she walked, when she ran, when her
hands had touched the sky, where the earth was so sweet in
her mouth she'd sucked it dry and the juice had run from
her lips and Mommy had told her not to eat it any more.
And, Jackie remembered, that after she had eaten the dirt
every day, when Mommy was away at work, her belly had
started getting bigger, and she'd got sick, so Mommy had
gone to the doctor for some medicine and then she'd said to

Jackie, 'Open up your mouth, swallow it down for me.' Then Jackie had started screaming, but Mommy was yelling too, so Jackie had to swallow the nasty medicine, even though it tasted like a stink.

One night, when the moon was like a slice of melon peeping through the spaces of her fingers, and the lamplight was flickering through the crack of the outhouse door, the shadows had come again and this time they'd danced inside her belly. Then there was a groaning and she'd pushed it away, pushed and pushed till she had to stand up because a worm had come out, all white and curling even as it hung between her legs and fell into the toilet. This time, Jackie decided, whatever happened, even if it hurt in her tummy, she'd keep what she was doing a secret, she wouldn't say anything about what she had eaten, not even to her mother.

Jackie tilted the pot. The black paint glistened. Jackie thought of the Golly-men dancing, she thought about their faces, and the taste of the sweet tinned milk. Would black paint taste like the earth? Would the earth-shaded darkness shine starlight on her skin?

Jackie put the pot to her lips and gulped it – cool on her lips, the dark cream sliding down her throat so easy. Now all that black paint was inside her, she'd be more than half a thing. She stroked her belly.

PART THREE

JACKIE – THE MOTHER

March 2004

On 12 March 1986, I had my own baby daughter. After Eleanor was born they laid her on my belly. The lights were in my eyes and the place was noisy, the way it is in most delivery rooms, but she hardly murmured. She just laid there, this little face, with her eyes looking around. She seemed to be searching for something. I put a hand on her back and felt the heat from her passing through my fingers. Every now and then an arm or a foot would start kneading at my belly. She could have still been inside me, the way our hearts were still beating through the one cord. Then she looked up, raising her chin, as if in all the commotion she'd only just noticed who I was. I smiled. She had such dark eyes, no colour in them yet, and then there it was, this wave of emotion, this overwhelming certainty that I had known and loved this child forever.

As the midwife lifted Eleanor I felt her hand was pulling at something more than the cord or the insides of me, she was pulling at a line of women, at the never ending line of mothers and daughters who'd left the strands of their lives running through my baby and me. I wanted to keep hold of that feeling, share it with my daughter. It was then I decided to find out what had really happened to my mother and me.

It took some time. It was slow at first; making phone calls,

waiting on files, but one piece of information l
one memory opened onto the next until I be
things I hadn't thought about for years, goin
layers of insignificant untold moments that m
And after a while it seemed as if I could almos t
the years like a book, picking my way from
another. I discovered wounds that hadn't hea
that had been planted, shadows I never realise
even the smallest things became important: the w
left tissues screwed up on the table, the flowers
mantle, a photograph, a letter, the texture of t
front room. And as my search went on and
older, there was more to share. I began to lo
the times when we could talk about the past.

When Eleanor was eighteen, I began to tell her
winters were colder than now, the way that fros
into forests on the insides of the windows and i
catkins from the sills and pipes so there was neve
of painting glass at Christmas. But it wasn't jus
sharpened the air; the smog that choked the rest
the life out of places like Deptford because the p
already thick with smoke from dockyards and fact
the fog straight from the river up into the streets
and pooled. I remember the smog was so thick
people carried torches when they went outside
you hardly saw a face or heard a decent word exch
trailed children behind them like wraiths while the
sang lewd songs and rapped their boots on th
lurched towards the kerb, blind and brazen, s
week's labour and the day's fresh beer even in t

* * *

March 2004

On 12 March 1986, I had my own baby daughter. After Eleanor was born they laid her on my belly. The lights were in my eyes and the place was noisy, the way it is in most delivery rooms, but she hardly murmured. She just laid there, this little face, with her eyes looking around. She seemed to be searching for something. I put a hand on her back and felt the heat from her passing through my fingers. Every now and then an arm or a foot would start kneading at my belly. She could have still been inside me, the way our hearts were still beating through the one cord. Then she looked up, raising her chin, as if in all the commotion she'd only just noticed who I was. I smiled. She had such dark eyes, no colour in them yet, and then there it was, this wave of emotion, this overwhelming certainty that I had known and loved this child forever.

As the midwife lifted Eleanor I felt her hand was pulling at something more than the cord or the insides of me, she was pulling at a line of women, at the never ending line of mothers and daughters who'd left the strands of their lives running through my baby and me. I wanted to keep hold of that feeling, share it with my daughter. It was then I decided to find out what had really happened to my mother and me.

It took some time. It was slow at first; making phone calls, waiting on files, but one piece of information led to another, one memory opened onto the next until I began to recall things I hadn't thought about for years, going through the layers of insignificant untold moments that make up a life. And after a while it seemed as if I could almost leaf through the years like a book, picking my way from one page to another. I discovered wounds that hadn't healed, thoughts that had been planted, shadows I never realised existed until even the smallest things became important: the way my mother left tissues screwed up on the table, the flowers she set on the mantle, a photograph, a letter, the texture of the sofa in the front room. And as my search went on and Eleanor grew older, there was more to share. I began to look forward to the times when we could talk about the past.

When Eleanor was eighteen, I began to tell her my story, 'and winters were colder than now, the way that frost made fronds into forests on the insides of the windows and icicles dropped catkins from the sills and pipes so there was never any thought of painting glass at Christmas. But it wasn't just the cold that sharpened the air; the smog that choked the rest of the city took the life out of places like Deptford because the piers and yards, already thick with smoke from dockyards and factories, funnelled the fog straight from the river up into the streets where it drifted and pooled. I remember the smog was so thick that year that people carried torches when they went outside and even then you hardly saw a face or heard a decent word exchanged; women trailed children behind them like wraiths while the men got drunk, sang lewd songs and rapped their boots on the road as they lurched towards the kerb, blind and brazen, smelling of last week's labour and the day's fresh beer even in the afternoons.'

* * *

The house we moved to that winter of 1962 stood at the apex of two of those streets in Deptford. It had once been a shop, but it had closed for business, and the windows had been smashed long before we arrived. The front door should have opened straight onto the pavement, but it had been nailed shut, so we used the door by the backyard instead.

That night we slept in the front room with mice running all around us. It seemed as if we, not the mice, were the intruders there; the gas and electricity had been disconnected and the other family hadn't moved in upstairs yet. We spent most of that night huddled together, telling stories to each other, until we got too tired to care about the scratching that was going on. I remember there was a hole punched through the floorboards of that room, a gash where the wood had been ripped up for burning by the tramps who'd lived there before us. I couldn't bear to look down that hole in case I saw what lay underneath; in my child's mind I knew it was the Mouth of Hell, an opening to the Other Side.

Later I dreamt of the ever-hungry demons I imagined lived under that house, of them and the shadows whose laughing faces so often tormented my dreams. I remember waking up screaming, insisting they were real. Even in the morning I couldn't go near that hole because I thought I might fall or be sucked into damnation, so I stayed wrapped in blankets, waiting for my mother to carry me where I needed. My mother had the windows and floor fixed straight away, but our neighbours put petrol and faeces through the door, smashed the windows, and chalked swastikas on the pavements so everyone would know where the coloureds were living. At first my mother cleared up the mess and had the glass replaced, but when the same thing happened again and again she decided we'd live with the windows boarded up. And even after all these years, so many pictures come to mind – like the way in winter, the step by the kitchen always shone like glass from the drip-drip spill of frost melting from the roof so I'd have to watch my step if I ran to the door. And then I see my mother, coming towards me, just the way she looked most evenings, her quilted dressing gown covering her shabby day clothes, her uncombed hair tied back into a scarf, her bare feet turning blue on the lino floor and I smile, because she's smiling at me, holding my baby brother on her hip. And I wish I could have told her then what it means to love her now, but I'm seven years old and all I can think of is the TV show I'm missing and how the chips are growing cold in my arms.

'C'mon,' my mother says as she walks towards me. 'Good girl, shut the door; you're letting in the cold.' She shoves the door with her foot and plants kisses on my cheek. 'Lord,' she shivers, 'put the food on the side, I'll do the rest.'

The kitchen is long and narrow, more a corridor than a room, no cooker, but a cupboard and a window looking onto the backyard. My eyes skim the cluttered surfaces, past last night's dinner and the patches of wallpaper peeling at the corners.

'Go to the front room,' my mother says, 'you look half asleep.'

The daylight has already seeped from the edges of the boarded-up windows. I flick the light switch as I pass it.

'Where's dinner?' Teddy asks from under his blanket.

'Mommy's bringing it.'

Teddy sneezes and drops his hanky between the baby's cot and the low wooden table.

'You keep an eye on Roy,' my mother calls and puts the baby on the bed. 'I'll bring the chips.'

'Don't forget the sauce,' Teddy shouts as my mother goes through the door.

I take off my coat and drop it on the floor. The bed groans as I lean towards the baby. He's lying on his back, kicking his legs, smiling with his brand new teeth as I take his fingers in my hands.

'Come and get it!' Mother shouts. I can't move too fast, I've got the baby, but I don't mind, there'll be enough for me. That's how I remember it; or sometimes it begins like this . . .

Even though it's spring, the ground is set like concrete. I'm standing outside the back gate, waiting for my mother to get her coat and finish dressing the baby. I'm wrapped against the sudden coldness of the day in a layer of almost-fit-me jumpers and a scarf that wraps twice around my neck but I lift my face and let the sun lick the cold from my chin.

The street is almost silent, or as quiet as it gets; front doors shut tight against the rise of the morning with the echo of the milkman's voice ringing from the arches of the railway bridge as he sings and clinks bottles through his fingers. Most mornings his whistle was louder than the birds in the church-yard trees.

'C'mon darling,' my mother bumps the pushchair down the step. 'Stop dreaming, hold onto my coat.'

We speed through the alley of the churchyard, pushing the trolley where my baby brother sits, his head heavy with sleep so the rabbits on his hat hang floppy by his ears.

Suddenly the streets are filled with people.

'Thruppence a pound! Get your Brussel sprouts!' the barrowman calls.

'I'll come back,' my mother smiles.

'That's what you always say!'

He shouts and she laughs as we push our way into the tread-tread feet of the crowds who come to walk those Saturday morning market streets.

If I close my eyes I can still see Deptford market in the 1960s; and there's that scent of wool, old clothes and sweat . . .

My mother calls me; I can't take my eyes from the flowers, the brooms, the buckets of sweets, the plastic windmills, the horse mess in the street and the chickens hanging by their necks at the butchers' shops.

'Hurry up!' My mother's coat tugs against my fingers.

'And now my friends,' a man is standing on an upturned box waving his arms. 'My good friends, how will we deal with this problem if you elect us?' He points a newspaper towards the market stalls and makes a sweep across the street. 'Well, those that weren't born here can simply go home. We'll help them boys, won't we?' The crowd roar, 'yes', 'you bet!' The man continues: 'That's right, we'll assist them on their way. We'll even let them take their youngsters with them, but the half-caste,' and I wonder if he's looking at me because he's leaning so I can see the veins at his neck, 'the half-caste, at the age of eighteen, should be given free passage to the country of his choice, or be allowed to remain in Britain enjoying all the rights and privileges of other people.' The crowd murmur dissent, but then the speaker raises his hands. 'Except for the fact that he should be made to undertake sterilisation –'

'Hear, hear!'

I tug at my mother's sleeve, 'What is sterilisation?'

'These are bad people,' she pulls my hand. 'Come on I said. We shouldn't be here.'

'Am I a half-caste?'

'I said don't listen to them; they don't like coloured people anyway.'

'Why?'

'Not now Jackie; they're just ignorant.'

'But what does it mean – half-caste?' I'm asking, but it's a test, I already know the answer.

'Well, it's when one of the parents is coloured and the other is white.'

'Is my daddy white?'

'Who, darling?'

'My daddy,' I ask again. 'Is he white?'

'What do you think of that one?' My mother turns to a shop front. Its windows are set for First Communion shoppers, stacked to the ceiling with white veils, green bow ties, satin dresses, diamante slippers and a choice of matching rosaries. 'This one would go really well with that veil,' my mother points to a flowery headdress. 'Next week I'll pick you up from school and we'll get your clothes.'

I nod. 'But my daddy –'

'Come now, you'll be late.'

I grab my mother's coat-tails as she heads towards the church.

'All right, darlin', you can go in by yourself. I'll meet you here when you're finished. Say goodbye and give me a kiss.'

To me it was Our Lady's Church of the Yellow Bricks but its real name was Mary of the Assumption. The church is still there; squeezed like an act of penance between Deptford railway station and the High Street shops. From the outside the building has the look of the Irish congregation it was built to serve; it's a working design, with a paved entrance, straight lines, and practical, arched doorways. But at its heart, the light of the sacrament shines at the altar, flickering between half-size statues of Saint Joseph and the Virgin Mother who stretch their arms as they stare past the candles that burn every day at their feet.

'Jackie,' Father Fagan calls as I walk up the aisle. 'Well done girl. Come in, come in, it's good to see you. Take a seat; I think that means we're all here.' Father Fagan's sing-song Irish brogue has a way of making me feel especially welcomed in. His eyes scan the pews.

'Right now, shall we begin . . .'

Thoughts of white dresses with matching embroidery and satin slippers tempt my mind away from the proper contemplation of eternal redemption. Dear Jesus, I pray, keep me pure, without sin, so I can live in Your home with my mommy forever.

'So, there you are,' Father Fagon goes on, 'Jesus had died, and then He got up again, not like a ghost, but the whole living body of Him was walking around as good and warm as you and me, and that is what will happen to us all on Judgement Day; if you die without sin you will live with Him and the saints and the angels and all the good people who you ever loved on God's Earth will be there with you. Now, what a gift that is!

'And next week,' Father Fagan continues, 'when you have had the body of Christ, you will understand the miracle of the mass and I know you're ready for Him because you're all such good, dear children and you've been working so hard, not just here but at school as well.'

I'm praying that when I die it will be just as I come out of Confession and when I'm so old I won't mind too much.

'All right,' Father slaps his hands together. 'That's it for now, but I will see you all for your final Confessions. I forgot to say,' Father raises his voice, 'if you're part of the dance group, please go to the hall now, the rest of you can go. Well done everybody.'

'You're with the dancers aren't you Jackie?' Father Fagan puts a hand on my head and I feel the sin of pride stirring in my chest.

'Yes, Father.'

'That's good, that's good. I think I will come and have my tea with you today.'

Father Fagan rests his hand on my shoulder and walks behind me.

The Church Hall is a large shed attached to the back of the church with a life-size picture of Saint Patrick in mitre and robes painted across one end of the wall and an Irish tricolour unfurled on the other. Along each side of the room rows of chairs have already been filled with mothers and children. The other girls look so pretty with their pink freckled faces and green plaid kilts. The boys have white shirts and grey shorts that reach to their knees and the prize-winning dancers have a green and gold sash tied across their chests but all of the girls preen and prattle, shuffle and laugh, while their mothers spit and smooth their hair neatly down onto their faces or pull their curls straight beneath black bands.

'Well, hello to everybody.' Father Fagan waves his fat hand. The mothers stand up from their seats as he passes, flushing in turn as he presses his pink putty fingers hard into their hands. By time the music starts Father Fagan's face is glowing with the pleasure of it all and then he sits, resting his belly on his knees, as he taps a foot to the music. We bow to each other, girls on one side, boys on the other. First our feet step heel and toe, then we twist-tap-spin, twist-tap-spin and soon I'm panting to keep up with the hands clapping, music stamping, flapping of the gold and green flags of Saint Patrick as the jig whirls us harder and faster round the hall.

'Well done, dancers! Hoorah!' Father Fagan shouts and the mothers join in.

My mother is outside the door.

'So you're off now then Jackie? Well goodbye, dear.' Father leans towards me, 'You've done so well since you came to us haven't you?' I can smell the drink on his breath and I notice how the veins around the swelling of his nostrils run like blue threads when his face turns red. 'It will be grand at Communion next week, eh?' Father Fagan squeezes my cheek. 'I'll talk to your mother, but goodbye till then.' He waves, 'Be good!'

I can hardly wait a week. I say my prayers each night, just like Father Fagan told me to, so I will be ready to receive the body of Christ and be redeemed from my oh, so many sins.

Deptford, London
May 1962

My name is Jackie Brown and I'm eight years old. I live with my mom and my two brothers at 172, Deptford Church Street, Deptford, London, SE8, England, the Earth, the Universe. I used to live with my Great-grandmother in Jamaica which is an island a long way from here. In Jamaica the people are coloured but they talk English and wear clothes. We came to England on a boat and whatever people say, it didn't have bananas on it, it just had people like me in it. I had my fifth birthday on the boat. They made me a cake and sang happy birthday. Everyone was sick except for me.

I have brown skin and eyes and curly brown hair. My mom combs my hair into plaits. I'm not very tall but I can run fast and I can do all the sums at school. My mom says I'm clever for my age. I can read better than anyone else in my class. My mom is the best mom in the world.

One of my brothers is still a baby, he is quite funny but he can also be annoying and his nappies smell. My older brother is called Teddy. He's really clever. My big brother says the Earth is just one of millions and millions of stars in our galaxy and there are thousands of galaxies in the universe. I have a big sister who lives in America. I don't really know who she is but my mom is always saying how much we all love her and that we have to remember her all the time.

My favourite game is pretending I'm Supergirl. I like playing with my big brother and my cat. My favourite colour is yellow. When I grow up I want to be a doctor.

On Thursday I had to go to church to give my Confession before I have my First Communion. Father Fagan says this will be the most important week of my life. It was dark in the church and there were only two people waiting for Confession with me. There were lots of shadows dancing on the walls from where the candles were burning. I'm scared of the dark when I'm by myself so I have to be careful where I go.

Before I went into the Confession Box I lit a candle to pray for my eternal soul like Father Fagan told me I should. Mommy gave me the money. All I could see through the window inside the Confession Box was Father Fagan's shadow. He had his hand on his face and his eyes were closed as if he was tired or something was hurting.

I said, 'Bless me Father for I have sinned, it is a week since my last Confession.'

I was really glad that I remembered the words. I had my new rosary to help me pray. It looks like a chain of little wet pearls or orange pips, and there's a silver cross on it. Even though it was dark I could feel the beads in my hands getting sweaty. My mommy bought the rosary at the same time she bought the dress, the veil and the crown for my First Communion so that everything would match. The shop we went to had lots of dresses. When I tried on the dress my mommy said I looked really beautiful, like a bride, and she always tells the truth. Mommy says that on Friday she will straighten my hair so it will be ready for the service and the procession on Saturday morning.

When I was at Confession I was so busy thinking about my dress I almost forgot what I was supposed to be doing until Father Fagan said, 'Tell me all your sins.' I tried to remember but when I began to speak it felt as if there were still some sins hiding and that made me think, can a person have secrets even from themselves?

Father Fagan gave me three Hail Mary's and one Our Father to say as penance and then he blessed me. I said penance in front of my candle by the statue of the Virgin Mary. I like praying to the Virgin the best because she was God's mother.

When I close my eyes I imagine how my soul looks now it's all clean and I'm ready to have Jesus inside me.

Deptford, London
June 1962

A corner of the front room is where we shelter – our Fortress of Solitude, its white walls are hidden behind the multi-dimensional force-field that shields us underneath a pile of blankets and clothes. Teddy told me.

Now we can leave our everyday lives – Teddy says we've spent enough time in Smallville, so we strip to our capes and fly from the city, across to the ice caps where we can play and have a feast on aniseed balls and sherbet dips as we watch the projections of our own home-planet that are stored inside the crystals of our Fortress. In our hideout we can remember who we really are because nothing there is hidden, everything that's ever happened and everything that will happen in the future exists at the same time in different dimensions.

When I close my eyes I think I can see my soul like a shiny heart that's been made dirty by my sins. That thought makes me feel so afraid until Teddy reminds me who we really are – the last representatives of a once proud people, the children of Jor-el, invincible, but light years away from our real home-planet. Teddy says only we escaped the earthquake that destroyed our home-planet so now nothing can hurt us. We are protected by our super-hero powers and our lifelong mission to protect mankind. That's how I know we'll survive, even when villains try to defeat us, even though our past comes back to haunt us we'll survive because we fight for freedom, justice and the American way.

I lean and dip a sticky finger into the candy. Teddy turns the page of the comic strip book.

Here, he points, the next part begins.

March 2004

'Of course it was strange coming to England' I told Eleanor, 'though as far as I was concerned it wasn't England I'd come to, it was my mother – compared to that, everything else was insignificant. I'd missed her so much. I'd have gone through anything to be with her, though of course things had changed, I was older and she was pregnant and that meant we had to leave her again, after all, we didn't know anyone in England, we'd only been here five months when Roy was born, so we had to go to The Hollies. My mother arranged it. I think I was more excited than anything; I was looking forward to the baby and being a big sister. I don't remember being worried at all, except perhaps on the first night they took us. You see, that time my mother had prepared us, told us exactly what would happen when she went into labour. Me and Teddy had our bags packed waiting at the door next to hers so it felt as if we were going together. And The Hollies wasn't bad for a Home, we only had to stay a few weeks and then we were back at home with mother, and for a while our lives went on pretty much like before.'

Deptford, London
June 1963

The radio is on. I'm sitting in the corner of the sofa because it's Sunday and the station is playing my favourite programme.

The lady on the radio says, the time in Britain is twelve noon, in Germany it's one o'clock, but home and away it's time for *Two Way Family Favourites*.

I have a colouring book and a pillow beside me. I listen for the song about the toothbrushes falling in love, or the runaway trains going over the hills, and then there's 'Puff the Magic Dragon'. The records I like won't get played till the end. I colour in pictures while I'm waiting – the theme from 'Rawhide', then 'Sparky's Magic Piano' and then at last it comes – the roll 'em, roll 'em rhythms of my favourite record where a gang of dead cowboys have to haunt the prairie forever and sing . . .

My mom isn't crying today but she still isn't talking to me. Sometimes she doesn't speak for days but I know she still loves me, it's just that her head gets so full of sadness and remembering with all the things she's doing to try and find my big sister Pearl that she forgets I'm here. Even from the sofa I can feel it.

I put the pillow on my face so I can hide from the music but still see my mommy. Yes, she's still there, sitting at the table looking at those letters. I know where they're from because she reads them all the time and now I'm nine I can read them as well. They're from Dr. Barnado's, the American Red Cross, Wilson's Private Detective Agency and the Salvation Army, anyone she thinks can help find my big sister.

April 2004

'We had left America but the truth is America had stayed with us just as much as Pearl was always a presence. In my mind the two were linked,' I smiled at Eleanor, 'my mother never stopped talking about either. At the time I couldn't remember anything about Pearl but I had one memory of America, though it's so faint now, I can't be sure it's real. I'm on the tarmac with Teddy, we're standing by the aeroplane, the propellers are still turning then we start to walk across the runway. I must be very small; even when I look up I can't see the face of the lady who's pulling at my fingers, but I know she must be pretty because her hands are pale and pink and she smells of talcum powder and flowers. When I turn I can see my mother walking with the men who brought us.

'It's strange; even though it's a melting sun I'm wearing a woolly green coat. I remember there was a heat haze rising from the ground. The lady told us we weren't allowed inside the Waiting Room. Teddy said it was because the sign read 'White' on one side and 'Colored' on the other so the three of us had to shelter in the shade of the building. We ended up faint from the heat, because the air hostess couldn't go through one door and we weren't allowed to use the other.'

*   *   *

Everything else I knew about America I got second-hand from my mother, she showed me how words could make worlds; she talked of dance places, even in Harlem, where she couldn't get work because of her colour, she told me how the police had locked her in a cell and put an electric current through her head, how when she'd gone down to the South with my father and the other protestors, the Klan had burnt crosses, just to remind everybody they could always organise a damn good lynching. A lot of what she told me I barely understood, but wherever she went, I loved riding on the stories of her imagination, living on her dreams of America. Didn't matter, Mother said, that she couldn't get there any more, because she knew one day, when I was grown up, I'd find my way back to that Emerald City where Hope and Crosby songs could always bring rest to the lines of weary Dorothys who like her, had to wait for hours in the scorching sun, for a bus to take them on roads to be housemaids, or singers, or to climb stone steps, never mind the dogs snapping at their feet, they'd stay ruby-slippered in their protests. these were the dreams of America I got to see – the ones that filled my mother's life, and the night I'm thinking of now is no exception because even though we were sitting in Deptford in 1963, it's the word from Alabama that had us staring at the television screen, as if the place itself was electric.

'Governor Wallace of Alabama had previously talked of putting himself between the schoolhouse door and any attempt to integrate Alabama's all-white public school system . . .'

The camera zooms towards this Wallace, a man with a well scrubbed face and the voice of a librarian. My mother sucks her teeth, opening her mouth as if she's ready to speak or spit, and then the scene shifts again, an old man is sitting in a street in a place called Saigon. I hardly had time to take a breath before I saw it was petrol they were pouring on him and the next thing I noticed he was striking a match. I remember even now how his body toppled over, crisp and cross-legged, as the fire finished eating at his face. Later, they found the heart of that man, charred but still whole. I thought even though it was black, it must be his soul.

Deptford, London
June 1963

I woke up this morning when the light was just coming over the tops of the boarded-up windows. I turned over in the bed to talk to Mommy but she wasn't there. I thought, maybe she's in the kitchen, so I waited and I called Mommy, Mommy but she still didn't come, so then I got scared and got out of bed. As I jumped on the floor I heard Roy crying. I didn't go to him first of all, I went to Teddy, but he didn't know where Mommy was either, so we got Roy out of his cot, I changed his nappy, then we stayed in bed waiting for Mom to come home. After that I was getting really frightened, I thought I'd be sick, that's when I said to Teddy, 'I think you should go to the phone box and call the police,' because when someone disappears that's what you have to do.

That's why I'm not allowed to see my mommy any more.

The policewoman is saying 'Hurry up children, come on now quickly, there's a good girl, it's time to leave.' But I don't want to go, not yet. I need to say goodbye to Mommy and tell her why I got Teddy to phone 999, but the police lady takes my hand anyway and she pulls it.

'Come on,' she says again, 'the car is waiting.'

My feet are walking fast, one step after another, even

though I can hear my mommy crying and this time I'm sure I'll be sick because this is my fault, it happened because I made Teddy call the police. Or it happened because I woke up too early and got scared of being by myself. Or it may have happened because my heart was beating faster than I could think when I saw the bed was empty. I tried really hard not to be frightened, but we had waited such a long time already, until it was past nine o' clock, and by then I was absolutely sure Mommy was dead.

First thing was the policeman knocking at the door . . . The next minute my mom came back home and then everyone went quiet. I was shaking by then, my hand was trembling as much as my teeth when I saw the way everybody was standing in the doorways, looking at each other, till my mom started screaming let me have my children.

I wanted to get to my mother so I could make her feel better, but the policewoman caught me by my nightdress and pulled me, then someone else held my mother back, I could see it, I could see it.

I really wanted to scream, but even though I was crying in my head, I didn't let the tears fall down even once, I remembered that Mommy always said I should learn to be quiet in front of strangers. That's why I didn't look at Mommy, or say goodbye even when the police took us away. So now I'm sitting in the back of the police car with Teddy and Roy beside me. My legs are sticking to the seats that are sweaty and shiny and smell like the polish they use at school. And even though it feels like the police should be arresting me, they don't use handcuffs or put on the sirens like I've seen them do on the TV.

I turn and look through the window as the car speeds off.

There are people staring and our house is getting smaller and Roy is shouting Mommy, Mommy as the car is getting faster and our street, and my school, and the chip shop, and everything else I know rush past me and I can't see anything I recognise any more.

Teddy puts his fingers on my hand and says, Don't worry, it'll be all right, as we go into the tunnel.

I don't know why he said that, because it's not me that's crying. I close my eyes so I don't have to see his face any more as the car sucks the road and the tunnel rolls its darkness all around me.

<u>*THE LONDON PROBATION SERVICE*</u>

<u>*PROBATION OFFICER'S REPORT to the S.E. LONDON JUVENILE COURT*</u>

<u>*on 2 August 1963*</u>

<u>*Confidential*</u>

Probation Officer: Miss Newman

Court: S.E. LONDON (GREENWICH) JUV

Address: 55 Lewisham High Road, Lewisham, S. E. 13.

<u>*CONCERNING*</u>

<u>*Full name*</u>

Theodore Brown	Born 1.2.50
Jacqueline Brown	Born 10.4.54
Roy Brown	Born 9.9.59

<u>*Religion*</u> — R.C.

<u>*Occupation*</u>—

Offence — 5.7.63, Greenwich Juvenile Court

Pilgrim State

In need of care and protection having a parent or guardian
not exercising proper care or guardianship, was neglected in
a manner likely to cause unnecessary suffering or injury to
health.

Previous orders of the Court — None

Family

Father Divorced in U.S.A.

Mother Dorothy Brown   48   Household duties

Children

TEDDY 13   S.E. London High School

JACKIE 9   Saint Joseph's R.C. School

ROY 3   Attends Rachel Macmillan Day Nursery

Circumstances

On Saturday, June 11, the police received an emergency call
from Teddy Brown. He said that his mother had gone out of the
house the day before and had not returned. The police went
round to the house at 10.00 a.m. and found the three Brown
children. The two rooms were in a filthy state with inade-
quate bedding. The rooms had the look of a junk shop,
stacked, in some places, from floor to ceiling with old
clothing and other miscellaneous objects. The Police Doctor
was called. At this stage Mrs Brown returned. She said that
she had not been out all night, she had gone out the previous
evening, returned at 11 p.m. and the next morning she had
decided to attend early mass and had left without disturbing
the children. The children were deemed to be in need of care
or protection. They were then taken to a place of safety.

When we got through the tunnel, out on the other side of the river, the car slowed down and the policeman said, 'Right, this is your stop Teddy, out you get.'

I didn't realise me and Roy were going by ourselves.

The policeman opened the door. 'Time to say goodbye to your brother and sister Teddy,' he said, 'there's a good chap.'

'Mommy will come and bring us home soon, you'll see,' Teddy smiled. 'Look after Roy as much as you can,' he said to me.

That's what made me cry, and once I'd started, I felt as if I couldn't stop until the policeman slammed the car door shut and I looked back and saw Teddy waving. I watched until I couldn't see him waving any more.

It didn't take long and the car was slowing down again. We stopped at a place that looked like an office or a school building.

'Go to the side entrance,' the policewoman pointed, 'that's where the reception is.'

We parked at the corner. There was a bush of pink roses climbing up the wall, their little faces scrunched up against the side of the fence so they looked as if they were tired of trying to get onto the roof.

This time the policeman didn't get out of his car.

'You do it Polly,' he told the policewoman, 'no need for me to come. I'll wait here, it won't take a minute.'

April 2004

Eleanor dropped the pages of the Probation Service report. 'How come you never showed me these before?' she asked.

'It took some time to find them and get them released; I've been looking since you were born. They passed Freedom of Information Acts here and in the States, that helped, but it still wasn't easy. And how was I supposed to decide what to tell you and when; it wasn't straight-forward, not for me; I wanted you to have your own life, not get dragged down by the past and the emotions I was going through.'

'Shouldn't I have had some choice about that?'

'Well, at first you were too young, then I was waiting for the right time and later I suppose I'd just got used to skimming over things when I talked to you – it seemed easier that way, and after all, we were happy. I'd coped.'

'But that's not the point,' Eleanor insisted.

'I know, you're right.'

'And just because you coped doesn't mean there wasn't a cost . . .'

I let the silence wash between us.

'But there's a cost to everything. Even now, the only way

I can come near to some of these feelings is to think how it would have been if those things had happened to you; the problem is when I do that, it seems too awful.'

'But it was awful, Mum. I can't imagine what it must have been like for you.'

'Then I've succeeded, at least to some degree, and not just me; after all, the reason your grandmother came to this country was to give us all the chance of a better life and when I look at you I know whatever happened in the past was worth it.'

Eleanor leafed through the papers.

'How did you feel when the police took you?'

'I think I blamed myself; that's what children do.'

And there it is, that old pain, ready to stick its rusted fingers back inside me.

'Each time I was separated from my mother it hurt and I was never prepared, not really, you can't be. But even as a child I don't think anyone could tell I was distressed, I was never delinquent or neurotic, or a self-abuser. That's how I survived, at least that's part of it. You see, I've never doubted my mother loved me, and that feeling was so strong even now, she still sustains me. I think about her every day. But to remember like that, to hold her love that close for so long means I can't focus too much on the pain, and maybe that's been a good thing because I've done alright, don't you think?'

The police took us to a Reception Centre, a Home that takes children into care before a decision can be made about their long-term future. It was large building, big enough to house more than fifty children in two adjoining blocks with a nursery on one side and a Home for older children in the other.

As I climbed from the car I remember staring at the windows, looking at the grime that had settled on the glass. A breeze blew grit into my face and I covered my eyes as the policewoman led us into the hallway.

'Hello there, I've been expecting you. I'm Miss Partridge. I'll take the children now, thank you.'

The policewoman said goodbye and disappeared through the door. I stared at my shoes.

'It's Jackie and Roy Brown, isn't it?' Miss Partridge leant towards us. 'My job is to take care of you while you're here. I look after the senior children and Mrs Blythe is in charge of the nursery.' Miss Partridge pointed to a younger woman waiting at her side. 'First thing to do is get you registered; it won't take long, then we'll take you upstairs, give you a bath and get you a change of clothes so you can get settled in.'

'Want Mommy.' Roy sat on the floor.

'C'mon, get up.' I pulled his hand.

'Don't you worry about your brother, it's Mrs Blythe's job to look after him now. He'll be staying with her in the nursery.'

My hand gripped Roy's fingers.

'Now come on, dear. We don't want any fuss do we? I know your mother would want you to look after your brother but I promise we'll take good care of Roy and you can see him whenever you like, he'll only be next door.' Miss Partridge looked like the school dinner ladies. 'That's it,' she said. I dropped Roy's hand. 'Well done, there's a good girl.'

Mrs Blythe lifted Roy into her arms. 'There you go little

man, I've got a lovely train set to show you, would you like to come and see? Wave goodbye to your sister, that's it; you'll see her soon.' Mrs Blythe carried Roy through the door.

'Right.' Miss Partridge spoke cheerily. 'You'll be staying with the big girls, but first things first: a bath, then I can show you your room. Follow me.'

Miss Partridge opened the door onto a long corridor and led me into a washroom with a row of sinks and toilet cubicles set along the length of it.

Miss Partridge took an apron and tied it round her waist. 'Now, this will be an adventure for both of us, won't it?' She unwound my plaits. 'Goodness,' she laughed. 'It's soft, like cotton wool. I thought it would be like a Brillo pad. Bend your head, that's a good girl.' I leant over the sink as she poured a jug of water over my head. 'Is that all right for you? The temperature I mean.'

I wrinkled my nose. There was a tingling sensation at the edge of my scalp and as the smell of the shampoo caught in my throat, I coughed.

'Don't worry, it won't take long and I'll rinse it off. We have to do it special the first time anyone comes you see, to make sure your hair's nice and clean. Guards against infection and that sort of thing. Right m'dear,' Mrs Partridge rubbed my hair in a towel, 'into the bath and give yourself a good wash, you know, all the important bits. I'll be back in five minutes with some clothes.' She picked my dress and underpants from the floor.

I was not used to being by myself. As the bathroom door closed I remember thinking how quiet this place was. At home I bathed in the living room; it was a family ritual. Every

Saturday evening my mother would unhook the tin bath from the wall in the kitchen, then she'd bring it to the front room, heat the water on the stove till it was good and hot and she'd pour it into the tub singing 'We're washing in the Jordan' till the top of the water slopped over my knees.

I stepped into the white enamelled bath and wondered what my mother was doing now.

'Coming, ready or not!' Mrs Partridge called as she opened the door. 'Right, these will do I think.' She put a brown dress and a set of underwear on a seat by the towel rail. 'I'll leave you to get dressed; I'll be waiting outside till you're ready. Don't be too long.'

The dress had pearl buttons shaped in little hearts and pretty red smocking stitched around the bodice and the neck. I noticed S. Bullock, Langley House was sewn in black thread onto the label but the knickers had A. Smythe inked in black on the waistband.

'I've done well this time,' Mrs Partridge said. 'That dress almost fits you. This way, then. We've put you in with the big girls in room 4; that's Janice, Sandra and Deborah. I'll introduce you to the gang.'

That first night, I hardly slept. The trees seemed angry, drumming their branches on the windows all night and the moon was playing shadow puppets against the walls. I put my head beneath the sheets so I wouldn't have to see the way the flowers on the curtains crawled spiders towards me. I didn't sleep until the wind had stopped talking to the trees but it seemed that as soon as my eyes had closed Miss Partridge was pulling back the curtains for the morning. I sat up straight away, calling for my mother.

'Mommy!' the girls chorused.

'That's enough of that,' Miss Partridge said. 'Time for breakfast. Janice, you show Jackie the ropes. Deborah, come on, I said get up now.'

Deborah was laying on her belly, her arms lolling across the pillows, her hands resting on the floor.

'All right Miss,' Deborah moaned. 'Just leave me alone. I'm doing it ain't I? Just leave me for a minute.'

'All right to you as well, madam; just make sure that next time I come in you're not still in bed or you'll be losing more privileges.'

Miss Partridge walked out of the door.

'Yeah, yeah. Silly cow.' Deborah spat as she spoke, swinging her legs to the side of the bed. 'Here, wass-yur name,' Deborah scratched her head and turned towards me, 'what you been put in 'ere for?'

I undid the buttons of my nightdress. The skin on my arms was cracked and flaking from my wrists to my shoulders.

'Here Darkie,' Deborah continued. 'I thought I was talking to you, or can't you speak English where you come from. I said what you in for?'

'I don't know,' I answered, 'they took me from my mommy . . .'

'Oh, that's terrible ain't it . . . they took me from my *mummy*, m-u-m-m-y; that's how we talk in this country, Darkie!' Deborah laughed. 'I put myself in here,' she lifted her head defiantly, 'better than living with my Dad any day.'

Suddenly Miss Partridge was at the door.

'Deborah Cummings,' Miss Partridge shouted. 'Leave the new girl alone and get yourself dressed otherwise you and me will be doing some talking in the office.'

Deborah scowled, picked up her dressing gown and slouched into the bathroom.

'Jackie,' Miss Partridge spoke softly, 'come with me and I'll show you where to have breakfast; you'll be seeing the doctor later, no school today, we need to give you a full assessment.'

<u>Assessment: Langley House Reception Centre</u>

<u>Date: August 13, 1963</u>

<u>Name Jacqueline Dorothy Brown</u>

<u>Medical Examination</u>

Jacqueline is below average height and weight for her age, however she appears to be in good general health although the skin on her arms is badly inflamed. Jacqueline says she had never suffered from this condition until she came into care. I am treating her for eczema.

There are no unusual signs of bruising or scarring to her body.

<u>Psychiatric Assessment</u>

Jacqueline appears a well-adjusted, intelligent child of well above average I.Q. When I met her she spent most of her time asking me when she would be allowed to see her mother. Jacqueline's relationship with her mother seems very close, and she says she misses her family very much. I suggest she should be allowed supervised visits from her mother on a weekly basis, but she should not be returned to her mother's care, even for a short period, until the courts have come to a decision.

Langley House, Hackney, London
September 1963

My mum comes to see us every Sunday. We have an hour's visiting time in the dining room from half past two to half past three. It's the best time of the week.

Last Sunday Mummy brought me sweets, a notebook and some colouring pens. She sees Teddy on Saturdays. My mum says Teddy hates the Home he's in and that he misses us all very much. Sometimes, at visiting time, me and my mum have to talk very quietly so no one else can hear us.

I mark each day in my notebook with a grade from A – D. Most days gets a C except for Sundays of course, and that almost always has an A.

My mum says they've set a date for us to appear in court, it's not till November because they need more reports.

When I first came to Langley House it felt strange, but now I've learnt the routine it's better. At eight o'clock there's breakfast and after that I get ready to go to school. When I come back from school I'm always hungry but I have to wait for dinner – we're not allowed to have a snack just because we want to. If my name is at the top of the list it's my turn and I have to help clear the dishes and wash up. We're allowed to watch the telly in the evening. Apart from Sundays, Saturday is the next best day because that's when they give us pocket money. There's a tuck shop in the Home so we don't even have to go out to go to the shops, but if you've been naughty, which means cheeky with the staff or lying or fighting, they take your money away. I haven't had my pocket money stopped once yet.

I miss my mummy and my brothers very much. It always makes me want to cry on Sundays when my mum goes home but the worse time here is at night. I try to go to sleep quickly because otherwise the big girls come to bed and they always want to start playing with me.

April 2004

'The truth is, I thought I got exactly what I deserved; it may have been Teddy who rang the police but it was me who made him do it. Not that my mother said anything, she wouldn't, she didn't need to; I knew I'd done wrong.'

'But you were a child!' Eleanor said.

'Yes, and we'd been left by ourselves and the police were right about the conditions at home, but at the time that's not how I saw it. Even now there's part of me that feels uncomfortable about calling the police. That's something I love about you – you never seem to have a problem showing your feelings or asking for help when you need it.'

Eleanor smiled. 'I like it too; it's a gift.'

We smiled.

'And one to be respected,' I hesitated. 'Though perhaps, when I was a child, hiding emotions protected me as much as feeling guilty sometimes did – it helped make sense of what was happening, you know, as if I was being punished. At least that way I could fool myself there was some justice to it all.'

*   *   *

The nights were the worst.

'Here, Darkie,' Deborah said. 'It's time for us to do some playing.'

Deborah got out of her bed and pulled the curtains so the light from the streets shone into the room. Deborah was the biggest of the big girls. Her breasts were large, almost as big as my mother's, even though she was only thirteen. They bulged and jiggled like jellies squeezing from the top of her candy-striped pyjamas. It was time for Deborah's fun to begin. First she tells the story of why her dad is in prison. I stick my fingers in my ears, popping them in and out so I don't have to hear. I don't want her dirty words dripping in my ears.

At last Deborah says, 'That's it, the end.' The girls sit up, rub their legs and smooth the covers. 'Now everyone has to tell a joke, or do a trick. If you manage to make me laugh you get a life, if not you have to pay a penalty. Did you hear that, Darkie?' Deborah stands, bounces on the bed and sits down again. 'C'mon then, and remember, don't make a noise, keep it like a whisper, or you'll have that old cow coming up.' She puts a finger on her lips, 'If you're going to laugh you have to stick a sheet into your mouth like this.' And she shows us how to do it. Sandra puts the sheet over her face so all I can see are her eyes. Janice is laughing already.

'Hush!' Deborah draws back her hair. 'Tonight I'm starting off first and it's a new joke so everyone has to listen. What did the elephant say to the naked man?'

'Put something on?'

'No.'

'Cover up?'

'No. Do you give up? You'll never get it.'

'All right.'

'He said, how do you breathe through something so small?' Deborah covers her mouth and the other girls laugh. 'What's the matter, Darkie,' she turns to me. 'Don't you like my sense of humour?'

I lay still.

'Right, Janice. Your turn.'

'All right,' Janice wipes her nose on her hand and sniffs. 'Here we go. What's worse than getting raped by Jack the Ripper?'

'I know this one,' Sandra says. 'You told it before you silly cow.'

'I know, but I was hoping you'd forget.'

'Hard luck you dope, not a hope!' Sandra laughs. 'Go on then, tell us what's worse then being raped by Jack the Ripper . . .'

'Getting fingered by Captain Hook!'

'Right,' Deborah whispers. 'We all knew that one and I'm not laughing so you have to do a penance.' The girls hug their knees, rocking to and fro. 'I say you have to run down the staircase, all the way down, touch the fire exit and come back again.' Janice climbs from her bed, creeps to the door and slowly opens it. Deborah continues, 'And if I find out you didn't go to the bottom, there'll be hell to pay!'

'Shh!' Janice opens the door. We hear her steps pit-patter down the stairs and then silence. The girls squeal again, waiting for the sound of Miss Partridge's door. I pray that it will open.

Suddenly Janice pushes the door, runs and jumps into bed, stuffing all the sheet she can fit into her mouth.

'Well done!' Deborah says. 'Right, Darkie.' Deborah's voice

is thick, she's taking time tasting this moment because it feels so good. 'Your turn.' Deborah clears her throat, 'Now we have tonight's star guest . . . our own, our very own Black and White Minstrel show; ladies and gentlemen, for one night only I'm giving to you . . .' Sandra stands on the floor and bows with a flourish '. . . only you . . .' Deborah's trying not to laugh, 'the entertainer what everyone loves and is waiting for, your very own – Jackie Brown!'

'Why, why –' but the words won't come.

'Right,' Deborah comes so close I can smell the toothpaste on her breath, 'did you hear me, Darkie? I said give us a joke or it's a penalty, I don't care which.' Her tongue flicks spit onto my lips.

'Why,' I stutter, 'why did the tomato turn red?'

'This is brilliant,' Deborah says. 'I can feel a penalty coming on already; fanny-tastic! Get on with it you little louse, come here thinking you're better than the rest of us 'cos your mummy comes to visit you every week.' She's pulls my hair. 'Your mum's so poor she has to chase the rubbish men just to do her shopping.' I bite my lip. 'And she's ugly; ugly and stupid and they're going to lock her up,' she pushes me back onto the pillow. 'She washes toilet paper and hangs it out to dry and that's why you stink, stink, stink!' Deborah grabs my neck. 'Finish the joke you silly bitch or I'll chuck you out the window.'

'Brilliant,' Janice says.

'Do her!'

'Last chance,' Deborah calls, 'or you'll be out of the window!'

I wipe my face. I'm thinking how Mummy will cry when they tell her I'm dead.

'Because,' now my whole body was shaking, 'because it saw . . . it saw the salad dressing.'

Deborah loosens her grip.

'That's rubbish!'

'Penalty! Penalty!'

'That's it, you're right aren't you my little darlin's; it's a penalty. What shall we give the little scrubber?'

Janice is jumping up and down while Sandra beats her head on the pillow so it makes a thud-thudding noise.

'Penalty! Penalty!'

'Penalty for Jackie Brown.' Deborah lifts a cup from her bedside table. 'I know what,' she turns to the girls. 'I'm going to get some water from the toilet and when I come back you have to drink it.'

'Yes!' they're squealing. 'Make her drink it.'

'Dirty cow.'

'Drink it, drink it.'

'What is going on here!' the light flicks on; it's Miss Partridge in her dressing gown with a torch in her hand. 'I said what is this noise about?' The torchlight sweeps across the room. 'And why are people out of their beds? Young lady,' Miss Partridge points the light towards Deborah, 'I've had enough of your shenanigans. Tomorrow morning first thing I'll see you in my office and I want the rest of you to know that I heard everything that went on and I'm very upset, very upset indeed. Now, for the rest of the night I'll be leaving my bedroom door open, and I don't like doing that, it makes me very upset. So if I hear a squeak, I mean the least whisper of a voice, before I come and wake you in the morning, there'll be trouble; have you all heard me?'

Pilgrim State

Confidential

Probation Officer: Miss Oldman

Court: S.E. LONDON (GREENWICH) JUV

Address: 55 Lewisham High Road, Lewisham, S. E. 13.

Home

I went to visit Mrs Brown at her home, two rooms in an old shop in Deptford. There is a large front room with a double bed for Mrs Brown and a cot for Roy; the bedding appears clean and adequate. The room itself is clean and tidy, clothes are put away in wardrobes and food is set out neatly on the table. Some of the windows are still broken and boarded up but ventilation appears adequate. The second room is slightly smaller. There are two bunk beds for Teddy and Jackie, these beds are clean and the bedding adequate. There is a spare bed in the room — Mrs Brown tells me that this is for the children to play on. There is a gas stove in the room which is clean and in working order. There is a sink in the corridor and an outside lavatory. Another family is said to sleep upstairs. Mrs Brown has obviously made great efforts in the last three weeks to clean these rooms and considering the very poor material she has had to work on I think her efforts are commendable. She pays £2 10 shillings a week's rent.

Jacqueline Walker

<u>General</u>

Mrs Brown tells me that before she came to this country she
worked as a pharmacist. Since the family moved to England,
Mrs Brown has been unable to find work that would pay
enough to cover the cost of the out of school care she
would need for the children. When the youngest child Roy
was born in 1960 the older children were taken into care
for a voluntary period of six weeks to allow Mrs Brown the
opportunity to recuperate. The Brown family have lived in
various different parts of London and have been in Deptford
since 1962. There seems to be a very strong bond of
affection in this family. I have gained the impression
during the past three weeks of visiting the family home
that Mrs Brown is a very unhappy woman who is possibly in
need of a good deal of support herself. Mrs Brown seems
somewhat depressed and isolated although she appears devoted
to her children and has taken a good deal of interest in
their progress at school. At the moment, her overriding
concern is whether or not the children will be allowed to
return to her. Mrs Brown feels 'everyone has it in for her'
and has found it difficult to discuss her plans fully with
me as she seems to have a deep-rooted distrust of any form
of authority, perhaps based on a misconception of the role
of the social services and the situation she is in.

Mrs Brown is an intelligent woman who is obviously
suffering from anxiety and shame about her situation. She
tells me that the rooms got into a mess because she was
unhappy about being separated from her eldest daughter and
she had also been expecting to move. She says her health has
become fragile and that she has been suffering from shortness
of breath which is why she had been unable to clean the

house properly. She mentioned a number of times that she is lonely and has found herself unable to make friends since arriving in England. Mrs Brown also said that the family have been the victims of continual racial attacks since moving to Deptford and that is why the windows have remained boarded up. This has made her afraid to go out and she worries about the welfare of the children when they are outside the house. I think Mrs Brown has become increasingly dejected by the rather depressing environment she lives in.

The accommodation at 172 Deptford Church Street is due for demolition this December. I have been in touch with the Housing Department and I understand that they are bound to re-house Mrs Brown before that. Whilst the house is extremely old and rather depressing, I consider that in its present condition it is fit for the children to live in until the new accommodation is available.

Teddy

When I saw Teddy at Wood Vale Remand Centre he struck me as a pleasant, intelligent boy who is mature for his age. He told me that he is very unhappy at Wood Vale. He was extremely concerned about his mother's welfare, he mentioned that her health was not good and he was anxious to be allowed to return home to help her. He enjoys school and his ambition for the future is to be an architect. Although he is the eldest boy, the separation from his mother seems to have upset him as much as his younger brother and sister. He told me that he would be glad to have an opportunity to speak to the magistrate on behalf of the other children if this were possible.

Jacqueline Walker

Jacqueline

Jacqueline appears to be a well-adjusted little girl who is extremely attached to her mother. When I saw her at Langley House she told me she was missing Teddy very much and she hoped to be allowed to return home as soon as possible.

Roy

Unfortunately Roy has mumps and I have been unable to see him.

Conclusions

The court will probably feel some concern about the safety of these children and a good deal of doubt as to the advisability of letting them return home. Material conditions are poor and Mrs Brown is an inveterate collector and she can, at times, be difficult to work with. This attitude has given rise to some concern. However, I have discussed the future with Mrs Brown at some length and I think that she realises that if the children are allowed home it would be under supervision and she would not be permitted to let things get into the state that they were in when the police were called. It is very difficult to determine what would really be in the children's best interests in this case. However, the Court may consider that in view of the fact that Mrs Brown is willing to co-operate if Supervision Orders are made, and that the children very much want to return home, that such Orders would be in the children's best interest.

Greenwich Magistrates' Court
November 1963

I've already been in a Home when my baby brother was born, but that time my mother didn't cry. That Home was called the Hollies. It was quite nice and it didn't take long before my mother came to get us. So even though I'm only nine and a half years old I already know all the names I need for living in a Home. First of all there's the Police, the Borough, and the Children's Department and sometimes there's even the N.S.P.C.C. Then there's Psychologists, Psychiatrists and Doctors as well and that's not counting Child Care Officers, House Parents and where I'm living now, a Home (not the same as a real home which is spelt with a small 'h'). I know about IQ tests and Case Conferences, the Children's Committee and Supervision Orders. All these people are there to help the court decide if I'm going to go back and live in my home (no capital letters), or go back to the Reception Centre, a Children's Home, a Foster Home, or even a Remand Centre (except really that would be for my big brother, not for me). Nobody has actually asked me what I want to do.

There's a lot talked about care. I'm in Care. There's Care and Protection and Care Orders but I just want to be with my mummy, that's all I care about.

I saw my mum when she came to the court. We were

sitting on some benches by the corner. She had taken a lot of trouble with her hair, she was wearing her best green dress and had lipstick on. She waved and blew us a kiss. When she turned to go inside the court I could see she had her fingers crossed behind her back, that's her signal for us to be lucky.

Last Sunday Mummy told me to be ready to run if the judge says we have to go back to the Home, she whispered it to me. She said she'd meet us round the corner and then we'd go somewhere the police would never find us. In some ways I can see that running away is a good idea, but when I think of the police chasing us it makes me scared because I don't know if I'll be able to run that fast. Teddy told me that all the other boys who live at the Remand Centre with him have done things like stealing and beating up people. He says he can't bear to go on living there any more so I *have* to promise to be ready if Mummy tells us to run.

Waiting for the court to make a decision is worse than being at the dentist. I watch the clock and kick my legs. Teddy is talking to Roy, sitting next to me is the lady from the Social Services. She's the same woman who visits my mum and writes reports. My mother says she's not even married, hasn't got any children of her own and she's too young to know her own business let alone start interfering with anyone else's. Mummy told us not to speak to her because the Social Services can't be trusted. I try not to talk to her while I'm waiting but it's hard because she's sitting next to me and there's no one else to hold my hand.

Each time the clock goes tick I think the judge must be making his decision.

I grab Roy's fingers to make him stop with all the scratching he's doing on his face. Now the door opens and the lady stands up.

Teddy whispers, 'Get ready,' into my ear, I nod but the truth is, I feel sick, like I might throw up my breakfast or cry. I try to think how we'll be like a gang of outlaws if we have to run, just like the ones on the films or the TV.

April 2004

' The court decided to return us to my mother but to put us under a Care and Protection Order. Soon after we got home we got a letter from the Housing Department saying there was a two-bedroom flat we could move to in Greenwich, on the Meridian Estate, by the river.'

The Estate had been built in the late 1940s to house the poor people from Docklands who'd been bombed out in the war. Each block had a balcony and a walkway that led to the rubbish chute and the main stairwell that opened onto a courtyard with sheds in the middle.

When I remember that yard it's always filled with people, like an ancient amphitheatre, with the women, their heads piled high with curlers, shouting to each other, calling from the balconies, yelling for their kids who bawled, or skipped, or played football down in the arena. 'Forty-forty; whoozit?' a child would shout and then the circus would begin, everyone running or hiding round the back of the bike sheds, smoking dog ends and swigging cherry fizz. There were nine or ten of those four-storey blocks on Thames Street, with the river running on one side and the High Road traffic speeding up and down the other. If anything, the fog seemed thicker there

than in Deptford, perhaps because the flats were so close to
the water, or because the mist got trapped in the loop of river
that bulges from the Isle of Dogs into Greenwich Reach. But
even with the fog and the traffic, the place lifted me, giving
me a landscape where at last my thoughts could breathe and
for the first few months I gulped that air. I spent hours every
day sitting by the window of my mother's bedroom, or if the
weather was good I went to the pier where at last my imagination could stretch beyond the rooftops, searching for a
world as yet unseen. I caught colours like butterflies, hitched
rides on black-bottomed dredgers, red-sailed barges, slick
white schooners, gun metal sweepers and the blue police motor
boats that flashed their lights into the breeze, bouncing their
bows on the turning tide of river as they sped downstream.
At times the ebb tide was low enough to leave the mud flats
high as sand drifts, the ground rippled with footprints from
the sea. Then we'd go down the pier steps and chase gulls on
the river bed, or search for firewood, or dig for coal, or
treasure. Could we reach Australia before we would have to
turn for home? Or sometimes, if the river was too high for
playing, a moon pulling hard at the hem of the water, we'd
run to the foot tunnel and go down the lift shaft, only putting
on our skates when we knew we could speed past the lift man
so he'd chase us and shout, 'Ere, you bleedin' kids, you should
know better,' and we'd laugh.

The men from our estate used that tunnel every morning
to go to work at the dockyards across the river. If it was
school holidays, and we were early enough, we'd catch them
cussing and joking and coughing up their lungs so they'd have
to leave their fag ends smoking on the pavement and we'd
collect them and sell them to the boys behind the bike sheds.

And when we got to the other side, to the Isle of Dogs, we'd take off our skates, climb onto the walls, and look back towards where we lived, to the river and the park with the Observatory beaming like a bauble on a Christmas tree, at the Palace and the hospital and the other great white buildings, at the red brick shadows of the council houses, and the rigging of the tea clipper dry docked by our estate. We'd chase and holler and count all the spaces till we found the windows of our little flat, lit like a doll's house, at the heart of my own world where the river sent its watery arteries, filled with commerce and cans and every kind of business, pumping its life blood through the city and into me.

When we first saw our home, the flat was empty and clean, each newly decorated thing shining and the scent of fresh paint hanging in the air like spring. The hallway was dark, but wide enough to take a secondhand piano my mother bought from the junk shop around the corner. And even though the front room and my mother's bedroom weren't large, they were bright and airy, with windows that looked onto a spread of grass, a line of hedges and further on, if I craned my neck, I could see the wall of the river path. For the first time in my life we had an inside bathroom and hot running water with drainage; no need to think of how to scoop the dregs from the bathtub any more. The front room was big enough for a small sofa and a dining table. But best of all was the fireplace with the brown tiled shelf where my mother placed photos and things we'd made at school. In winter she'd try, if there was the money, to keep a coal fire burning all day. My mother never trusted electricity, so the electric iron stayed packed, all shiny and new, in its box somewhere. She kept the old black irons on the hearth all through the year, heating them on the stove in summer; in winter she'd put them straight on the coals, rubbing them clean before pressing our clothes. The room and the kitchen by the front door were always dark; they had small windows facing the courtyard, set too high to see out. Even on the brightest days they were shaded by the overhanging floor of the balcony above them. My mother bought bunk beds and put them in our room, Teddy on the top, and me underneath, and that was where I was supposed to sleep, though if I could help it I always tried to end up in my mother's bed at nights; there was such comfort there, sinking into the middle of her double-size sheets.

Two carved wardrobes, big as sheds, bought from the junk shop, took up most of the space in her bedroom. Sequins and satins, petticoats and skirts were rainbow bunched in strict colour order inside one wardrobe; furs and woollen coats were stored in the next. I never saw her wear most of those clothes, but my mother was a collector and she was on a mission; she scoured every secondhand stall, every jumble sale or junk yard in the district to save and restore these cast-off beauties, and I'd go with her. We'd arrive early for a jumble or a market, stand in a queue in any weather, always disappointed if we weren't the first to get in, though my mother had a talent, even if we were late, for finding whatever was best. I took my lead from her and I was a quick learner so it didn't take long before I was picking through piles of clothes for myself, and I did pretty well. I was dressed in a fine, if at times, a somewhat eccentric fashion and I developed a sense of style, though I must admit, my fancy could at times go to extremes.

With both of us devoted to this same undertaking we ended up living in a Noah's Ark of the garments trade, except there were always more than two of each kind of a thing, kept for the day, my mother said, when she knew they would be needed. She loved those clothes and knew them by name, cooing and calling as she checked the condition of each one; here's the Russian sable, she'd say, and the sheared mink coat, I was lucky to get that one, and here's the silver fox stole, the wrap, the cape, the muffs, the mittens. It didn't matter how insignificant they were, she could tell them by a touch, by a smell and by the time I was ten, I could tell them apart as well as she could. I'd whisper their names as she brought them out to show me. And when she'd done all she could in the first wardrobe, she'd turn her attentions to the next, tending to the silks, sponging down the satins, or stacking the drawers with camphor balls to keep the moths away. We'd be having so much fun on those evenings that most times we'd forget there was a world outside those wardrobes and I'd fall to sleep on her bed. But if I was unlucky, and she got distracted, she'd insist that I go to my own room, then I'd wheedle my way to my brother's bed so I wouldn't have to wake up by myself if I had nightmares.

Greenwich, London
November 1963

I'm a dreamer.
I dream every night.
I dream the same dream over and over.

I dream I'm on Popeye's ship, a cartoon drawing of a black and grey school girl. My clothes are wet and my fingers are sore. I have to keep hold of the mast because there's a storm, the waves are gigantic and the water is coming all over me. Or sometimes my dreams are like a movie, all purples and greens, like *The Ten Commandments* or *Ben Hur* with angels playing trumpets and thousands of people in the streets. But tonight there's a new dream. This one begins with me waking in bed next to my mother but I'm cold. The sheets are pulled down so I sit up to reach for them but as I turn I see my mother's soul floating from her body. I know it's her soul because I can see straight through it while her real body is lying on the bed sort of crumpled up and empty. When my mother's soul smiles I see her eyes are like the Virgin's; they're looking up to heaven, not at me.

April 2004

' **M**y mother could enjoy herself just from being alive. She didn't just dance and sing, she played the piano and told stories and she laughed all the time, that's how I remember her. She knew how to celebrate, she didn't need an excuse to appreciate a performance or to become part of one. Along with the clothes, she had a collection of 78 records and a wind-up player. The records weren't just the jazz and dance music from her youth, there were film scores of the thirties and forties, popular hit parade tunes, Big Band sounds and a varied selection of her favourite classical tunes. Teddy and me learnt words from Gilbert and Sullivan, Bizet, Cole Porter, Irvin Berlin. Like Mother our musical tastes knew no bounds. We could give as cheerful a rendition of 'Three Little Maids From School' as 'Shaking the Blues Away', depending on what my mother chose to hear when we insisted she needed a treat.'

By the time I was nine I'd choreographed and danced both leads in *Romeo and Juliet*, died gracefully in *Swan Lake* and learnt how to shake my hips to *Carmen Jones* so it was no surprise one afternoon when my mother came home and told us she had auditioned for, and had been chosen to play, a walk-on part as a jazz singer in a three-day run in a fringe

West End play. Even better, as far as I was concerned, she had to wear an evening dress and provide her own costume. It was a passport to heaven. There would be dressing up and rehearsals, putting on make-up and at long last a proper performance; would they give her flowers, would men fight for her favours? As far as my mother was concerned, everything was possible because at last the world was going back to the place it was meant to be – at her feet. But even better, as far as I was concerned, it gave us another reason to go shopping.

Though Deptford market could easily provide for our regular needs, it was obvious that a commission like this would demand days more work than usual. I was fortunate; it took my mother more than three weeks to get what she needed.

Mother had her favourite stalls, knew what she was looking for, and when at last she found it, we both agreed it was perfect: a coffee-coloured satin and sequinned fish tail dress with bulging lace petticoats, a plunging neckline and a taffeta train. I thought she looked like a dream, at last she'd be discovered and we'd end up rich enough to forget we had any needs. We paid the man, folded the dress carefully into a bag, and were about to turn for home when I saw a pink tutu and a pair of matching slippers peeping from a box under the stall. I wanted it. I needed it. It would be all my happiness, everything in my life would come to right, I knew, if I could only realise my own modest ambitions to become a prima ballerina. At first my mother was reluctant to part with the money, but it didn't take long to convince her that the few shillings it cost was cheap, considering how much I needed the outfit and my repeated promises that I really would be good for the rest of my life and I would never ever ask for anything again. I had plans to be a star and, of course she agreed, because as far as she was concerned, like her, it was what I was meant to be.

While my mother was out at rehearsals, I wore the tutu at home and practised. Teddy and Roy applauded. At last it was my mother's final performance and she brought me to the theatre. I had a front seat in the stalls but no interest in the play, the plot was slow, the words seemed to float over my head. There was no dancing or singing like on the films or the TV and where was Mummy? Each time the lights went down I leaned forward, hoping it would be my mother's turn to make an entrance. At last she had her cue, a scene in a nightclub. She had described it, but even my imagination hadn't prepared me for what I saw. She emerged from the darkness, the light shining as if it was coming from her skin. She was perfect, now everyone would see it; and she was mine. Under the stage lights her satin dress was burnished to gold, so she shimmered as she raised her arms and then she sang, not the way I heard her at home; she stood proud, erect, with a voice that caressed the air and I hoped, if I tried really hard and practised, one day I would be as good as her.

Greenwich, London
24 December 1963

It's Christmas Eve! I've been putting crosses on the days in my notebook every morning since the first of December. The tree is already in the living room. My mum bought it with the money she gets from the Post Office where she works. One day, Mummy took me to her office so I could meet everybody. I had to put on my best clothes and get the train from Greenwich to Waterloo Station. There were hundreds of people working with her. First of all I thought it was going to be interesting, but in fact by the time I'd been in her office for an hour I was worse than bored, I don't know how she can do that job. Once I was there I had to stay till the end and watch Mummy filling in forms. School is much better.

I helped my mum carry the tree into the living room and we both put the decorations on it. It's nice having things at Christmas but I wish Mummy didn't have to go to work every-day because she's tired all the time and she's never here when I come back from school so I have to wear the front door key on a string around my neck. I like the fairy best of all. She has a white dress and a crown on her head and wings that grow like leaves from the side of her body. The Christmas tree fairy looks like the picture of the Guardian Angel that Father Fagan gave me for my prayer book. Mummy held me up and I put the fairy on the top of the tree so she could see how happy everyone is. She looks like she is floating.

This year, as a special treat, my mother said we could have presents from a shop. Today is when we're going to the West End to see the lights and choose the toys we want.

It took a long time to get dressed this morning. Because it's so cold I had to fasten my coat to the top, put muffs on my ears and a scarf over my nose and mouth because the air will nip my face and the fog will taste like smoke.

At school, before the end of term, we did work on Niagara Falls. My mum has been there. She says it's a wonder to see. There are three falls at Niagara called Horseshoe, America and Bridal Veil. The fog is so thick from the river this morning that it runs over the top of the wall just like the Niagara waterfalls in the picture.

Today I saw a robin jump onto our window sill. I was staring straight at him and he was looking at me. He was so close I could see his chest moving up and down. You'd think he was trembling he was breathing so fast, but Teddy said not to worry, it was normal. I think the robin came to see our Christmas tree.

Don't forget your gloves, Mummy says, does anyone else need a wee before we go? And then we're out of the door.

The frost has made a pattern on the yard floor – we're almost the first to walk on it. I drag one foot along the ground as we go for the bus so I can look back and see where I've been. The sky looks the same as the river this morning, muddy greys with a dirty white froth, like the top of watery milkshake.

By time we get to Oxford Street the shops are already crowded, everyone rushing and smiling, carrying boxes and bags back home. The decorations are hung across the street, but they haven't turned the lights on yet. Mummy says we can stay here all day, we can have a Wimpy beef burger for dinner and wait till we see the snowflake lights get turned on before we go to the movies.

Today is for us, Mummy says, today is the day we can go where we want, and choose anything we'd like to do, all we have to do is ask.

This is the best kind of dream, but I'm careful not to ask for anything that costs too much. I chose a ballpoint pen with nibs that change colours and a book called *Ancient Myths and Legends* which has stories like the ones Mummy tells me when I sleep in her bed.

Tomorrow I can play all day and read my book.

Greenwich, London
25 December 1963

This morning it was Christmas so we woke up early. Father Christmas had left us a stocking filled with sweets. I know it's my mum who does it really, but it's fun for us to help her do the pretending.

Teddy and Roy have gone to play cars, I'm in the front room reading my book and Mum is in the kitchen. The door clicks opens.

'Hi.' Teddy says.

'Where's Roy?' I ask.

'I've left him in the pushchair,' Teddy shouts. 'C'mon Roy, get up.'

I look down the hall. Roy has his coat and hat still on and his face is turning red where he's getting too hot. He's trying to climb out of the pram by himself.

'You have to hold the pushchair for him,' I shout to Teddy, 'otherwise he'll fall out.' Teddy lifts Roy from the pushchair.

I take my eyes back to the story because I don't want to lose the page or have to get up and look after the baby.

'Car,' Roy says, holding his toy in a sticky hand right in front of my face so I can't see my book.

'Yes, car,' I answer. 'Take off your coat, then you can play properly with your car until dinner.'

'Roy car,' he says.

Talking to Roy can be a bit like filling in forms because he only knows a few words, so I say yes, and I give up trying to read for a moment and I unbutton his coat. 'Why don't you play with the car some more?' I say and point to the floor.

'Want Mummy,' he answers.

'Well you know where Mummy is,' I tell him, 'she's in the kitchen. Play with your car now or watch some telly and Mummy will come with dinner soon.' I go back to reading my book. I've got to the story of Demeter and Persephone. What I like about this story is that it didn't matter what anyone said to Demeter, she was the mother goddess; all she wanted was to be with her daughter and Persephone never forgot her mother either, even though Hades made her his queen.

I wish it was always Christmas. My mum is frying pork chops, I can play and eat sweets all day, then I'll be stuffed with food and happiness and ready to watch *White Christmas* on the TV – it's on every year.

Sometimes watching *White Christmas* makes my mother cry, she says it make her think of happy times. I only cry when I'm sad. We'll sit on the sofa and sing the songs. I know all the words about the days being merry and bright, and all the Christmases being white, and this day is bright, even though it's raining instead of snowing, everything is still all bright today.

April 2004

'Ⅰf the weather was fine Teddy and me would make a bread and jam picnic and we'd take it to the park. If it was raining there was always the Maritime Museum or the Observatory. At the weekends we bought tickets for Saturday morning pictures. If there was no money we had the library. Teddy must have taken out every *Just William* book the Greenwich Library Service held in stock and we took turns reading the *Adventures of Tin Tin*. I found stacks of Greek and Roman legends on the shelves of the children's library and I read each book till I knew the stories by heart but even better than all the reading, for the first time since coming to England, I had begun to make real friends at school.'

Saint Peter's was small, the size of a village school, housed in a clutch of flint and brick Victorian buildings sited at the edge of the Meridian Estate and the High Road. Even then it seemed incongruous there, squeezed between the traffic and the council estate as if the school was a remnant of the time when Greenwich had been a ship-building town at the boundaries of the ever growing City. There was a central playground area just by the street, a toilet block, an assembly hall, a series of higgledy-piggledy classrooms set around the winding staircase of the main building, and a couple of temporary classrooms housed in prefabricated sheds in the backyard. There were fifty children in each class and one class in each year group. Teachers came and went quickly; I can barely recall one who stayed for more than a few months. Thinking about it now, it's hard to see how so much learning went on at Saint Peter's, but it did; perhaps because there was so much variety. Saint Peter's attracted extraordinary people onto its staff; actors and writers, people passing through on their way to doing something else. Those who couldn't keep our attention we treated mercilessly and they stayed days or hours, not weeks, but I still remember Mr Springer. He was the first man I'd liked and known long enough to imagine I was in love with. He never raised his voice. If I could have chosen a father, it would have been a man like Mr Springer. He'd been a hero in the war, a Spitfire pilot. He brought his medals to school to show our class and kept us amused for days with stories of dog-fights above the dockyards and the Thames. He smelled of lavender water and bath time and when he smiled, which he did all the time, his skin wrinkled up like fine tissue paper. Today Mr Springer would be called eccentric, but at the time I thought him a wonder of creation. He wore a floppy bow tie, more like a scarf, which he wrapped around the collar of his almost white shirts. His ties were always silk and brightly coloured, usually of some gaudy pattern, and he changed them each day, to match the weather or the way he was feeling, he told us. He wore a corduroy jacket with leather patches at the elbows and deep sewn pockets where he'd keep things he'd brought in to show us: shells, fossils, or some exotic trinket he'd found at the bottom of some old box at home. He told us he was an artist not a proper teacher, explaining that he only worked in schools when he needed the money. I was convinced that this must be true because even though he was old he looked like the artists of my story books with a pencil moustache and a swathe of grey hair, curled at the ends, which he kept beneath a beret when it was cold. Mr Springer was a performer, a clown, a conjuror; our own Pied Piper. Each lesson was planned for our amazement and enjoyment. He taught us what interested him, took us wherever his mind wanted to go, and we were happy to follow. When he decided we'd do maths he'd talk about shapes and colours. If it was history time he'd bring in pictures or paintings of places he'd been that we'd never seen. If it was writing practice he'd explain how metaphors worked, or he'd make up poems from words we shouted out from books, or he'd give us the space to work on our own day-dreams. He could rustle up a story at the end of a day without turning his face to a book. I thought he must know every tale that had ever been told.

We worked on arithmetic, or history, or spelling in the mornings but every afternoon we'd paint, mix colours, write and read stories; he showed us how we could plant words or pictures on paper like seeds and I bloomed. I made friends, I played in the playground, seeking out all the running, bouncing, skipping games I'd spent so many years watching other children do. At last I had secrets to keep and favours to beg. Some girls might run faster than me, but I could beat them in the clapping games, I could remember all the words of the skipping songs and even better, I could do handstands against the wall. I went on school trips, sitting at the back of the bus with the other big girls, singing ten green bottles as we watched the city disappear, watched the towns give way to the flow of the oh, so much green. I pressed my face to the window, making mists on the glass, played noughts and crosses with my fingers, searched for forests to make my way into, or counted the trees that stood tall and by themselves on the brows of the far off hills. Sometimes the coach would slow down by a hedge and I could watch the way the cows twitched flies from their backs or how, when they were heavy with milk, they dragged their udders so close to the ground that their teats dropped like fingers through the long, lush green. By time we'd been in the coach for two hours we'd be on our fourth verse of 'You'll Never Get to Heaven', speeding along the patchworks of fields and forests, bound to the land by ribbons of hedgerows that drifted and frayed into the open, wind-swept cliffs as we got closer to the sea and the long awaited stretch of beach.

Greenwich, London
January 1964

The fog was so thick today. I couldn't even see the river though I could still hear it, and there was no difference between the ground and the sky and everything was hushed, as if the fog had wrapped the earth in cotton wool. Everybody outside looked like a shadow, I could hardly tell one person from another till I got really close. When I was far away, trying to look in through people's windows, all I could see at first was the glow of their light bulbs. The insides of the rooms looked murky like a reflection in a pool. It made it seem as if everything going on outside was in a different world to what was going on inside the houses, but as I got closer the things on the inside looked almost too sharp and clean.

Me and Teddy had to take a torch to go to school and though I've always thought I knew the way really well, in fact I tripped on the kerb and hurt my knee so badly that when I got to school it was still bleeding and one of the dinner ladies had to put a plaster on it.

Ever since Christmas my mum hasn't been well. First of all she said it was a cold that had gone to her chest but even after two or three weeks it hadn't got better and then she had to go to bed because she could hardly breathe. Me and Teddy made her mint tea. When she went to the doctor he told her she had asthma and gave her an inhaler. I didn't know what having asthma meant so I looked it up in the dictionary at the library. It said Asthma (Az-muh) is a chronic disease that affects the airway. The inflammation (IN-fla-MAY-shun) makes the airways sensitive. When the airways react, they become narrower causing less air to flow through the lung tissue. This may cause symptoms such as coughing, chest tightness, and trouble breathing, especially at night and in the early morning. The dictionary was right.

My mum says asthma can't be cured, but it can be controlled and that's what the inhaler is for. We aren't allowed to clean or even run around the flat because she says the dust goes straight into her lungs and chokes her. I don't miss the cleaning.

Greenwich, London
February 1964

It's evening time and we're watching TV, a film of the fight that happened yesterday.

'Hush now,' Mummy says.

The men are shaking their fists. One is Cassius Clay, he's a boxer and my hero. Last year he had a fight with Henry Cooper and my friends ran around the playground shouting Cassius, Cassius, while others were yelling Henry, Henry, depending on what team they were in. Everyone at school said they were going to watch the fight tonight because it's the Heavyweight Championship of the World.

'I'm gonna float like a butterfly, sting like a bee, your hands can't hit what your eyes can't see,' says Cassius Clay.

Cassius laughs and that makes me smile too because the way he speaks makes everything sound really good with all the rhyming at the end of his sentences.

The camera goes into the boxing ring and the men start fighting. I hide my eyes behind my fingers so I don't have to see how they punch at each other's faces so their eyes start to bleed. Everyone is shouting and yelling for more, more, more and the bell rings again and it's over – Cassius has won! I clap my hands. He *is* the greatest, he *is* the best, I keep shouting, bouncing on the sofa till my mum says be quiet because she's trying to listen to the TV and if I get too excited it will make her chest wheeze, so I sit down.

The reporter says Cassius Clay wants to be known as Muhammad Ali in the future.

I ask my mother, 'Why did Cassius change his name like that?'

'It's because he's in another religion, he's not a Christian any more,' she tells me.

'But that's terrible,' I say and 'I'm really surprised because if he's not a Christian he won't go to heaven, Mummy. Will he, will he?'

Mummy says, 'It's not as simple as that, he doesn't want his name because it came from his slave master.'

I ask, 'What's a slave?'

Now my mum bites her lip, which always means she's thinking or cross or something important is going on in her head.

'It's when someone owns somebody else like they're a cat or a dog,' she says, and then she stops for a while before she continues. 'Years ago, white people went to Africa and took coloured people and brought them to places like America and Jamaica to do the work.' Mum says that in slave times the master that owned you could sell you or your children if he wanted, and you could do nothing about it, you'd never see your family again.

I think that must be the worse thing that can happen to anyone, to lose their children or their parents, so I ask my mum if that happened to anyone in our family.

'Yes,' she says, 'definitely, lots of our ancestors lost their children that way.' And then she starts telling me about the past again. 'When I was young I used to love listening to the old women sitting on the veranda in the evening telling stories

229

of themselves and the old days. You know you can learn as much from listening as from reading. They used to say that the first African from our family was a storyteller, a special man in his own country. He was stolen from his village and sold to a plantation where he became the carpenter and the fiddler of the estate. Being a carpenter was one of the most important jobs you could have as a slave, because they had to teach you how to measure and do sums and you got to work in the Big House, that's how he taught himself to read. He'd be working in the master's house and when he thought no one could see him he'd get hold of the Bible.'

I think that African must have been really smart, because he worked out the words for himself. Mum says he taught himself Latin from that Bible as well as Greek but he was lucky, if his master had found out, he would have been sent to the boiling house which is where they made the sugar and that, Mum says, would have been the end of him.

My mother sat back and was quiet for a while and then I thought – my mum lost her mother and a child as well, not through being sold at an auction or anything like that, but she wasn't allowed to see my sister any more and her own mother died when she was little. That's enough to make anyone feel sad.

My mum's eyes started looking far away and she stopped speaking until suddenly she looked at me and said, 'You need to listen very carefully to what I'm telling you because even though all this slave stuff seems like it happened long ago, it's closer than you think.'

Then she says that the mother of my great-grandmother who looked after me in Jamaica, was actually born a slave. Her name was Sarah Cooke and she worked in the kitchen. She did well for herself because she had a daughter by the master's son and that was lucky because he gave her a house with some land. Her child could almost pass for white and that gave her a better chance to go to school and get an education.

Then my mother starts talking so low it's almost like a whisper. She says knowing this history means you can understand a lot of things that's happened to you already, like why Great-grandma wouldn't have Teddy living in her house. 'You see, white people don't need to brand our skins any more because some coloured people had the mark of slavery burned so deep that some of us still carry the scars on our souls.

'Now your Great-grandmother was a proud woman, but sometimes she was proud of the wrong thing. She didn't have much of that slave colour showing on her skin and she wanted to keep it that way, so she didn't welcome family coming close if they were too coloured. Teddy and his dark skin reminded Grannie of where she'd come from.' Mummy shook her head and then she said, 'History is a hard teacher darlin'. You can try, but you can't turn your back on the past and think it will go away, it stays in your head and it will play tricks on you if you don't know how to watch out for it.'

But I think, as I didn't know about slavery in the first place, how can I forget about it, and I still don't understand what it's got to do with me. What I remember about being coloured is white people spitting in my mum's face, and white people telling me I smell, and on the news the other day there was a story of these three little girls, one who had skin like me, who got blown to pieces when they were at Sunday school. I was scared for weeks after that because I thought, maybe the same thing could happen to me. But then again, people get hurt like that even if they're white don't they? For example, there was President Kennedy. He was white. Mummy told me President Kennedy got killed because he was making laws to help coloured people in America. On the TV they said the President was shot and his head shattered everywhere. After that Mummy took us to sign our names in a commemoration book at the American Embassy. We had to have a bath and get dressed in our best clothes. I was glad I had new plaits and the best yellow ribbons in my hair because an America TV channel called NBC took pictures of me writing my message in the book. I wrote to the people of America and told them how sorry I was for the President's wife and children.

My mum says that millions of people will have seen me doing that on their TVs.

Greenwich, London
July 1964

I'm a collector.
   I collect stamps from envelopes and from a stamp club too.
Belize, Barbados, Bahamas, Bermuda.
   I collect legends from the library.
Hercules, Theseus, Jason and Pandora.
   I collect colours and put them in my spelling book.

Blue

sky blue   midnight blue   navy blue   baby blue   azure
turquoise   topaz   lapis lazuli   indigo   ink blue

By the end of the term my school bag is splitting open because it's full of the recorder music for Greensleeves, a story I wrote about the Queen's coronation and a sheet of sums with red ticks and a gold star stuck at the bottom. I've lost the spelling book, but my head keeps hold of the colour words so I don't need the book any more and I managed to stuff the other things back in my bag.

We worked on speech marks, metaphors and similes at school today. Mr Springer said metaphors and similes are like drawing pictures with words and he gave us some examples like 'all the world's a stage,' and 'my love is like a rose'. It makes your writing more interesting. I'm going to try and use metaphors from now on when I'm writing stories.

At the end of school my friend Margaret came running to me and said, 'So what you doing for the holidays? Do you want to go to the pictures tomorrow?'

Margaret lives on my estate. She is really pretty. Her skin is dark and shiny. My eyes lick the velvet chocolate of her skin. She's bigger than me, which isn't hard, but she's even taller than the boys in our class. Margaret's hair is black and shiny like liquorice, oiled at the front and plaited down her back so it hangs in two long tails. It goes all the way to her waist. My hair is conker brown and fuzzes around my face like a halo. Margaret can run faster than anyone I know. Sometimes I think she's a lost princess, escaped from the lands of the Amazon queen. I read about the Amazons in a poem at school, 'Hippolyta, the long limbed huntress, the warrior bride of King Theseus.'

The Amazons were a totally female society. They never had husbands because they didn't need them, they did everything for themselves. If Amazons had children who were male they gave them away or killed them. My mum is like that, she manages without a husband, though of course, she loves my brothers and would never hurt them. I don't know what it would be like to have a dad. In fact I can hardly imagine I ever had one, it's as if all of me was made by my mother. There are times when I try to think what having a dad would be like, but I don't get very far. Lots of my friends with dads get shouted at or smacked, or their dads come home drunk, or go running off with other women all the time and that makes me think, maybe I'm better off without one. One night we went with Mum to the pub at the corner to get cherryade and crisps. We had to wait outside. When my mum came out this man came after her and started getting funny, asking if he could come back to our flat. My mum told him no again and again, but then he was shouting and his face was getting red. Teddy had to make him go away. That man made me feel really frightened. In the end I think I'm happiest with our family just the way it is. Mum says when I'm old enough she'll tell me all about my dad.

Vroom, vroom, the cars go by, choking the street so I cover up my ears till the rag 'n' bone man has caught up with us and he's driving his cart right next to me. The cookers and saucepans on his wagon rattle-crash-bang as he goes by. The horse claps his hooves on the road as if he's counting one two, one two. Margaret and me have to run as fast as our legs will take us to keep up with the cart then the rag man shouts, 'Rag 'n' bo-one, rag and bone!'

'Giddy-up,' I yell and I lift my knees till I'm galloping along as good as any old horse and I neigh. The rag man looks up for a moment, flicks the reins and speeds round the corner.

'Uhh!' Margaret yells. She points and laughs at the piles of horse mess that are left steaming in the street. 'Hol-lid-days!' Margaret shouts again, as if she's won the prize for the best work at school and then she spins on her heels like a top and says, 'So what you doing now Jackie?' But she doesn't wait for my answer. 'D'you want to come round the shops for a bit?'

Margaret always has money, she gets it from showing her minge to the boys at school. They go mad when they see it. Hers has hair. I don't like it when she shows it, but I do like her and Margaret doesn't care what anyone, even me, thinks of what she does.

We skip past the traffic, brrrmm, brrrrm, then we turn up towards Goddard's, our favourite pie and mash shop.

Goddard's is busy. The walls are always steaming brown and warm with the smells of pies and eels and the cigarette smoke that goes up to the ceiling. For the cost of my pocket money on a weekend spree I can get a ticket for Saturday morning pictures at the Odeon or the ABC and come back to Greenwich for a pie and mash dinner with mushy peas and hot, green gravy liquor.

Margaret pushes the door.

'Right,' Margaret says. 'Let's go over there.' She points to the seat by the corner.

We ask the lady for beef pie and mash then we sit on a bench, pick up our knives and forks and tap them on the table as if we're singing, 'Why are we waiting?'

'What you doing for the summer then?' Margaret asks.

'I don't know. I'll go to the pictures tomorrow morning if you want but I'll have to look after my brother in the holidays when my mum is at work.'

Margaret nods, 'I have to look after my brother as well.'

Margaret always has to do a lot of work in her house because her mum left home and her dad says she needs to learn how to be a proper woman. Margaret says she hates her mum now. My mum told me I need to learn how to play and laugh even more than I do because that is what being a proper woman really is and life is hard enough without making it worse.

Margaret lives at Rockfield House, me in Delaney, right at the other end of Thames Street, so when we say goodbye I have to hop-scotch run past the no-where yards of the blocks I've never been into till I come to the pub and turn into my flats. It's full of children playing but I can't stop because I promised my mum I'd be back when she got home from work. I open the door with the key from my neck, rub my eyes and drop my bag as soon as I get inside. After being in the sun our flat seems really dark and I can't see a thing till I blink and my sight comes back and then I run past the kitchen and slam the door – bang!

I jump on the sofa, switch on the telly and close my eyes while I wait for the picture to warm up.

'Jackie!'

I turn my head.

'Jackie.'

It's my mum calling. I wonder what she's doing back early so I shouted, 'What?' and ran into her room.

'Hello Mum.' But I didn't understand what she was trying to say. All I could hear was her gasping.

April 2004

When I tried to speak to Eleanor of how things had been after my mother got sick the truth is, I struggled to recall it. I could talk about anything else; my mother's views on the weather, or politics or religion – I think she had more opinions than anyone I've heard speak. I could describe the kind of clothes she wore, the way her eyebrows arched without being pencilled in, the colour of her skin, that easy way she had, her sway, that dark muscovado, straight from the juice, swinging rhythm of her hips, of her lips, her voice; how could I forget it – the heat of the tropics wrapped up in New York chic. My mother could fill a room to bursting just by opening her mouth; she licked my world into shape, caught words in her mouth and once she found the ones she liked, she savoured them.

'Perhaps in this neglected spot is laid,' she'd say, sweeping a hand past the debris of our room,

'Some heart once pregnant with celestial fire;
Hands that the rod of empire might have sway'd,
Or waked to ecstasy the living lyre.'

She lifted our lives with prose, or verse, old time hymns, jazz, or swing, she was never one to discriminate, nothing was spared, not a word. She wrapped rhythms around her tongue as if they were a mink stole and when she had them where she wanted she'd twist them, let them drip from her shoulders, till she became Billie, or Ella, or Mahalia Jackson.

Or she'd take an old song, something she'd learnt as a child, like the one she heard when she'd stood with her mother watching soldier-boys coming back to Jamaica from the First World War. My mother said the city was choked that day, streets so full that the crowds had to stand twenty deep at the corners. She recalled the heat, the sweat on her hands, the band drumming 'Tipperary' with the sun set to boiling in a Caribbean sky. Soon as they heard the drums the crowd went crazy, must have been a thousand flags were waving, their tails flicking and popping, happy as church-going ribbons. The crowd sang 'Rule Britannia' as loud as their voices would let them; schoolbooks had wrapped the memory of their beginnings in so much amnesia they'd forgotten it was their parents who'd once been the slaves. So they shouted out the lines anyway, cheering for their dear motherland, for their King and country, for the triumph of an empire that was so almighty it could keep their hearts blazing even through the winds of their own black history.

> Kitchener wa'an a bundle of grass
> Te ra ra boom,
> Kitchener wa'an a bundle of grass
> To stuff up the Kaiser's ass,
> Inky, pinky, parlez-vous

And she'd show us how the country women used to sing it, stooping and scooping her skirt and dancing lewd, swaying her hips, legs set like trees on the lino floor. If I was lucky she'd go on to tell us more stories, tales of Brer Rabbit, or Anansi the spider, or how, when she was small, the market women still wore their dresses so full that they could do wee-wees in the street without being seen, they just stooped down a hem's inch till their skirts trailed the ground and when they were finished they'd stand up again, and all that you'd see were the puddles they'd left behind. Or she'd say how all the dead people who lived in her street walked around as zombies, bold as you or me, or that Great-grandmother could tell the future just by looking in her mirror at night. And after all her stories were finished we'd get hungry for the Island, for the taste of fried plantain, of spicy meat patties, of sweet tamarind balls sucked till they turned sour. I wanted to tell Eleanor all this, show her every space that was left in my memory before I had to start at the ending, taking us to that room again, back to the way I'd found my mother that after-noon, sitting on the bed covers, the rose of her mouth turning blue as she flapped me away with her hands.

Greenwich, London
October 1964

I'm the watcher.

   I watch the clouds from my window.

   I watch the river and follow which way the tide is running by raising my hand against my eyes and measuring where the water is with my fingers.

   I watch for the fog rising and look at the world as it goes past the window so I don't have to watch my mother when she's not feeling too good.

I got a book from the library on *Legends of the Classical World*. There was a whole chapter on what Greeks and Romans thought would happen to them in the afterlife.

   In Christian stories the difference between heaven and hell is simple; heaven is white, full of light, with angels singing and flying around but apart from that nothing much seems to happen. Hell is all fire and sulphur with devils tormenting the souls of sinners. The Ancients believed the Afterworld had a geography, just like the one of Earth we learn at school. The part called Elysian was for heroes and the virtuous, Tartarus was like hell, a place of endless punishment. All through the Underworld there were mountains and rivers and pools that had wonderful powers. The river Styx separated the world of the living from the dead. If you were lucky enough to understand the secrets of the Gods, after you died you'd know to drink from the river of memory called Mnemosyne instead of drinking from Lethe, the river which made spirits forget what had happened when they were alive.

I think if you can't remember what has happened to you it must stop you being the person you were meant to be. Perhaps that's why the dead in Hades are called shades because they are shadows of themselves, not knowing who they really are.

The River Thames runs beside our flat. Everyday it looks different. I found a bottle once with a note inside it. Some water had got on the paper so I couldn't read what it said but somebody had taken the trouble to send it on its way without ever knowing if it would be found and read. I took it home to show my mother. She said bringing up a daughter sometimes feels like she's sending a message in a bottle.

When the tide is low I play on the beach that the water leaves behind, or I collect wood and left-over coal for the fire, or go hunting to see if I can find other treasure that has been washed overboard from a ship.

When the tide is high the river swirls against the banks, lapping at the sides as if it wants to burst out and spill onto the grass. The Thames is one of the most famous rivers in the world. Sometimes I go under the river, through the foot tunnel, on my roller skates. I have to hide my skates because the sign at the entrance says no bikes and no spitting.

Greenwich, London
November 1964

Roy has gone to sleep and the fire is going out. Teddy is drawing and the TV is on. I'd like to get more coal but there's none left in the bag. If there's enough money, Teddy will have to go to the coal yard tomorrow on his way from getting Roy from nursery. Mummy says we have to be even more careful what we spend now she hasn't been at work for such a long time. She hasn't been feeling too good.

I'm trying to read my book because I don't like *77 Sunset Strip* and there isn't anything else on TV.

Mummy has been in her room a long time, since before it got dark. She went to bed early today, she does that all the time now. Teddy doesn't want to play either, he's just drawing cartoons in his notebook. He doesn't look up, even when I talk and ask him to.

I wish I was more like Teddy, he's the best boy I know, he's kind and funny and he's never even scared. My big brother can do everything. He can ice-skate and jump in the air and land and still be smiling. He can do cartwheels and walk on his hands and make Vesta Chow Mein from the packet so the noodles are crispy on the top. Sometimes it feels as if I'm frightened all the time. For example, I'm scared of the dark, of strangers, of spiders, of mice and of water. Even though I like playing down the river, I think drowning or suffocating must be the worse way to die. Once, when I went to the swimming pool with my brother and his friends, they threw me in the deep end of the pool. I thought I was going to die but Teddy jumped in and saved me. That's why I'm never frightened when Teddy is with me. One day I think my brother will be famous like an astronaut or a politician or someone on TV.

Sometimes Teddy saves his pocket money till he has a one pound note. I spend money as soon as I get it. Once, when he had more than one pound, he shared it with me. I bought a torch that had a key ring on it and a do-it-yourself Pearllery kit. I made a bracelet and a necklace in one evening. But even though Teddy is the best boy ever, I still think my mother loves me the most because she always says I'm special.

One night, when I went into my mum's bedroom, when she'd been there too long, just like now, I saw her sitting on the bed. First of all I thought she was having another asthma attack but her hands were over her face and she never does that when she's trying to breathe. Then, when she looked up, I could see she'd been crying because tears were running down her cheeks.

'What's the matter Mummy?' I asked her, and then I said, 'Don't cry.'

This time she let me sit next to her because her breathing was coming in and out quite well.

'I'm crying for my mother,' she said. 'I miss her so much.'

Then I thought, how about that? How about the fact that my mummy, who is big enough to do whatever she wants, is crying for her own mother who died such a long time ago.

I said, 'Don't cry any more Mummy, please.'

It always makes me feel bad to see Mummy like that so I tried to find something to say that would help her feel better. 'What was your mum like?' I said, then I kept asking questions, and I kissed her again, and she put her arm around me so we could lie on the bed together.

My mum stroked my head, 'My best, best girl,' she said. 'If only my own dear mother could see you now, she'd be so proud,' and then she smiled. 'My mother was the most beautiful woman I've ever seen and she was clever as well, she could do just about any sum in her head and she was always kind, never smacking or shouting at us the way my father did. When she was around our house was alive with the sound of her singing.'

That made me think how much my grandmother sounded like my own mother. Then Mummy told me that she was only little when her mother died, just eight years old. That's not much bigger than my baby brother. The trouble was, the thought of my mother being by herself made me want to cry as well so I tried not to think about it and I kissed my mother again, and thought I'd better change the subject and I searched for something happy to say. I told Mum that one day I would get a good job that paid lots of money and then I'd bring her to live in my house and I'd look after her. I'd get her anything she wanted, bring it from the shops on my way from work, or I'd order it from a catalogue if I needed to, and she could stay in bed every day and never have to worry about getting up or having a job ever again, unless she wanted one. That seemed to work because then Mummy smiled and hugged me and said, 'I'll hold you to that. Thank you for trying to make me feel better.'

But I wasn't trying because I meant every word I'd said, so that night, after I'd done my prayers and was waiting to fall asleep, I made a promise to God that I'd work hard every day at school so that when I grow up I'll have enough money to look after Mummy properly. Anyway, what I told her must have been a good thing to say because it did make her happy and I got to sleep in her bed and I woke up the next morning without having any dreams.

Greenwich, London
February 1965

It's cold outside but if I sit by the fire I can stay warm. Sometimes now, when it gets too cold, me and Mummy sleep in the living room on the sofa bed.

Today the frost didn't melt and the sun wasn't warm at all. I could almost look straight at it. Even the grass was frozen so it looked as if someone had sprinkled icing sugar all over and the ground crunched like candy every time someone walked on it.

Teddy had his birthday last week. He says now he's fifteen years old he's almost a full grown man so I can't share his bed any more, but that's not a good reason because Mummy is a full grown woman and she lets me sleep in her bed all the time and she's much older than him.

Tonight, on the news, they said that someone called Malcolm X had been shot dead by other coloured men. My mum said it was terrible thing that the community was eating its own tail.

'What do you mean?' I asked.

'Coloured people shouldn't be killing each other,' she said, 'there are enough white people wanting to do that! And anyway,' she tossed her head, 'even if you don't agree with someone, it doesn't mean they should be dead.'

I asked what the argument was about and she said it was complicated, about politics, which was good because I'm interested in things like that.

'Why did he have such a funny name, "X". Where did that come from?'

I could see my mum wasn't feeling like talking but I took no notice and I asked her again.

'Well you see,' she said, 'Brother Malcolm stopped being a Christian, that's why he changed his name.'

Then I thought, that's another one; first there was Cassius Clay who became Muhammad Ali and now there's Brother Malcolm becoming an X; where's it going to stop? Perhaps I'll wake up one day and I'll become Jackie Y. I don't think that will happen, not really, because I would be too scared of not being able to get into heaven.

'Malcolm X says coloured people like us don't have real names, what we've been left with as our names are really the trademark of the family who once owned us. Our real names were taken from us when our ancestors were stolen from Africa.' My mother shakes her head.

Well, I never knew that, I mean, my mum has told me about slave times but I never thought about how African people must have had their own African names before they were made into slaves. And once my mum started speaking, it's was as if nothing could stop her, like the things that Malcolm X believed has reminded her of other things she's wanted to say for a long time and suddenly more stories were falling from her mouth.

'Me and your father met in October 1952. First time I saw him he made my heart leap. He was a good man. We were at a meeting, and they decided we should both go South to help the Organisation'.

So then Mum told me about the Civil Rights Movement that she had been in, and McCarthyism and the Communist Party and the way that some people, coloured and white, have died to make sure everyone can eat in the same restaurants together. Even my mum and dad got beaten up when they were on a protest. I hope when I grow up I can be that brave.

I wanted to ask her more questions about my father and politics but I knew if I interrupted her she might stop all her stories.

Then, suddenly she said, 'I am sorry for leaving you in Jamaica the way I did, it must have been hard, but you know, I had no choice. I had to get a job and find a place where our future could begin. The thing is, I couldn't have stepped away from you if I'd seen you crying.'

And that made me forget about asking more about my father because I wanted to tell my mother what had happened when she left me, the way I had cried each night, that I didn't want to eat, that it wasn't ever fair and all right to go away like that and not say goodbye, that I was lonely without her or Teddy, and that Granny was too strict and beat me every day for not eating my dinner. While I was talking I saw tears were coming in her eyes.

Mummy said, 'I want to show you something.' Mummy pulled down her nightdress, 'Can you see those marks across my shoulders, those stripes across my back?' I nod my head. 'Well,' she said, 'when I was just a bit older than you are now and I was becoming a woman, my daddy made me tie my breasts down with rope so the boys wouldn't see I was growing. Then one day he found me talking to some boys, nothing else, I was just having conversation, so he cut a fresh switch and he took me to his room and he beat me till my back was running raw.'

I've seen the scars on her back. My mum was lucky that time because my great-grandmother came round and saw what was happening and saved her.

'You see darlin', what I'm trying to say is that loving anyone is hard work, but knowing how to love, especially how to love a child, that can be the worst, most complicated kind of love there is. My daddy and your great-grandmother were hard on you and me, but that didn't mean they didn't love us.'

Mummy rubbed her hands towards the fire and coughed before she went on speaking.

'Daddy and Grannie were brought up on the edge of slavery times. They were dragged up with the whip on their backs and the words of the Old Testament slapped into their ears. It wasn't that they didn't love me or you, it's more that they didn't know how to love us any better than they did. And when I left you on the Island it wasn't because I didn't care, it was more that I didn't know how to say goodbye, or maybe I just couldn't face it. I know it was wrong, but it happened because I loved you and I couldn't do any better, not at the time.'

My mum's face didn't move.

I never realised that loving was something that needed learning as if it was maths or history, but thinking about it now I can see it must be true because it makes sense of how even my mother sometimes gets things wrong. And suddenly I see it's the same for me, when I don't understand how something works I can behave badly. So after that we sat and were quiet with each other until I put my arms around her and said, 'Mummy, I know you love me and you've always tried to do your best. Just promise that if you ever have to go away again that you will make sure to say goodbye and you will always come back. Promise me, Mummy.'

My mother said she promised, and she crossed her heart without hoping to die and I knew she meant it, so I put my head back on her lap and she kept stroking my hair and it was lovely. But I still don't think I'll ever change my name because even if it belongs to a slave master, I've had it for a long time and that makes it part of my history now as well as his, doesn't it?

April 2004

'By the time the first signs of spring were blowing from the river, warmer winds than those were stirring in me, and though I didn't know how it would happen, I could feel my body was changing and I began to look forward to what those changes might mean. Somehow, I thought, growing up would happen overnight. Maybe one morning I'd wake up and find my body curved with hips. I decided the best thing I could do was to get in some practice before it really happened. I took cotton wool from my mother's dressing table and stuffed handfuls of it inside my vest. I checked mirrors, I used my mother's lipstick, I walked like a woman, swaying my hips as I passed my reflection and I tried to imagine how it would look to be the grown-up me. But while I was attending to what was happening to my body, other things were going on in my head that I was less aware of; however much I loved her, I was starting to find my mother an increasing source of embarrassment. At first I tried to keep my opinions to myself but the breaking point came in the spring of 1965.'

My mother announced she had decided to have her own Easter parade. I protested. She laughed. What did it matter if I slammed a few doors, I'd come round to her way of thinking, and who cared if parading at Easter wasn't done in Greenwich; that was even better, she'd be the first to initiate it. She started by making us matching red blouses with little cap sleeves and smocking at the waist. On my almost flat chest the blouse looked demure, but on her more than hour-glass figure it was an eye-stopper, and she loved it. She wore her best boned corset underneath the red blouse and by carefully levering each breast into the cupped supports of the corset and pulling the ties at the sides until she could hardly breathe, the results she achieved were dramatic. Mother looked as though she had devised a way to defy every one of Newton's laws of gravity. The whole outfit, including me and my flat chest walking besides her, was designed to cause a riot, and it did. She thought we looked cute. We walked from Greenwich to the park gates at Blackheath and back again. She did the whole performance in her highest heeled red stilettoes, parading down the street as if she was on the catwalk. It was a miracle we didn't have an accident or cause one. While other, normal families were strolling in the park in practical clothes and flat shoes, my mother was shimmying her way up the hill and wobbling all the way back down again, smiling knowingly each time a man blew his horn or turned to get a better view. I was devastated, I protested more and more and as the afternoon went on, I withered. I wanted to curl up or disappear. By time we got home she was rubbing her bunions with satisfaction. I stormed into the bedroom. How could she behave like that I shouted, using me in that way, making us both look so . . . ridiculous. She took no notice. I had no doubt that having a mother like mine was not just an irritation, it was a downright humiliation; she talked too loud, laughed too much, and even if she managed to reach the highest notes she hardly ever sang the right words, and she was almost always out of key. It seemed extraordinary that it had taken me this long to discover that life with my mother was, in fact, insufferable. When she took us to the cinema or came to speak to the teachers at school, why did she have to wear *that* dress, with *that* hat – and her lipstick! I was coming to the realisation that I didn't have to do or be everything my mother wanted, but before I could begin to understand what this revelation might mean the fog came back from the river for the last time that spring and my mother was taken into the Miller Hospital at Greenwich. We stayed home. It seemed like a game at first, or something from a book; a South London version of *Swallows and Amazons* or better still *Little Women*, with me playing the part of Marmee. When we weren't at school we went to the hospital. They put my mother in a room by herself, perhaps because she coughed at night, or perhaps to make it easier for us to see her outside visiting hours. Sometimes my mother could barely speak for wheezing, then we'd sit by her bed and tell her what was happening at home. The nurses made us hot chocolate and patted our heads and my mother doled out money every day; just enough for food and coal if it was needed, and a shilling to feed the electric meter.

When I think of it now it seems extraordinary that the Social Services allowed us to stay home and look after ourselves, but they did, and for a while we managed quite well. I did the best I could, which in truth, was not very well, and Teddy did the rest. We went to school in mostly clean clothes and ate some kind of meal every day even if all we had to do was add water and heat to a packet, but after a week or so it got too much for us and Roy was taken into care.'

Greenwich, London
March 1965

My mum is coming home from hospital today. Teddy and me have cleaned up the flat so it will look nice when she gets back. Roy isn't coming back until next week because he's too much work and my mum needs a rest. When they took Roy away he hardly cried at all, he just sucked his thumb and kept calling my name. Teddy said we had no choice, we had to let him go.

It was a lovely, fresh looking morning. A day for going down to the river or playing in the park. On the grass outside the front room the daffodils have just opened up, they've been growing fast all week, I've watched them changing each day. So this morning I picked some and put them in a vase for Mummy to see. Mummy likes gladioli the best but I hope the daffodils will make her happy.

Everything is ready, Mummy told us she'd be home at three o'clock. It's two-thirty now so while I'm waiting I'm reading the story of Orpheus and his wife Eurydice.

Orpheus loved his wife so much that when she died he went to the Underworld to try and get her back again. In the book there's a picture that shows Orpheus going into hell with all these ghosts coming towards him. Orpheus played the lyre so well that King Hades and Queen Persephone said he could have Eurydice back as long as he left their land without looking behind him; it's a test.

When I went to the kitchen to get a drink I tried to pretend I was Orpheus in the Underworld and there was someone I loved walking behind me. I made it to the door without turning but it's hard to tell what would really happen because if someone I loved was dead and I hadn't seen them for a long time I know I would be tempted to turn around. Just as I was going back to the front room I heard a key in the door and Mummy was there. She rushed in and out, just shouting hello because she had to pay the taxi.

I was so happy to see my mum that I ran at her and she went shaky so I had to hold her really tight, but the first thing she said was, 'You could have cleaned up the house if you knew I was coming.'

She didn't even notice what we had done, or how pleased we were to see her. After that Mummy went to her room and closed the door. I was upset but Teddy said not to worry, that Mummy would be all right, she just needed time to settle down. Teddy was right because later she seemed to cheer up. I heard her singing so I knocked on the door.

'Come in,' she said. I walked quietly this time and lay on top of the covers gently so I wouldn't disturb Mum too much. Then Teddy came and asked my mum if there was anything she needed.

'I'm sorry about what happened when I came home. I know it must have been hard for you when I was sick and I want you to know I feel really lucky to have such good children at home to help me,' she wiped her eyes. 'And look at these,' she pointed to the flowers on the sill, 'how lovely they are. You two thought of everything.'

So then all of us were smiling and cuddling and my mother was stroking our heads, and everything was back the way it should be.

July 2004

'Even when my mother was out of hospital she was too sick to go back to work so we were living on Social Security again; that didn't help. It was cold enough to need a fire every day but at times, when the money ran out before the next cheque came, we were cold, and it was wet that autumn; the wind was the only thing that seemed to keep the rain off the windows. Because the air was damp my mother took to sleeping on the sofa in the front room every night but even then it was hard to make her comfortable. She'd try lying on three or four pillows, she'd stoke up the fire before we went to bed to keep the place warm; we went scavenging by the river to get as much wood or coal that we could find, but whatever we tried she still coughed all night, and even in the day she struggled for breath. Of course we thought we were looking after Mother very well, but it wasn't easy. When she was tired she got listless and withdrawn, when she wasn't exhausted she was irritable in a way we'd never known before. She'd yell at us from the sofa or lean against a doorway tapping her foot. She told us we were selfish, that she blamed herself for making us into such spoilt children.'

'Didn't that make you angry?' Eleanor asked.

'Yes, it did. But I'm sure what she said was true, after all, we could never do enough to help her; we were children. I think I just accepted the way things were. I distracted myself; and anyway I was getting older, things were changing for me too. I was getting more interested in what was going on outside of my family. So for most of the time I carried on as if my mother wasn't really sick, it wasn't hard, there were still days when she seemed hardly changed, when her symptoms were under control.'

Greenwich, London
March 1965

Today, when I came back from school, Mummy was still laying on the sofa.

'Are you all right?' I asked. She picked up an envelope that had stamps on it from America. I knew where the stamps were from because I have the whole set in the front page of my collection.

'They've found Pearl. The Salvation Army have found her and they've given her our address.'

I was so happy because for as long as I can remember my mother has been trying to find Pearl. My mum said she'll send Pearl money for a ticket to come and see us soon.

'How old is Pearl?' I asked.

'She's nearly nineteen years old.'

'Fan-tastic!' I said, because that means she's grown up. I jumped up and down. 'I'm going to tell my friends that my big sister is coming from America and maybe they can come and meet her.'

But I probably shouldn't have jumped around so much because it started Mum coughing again, and that night I had to sleep in my own bed because she was still not feeling well. She said I was too excitable and fidgeted too much.

The next Saturday Mummy took us to Waterloo Station to make a record in a booth to send to Pearl because she said my sister hadn't heard our voices for such a long time. We went in the afternoon. Roy stayed in his pushchair because he's too little to speak, but me and Teddy stood outside the booth and when my mum had put the money in the slot and finished speaking she told me and Teddy to send a message to Pearl. It was hard to know what to say, but when we'd finished and played it back, it was strange to hear my own voice like that. I never knew how I sounded when I was speaking.

April 2004

'That's the recording you've heard before; do you remember?'

Eleanor nodded. 'But it was some time ago and I didn't really understand the significance.'

'All things considered, it's amazing it survived. We were lucky that Teddy had the sense to put it on tape.'

I took the cassette and fed it into the machine. There was a pause and then the far-off voice of my mother began running underneath the furry static of the scratched vinyl recording.

'Hello Pearl, I'm so sorry I had to be away from you for so long, for six long years, but I know you missed me as much as I missed you and that we'll soon be together. I – I only wish your father was sensible and would let bygones be bygones and let us all be friends again. We have a lot more experience now and we should be able to forgive one another. C'mon Teddy, say something to your sister.'

'Hello Pearl, I haven't seen you for a long time, please come over as soon as you can, we're all anxious to see you.'

*'Hello, this is Jackie here, this is your baby sister
that used to be! I love you so much . . . and now I'll
hand you over to Mummy.'*

'Why does your mother say it was six years since she's seen
Pearl?' Eleanor asked.

'I have no idea, maybe she was confused, it must have
been pretty hectic with us kids running around, and we
didn't have more than a couple of minutes.'

'I'm surprised she could be so forgiving to Clifford.'

'Well, I think my mother was so happy to be back in
touch with Pearl she just wanted everything to be alright,
it was her dream, and she was determined that nothing would
spoil it. And the truth was, since she'd heard from Pearl
everything had got better, the days were warmer and her
health had improved, it was as if she'd found a second wind.'

Well, Mother said, it was true, maybe she could still feel
the scars but they were from the past and she'd healed;
hadn't she learnt her lessons, served her time, suffered long
enough for her sins to deserve a happy ending? She went
back into her wardrobes. Even from the front room I could
hear my mother talking to herself as she pulled out this
jacket or lifted that dress from its hanger and saw the signs
of her recent neglect; the dust on the shoulders, the holes
at the hems, the moths, dear Lord, the moths! But whatever
the damage to her wardrobe she was singing again and
however it sounded I was glad to hear it. Now each day
seemed to rush by, spurred on by the whirr and click of her
mending and making. Every table and shelf space my mother

could find was taken up with piles of clothes and material, packets of paper patterns, button boxes, different sized scissors and stitch-pickers, reels of binding and every-colour-you-can-think-of thread. As soon as she'd finished mending clothes she unpacked her sewing machine and began making things: new spring dresses for both of us, curtains for the living room, even a tablecloth. She'd bought a brand new electric machine, the kind that has its own light. That electric machine was voracious, it raced over garments, screaming as it went, churning out buttonholes, fancy embroidery and every kind of stitch mother could need or imagine. But my mother never used it. The machine she loved she got secondhand from Deptford market. When I was young I thought 'Singer' described the way that old machine purred when my mother pumped its treadle. It was a beautiful thing, and just like its name said, it sang while she sewed, anything my mother wanted, always keeping rhythm to the timing of her feet. Its lines were as graceful as a piece of fine sculpture, its black surface inlaid with little pieces of mother of pearl which fell in iridescent spirals from a wreath of gold vines that coiled their way around its enamelled body. I had two jobs when my mother was using the Singer, threading the needle and bobbin to save my mother's eyes and feeding the material through my hands so it landed neatly on the floor. When my mother had finished with the sewing there were letters to write, floors to clean; I can hardly remember the place looking better, clothes that had been dropped on the bathroom floor were washed, pressed and folded into drawers, the magazines and books that had been stacked behind doors or tucked out of sight by the side of chairs for months were thrown out or put away, beds were stripped, the kitchen was scrubbed to the ceiling till at last, everything was ready for Pearl's homecoming visit.

Greenwich, London
April 1965

L ast week was my birthday, I was eleven years old. I got a tin of talcum powder and a new school bag.

This is my last year at Saint Peter's Primary School. In September I will go to secondary school. It's Roy's last year at nursery as well, so it seems as if a lot of things are changing for us.

We had to get up early this morning because my big sister is coming from America. I like saying that, my big sister, because I've never even had a little sister before. I wonder what someone from America looks like.

I had a bath last night and put my clothes on the chair before I went to sleep so I would be ready to go to the airport. I'm going to wear my pink earrings with the silver clasps and the red knitted dress that my mum got from the jumble sale last week.

My mum says we have to tell Pearl how much we love her because she's been living without us for so long she has missed out on what we've got because she didn't have a mother or brother and sisters whereas we've been lucky to have each other.

Last week I bought 'Ticket to Ride', the new record by the Beatles, and now it's the number one hit. I saw *A Hard Day's*

Night at the cinema three times last year but I didn't scream.
I thought the girls that were screaming and crying were stupid.

We had to get two trains and the underground to go to
the airport. We stood for a long time at Arrivals watching
people come out. We stayed for more than two hours and
then Mummy said we'd better wait some more, but then she
started crying and people were turning and staring at her. I
said to my mum 'Never mind' and tried to cuddle her, but
she was gone already, busy in her head, the way she gets, and
then she listed the reasons why Pearl might not have arrived
which included:

1) that she'd missed the plane

2) that she wasn't very well

3) that she'd changed her mind

Number three was the worse thought, and after that we
went home.

April 2004

Suddenly the weather had turned to winter again, cold enough to keep me and Eleanor inside. As I opened the blinds that morning I saw the garden was covered with snow. It was so beautiful; deep enough to pull at the branches, and it kept falling for hours, coiling in the eddies that ran between the trees till the borders disappeared. It gave Eleanor and me even more reason to spend time talking together.

'I heard from the American Immigration Service this morning.' I picked up the envelope. I had wanted Eleanor to share my excitement but she seemed reserved.

'They say they have more information relating to my mother, that the departments will forward the documents directly to me. It's funny, even though I've been waiting for years I'm not sure how I feel.'

'Why not?' asked Eleanor.

'Sometimes life's easier to leave things as they are.'

'I think we should try to find out everything.'

'Yes, in the end of course I agree. But there have been times when piecing together what happened to us has felt more like a burden than anything.'

'But Mum, that's how survived. Look at most people who've been in Homes; they end up in prison or mental hospitals, abusing themselves or their children. Maybe you could have tried to forget what happened, avoiding the pain for a while, but not remembering would have meant cutting yourself off from your emotions.'

'And then I wouldn't have what I've got today,' I looked at Eleanor and smiled. 'I know it, and in the end, that's why I'll never let it go, I just need to remind myself sometimes.'

'Good,' Eleanor said. 'So tell me,' she stroked my head, 'how did your mother react when Pearl didn't appear at the airport?'

'I don't recall exactly, I don't think she said much, and it's funny, because within a day the flat was looking exactly the way it always did; everything on the floor, dishes in the sink, piles of things everywhere . . . But two days later, just after I'd got back from school, there was a knock. I was by myself and under strict orders not to let anyone in, so I stood in the hallway, looking at the shadow that was peering through the glass.'

Greenwich, London
April 1965

When I opened the door Pearl was wearing a hat, a neat, small hat that sat on the back of her head. It made her look like an air hostess. I could see why my mother had talked about her so much because it was true, she was tall and beautiful and her voice was deep and smooth. She sounded like a film star. I told her, 'Come in,' and we stood for a moment just staring at each other.

At first I couldn't speak, but neither did she, and whatever my mother had wanted me to do, it didn't seem right to tell my sister I loved her, not straight away, because I wasn't sure who she really was, so I stared even more, and she looked at me, till at last we both smiled.

That's when I first noticed that when Pearl laughs she likes to cover her mouth just the way my mum does, and I saw she has hands like my mother's with long nails too, although Pearl's were painted red.

'When will Momma be home?' Pearl asked.

'Not long,' I answered, 'she's only at the shops.'

I could feel my face burning because Pearl had noticed my dress. I'd come straight from school and there were stains down the front where I'd dropped gravy from my dinner. Pearl looked perfect, little gold earrings and matching shoes with her dark blue dress. She was looking around, as if her eyes were searching for something. I asked if she wanted a drink, I was glad when she said 'Yes' because then I could escape to the kitchen. When I came back Pearl seemed more relaxed and she smiled and brushed her hand across the sofa.

'I brought some presents. There's even one for you, would you like it now?' She opened her suitcase, took out a packet from the pocket of the lid. 'Here you go.' It was a box of Hershey bars. My brother had already told me about American candy, especially Hershey chocolate and pretzels. The way my brother had described them you would think they were the best sweets in the world, but now I've tasted them I think Cadbury's is just as good.

While her case was open Pearl said she might as well show me the presents she'd brought for everyone else. There was perfume called Manhattan with a fancy cut-glass bottle for my mother, a toy car like a Cadillac for Roy, and comic books for Teddy. I think I would have preferred a book, but I didn't have time to say anything because straight away Pearl was asking me questions about how long we'd lived here and what I did at school. The truth is, I didn't listen to a word she said because all I could think of was the way my throat was getting tight and how my voice didn't sound like it was mine any more, and the way the living room, which yesterday was my comfortable home, seemed so shabby that I wanted to pretend I didn't live there any more.

Pearl didn't notice I wasn't paying attention, or maybe it didn't worry her, because she kept talking about her apartment and how she worked in an office and was hoping to go back to school. I thought she looked a bit old for school, but she laughed and said that was what they called college in America.

So then I really blushed and wished someone else would come home to save me from having to talk to Pearl by myself, and at last, thank goodness, my mother came through the door, and there was lots of hugging and kissing.

It's funny how sometimes talking can make you feel more mixed-up than saying nothing at all, but the strangest thing was that with Pearl in the flat, everything changed, not just how I felt but how everyone behaved and how things looked. It seemed to me as if our family must have drunk a magic potion, like people do in fairy tales, because suddenly we started eating meals at the table, and we had to be quiet in the mornings, we even stopped watching TV all the time and, worst of all, we had to sleep in our own beds. I decided I didn't want to be my mother's best girl any more. Then I got clumsy, started knocking things over, and our flat, which had always been quite big enough, was suddenly too small, as if there was no space left for me. It seemed that I was the only one who noticed these changes so I began to go out with my friends as much as I could because they don't spend all day talking about America and how great everything is there.

No one seemed to notice or mind.

Greenwich, London
May 1965

I think I was lucky Pearl came this spring because as soon as she arrived the weather got warmer. It seemed as if the sun had been waiting for me to come and play so it could kick up its heels. And after all the cold and rain, even though it was only May, it felt as if it was summer already, except the flowers and leaves were coming out new so everything was fresh and still sparkling clean.

On the first Saturday after Pearl came to stay, Margaret and me went down to the river early, before my sister even got out of bed. We put our arms round each other's waist so we could roller skate without falling as we chased pigeons round the tea clipper ship. Then we raced to the park, ran up and down shouting to each other till we found ourselves dancing underneath the big old trees where the branches hang low so they almost reach the grass and we could lay underneath and pretend we were inside a tent. The flowers grow thick there and the air smells sweet. We had to shove our noses into the petals, take our shoes off, brush our toes against the petals till it felt as if they were our bedside mats. I could have stayed there forever, watching people's feet walking by, trying to imagine, just by looking at the

shoes, what the rest of their bodies looked like. Most of
the time, when we sat up, we saw our imaginations had got
it wrong, but it didn't matter because it made us laugh so
much! Then Margaret said she had enough money for
canoes, that I could be Pocahontas if she was Hiawatha,
so we ran to the boating pond at the bottom of the hill
and bought a ticket, and that's who we became, speeding
on the water, my thoughts keeping time to the rhythm of
the song, thinking little pounding thoughts each time the
paddle hit the water.

> My paddle's clean and bright
> Flashing with silver,
> Follow the wild goose flight,
> Dip-dip and swing.

And the world did stand still, and the clouds and the sun and
the wind, but I was fast as quicksilver, fast and bright, forget-
ting where I was and where I lived because for that time I
was Hiawatha, a beautiful Indian girl, fearless and careless
and free. I was so happy I couldn't stop laughing and it felt
that my life could be like that forever until the man from the
kiosk called out our number and said we had to bring the
boats back please. So time didn't stop, except in my head,
and although that may be good enough, in fact we only got
twenty minutes on the boats, which made the game too expen-
sive, so we never did it again.

On the way home Margaret said we could go to the shop,
that she would buy some sweets and keep the man talking so
I could put some into my pocket without paying. I tried, but

then I got scared, my hand was shaking, so I put the sweets back.

'Never mind,' Margaret said. And anyway, she still shared her chocolate with me and I was happy with that so I brought all those sweet moments home that afternoon and when I opened the door I was still smiling, especially as it was time for *Doctor Who*.

'You can have the TV on for a while,' my mum said, 'but you'll have to switch it off as soon as *Doctor Who* is finished.'

Even then I didn't complain, but before it was nine o'clock, my mother decided to send me to bed. She said there were things she needed to discuss with Pearl. I told her I didn't mind, that I would sit quietly, but she said their discussion wasn't for my ears. That's how it's been almost every night since my sister came home. Sometimes it's made me feel like biting my arm or kicking a wall, especially at night when I have to go to bed by myself. So this evening, when my mother said goodnight and it wasn't even nine o'clock yet, I was nearly crying, but trying not to show it, in case my big brother saw me and called me a brat. Even though I was trying to look normal, the fact is, my heart was pounding in my ears, and as soon as I closed the bedroom door the tears came down, steaming hot and running down my cheeks so I had to lick them before they went into my mouth. And when I saw one of Teddy's comics lying on the floor I picked it up and tore it into pieces. In fact I felt as if I wanted to rip it with my teeth, I was so angry, I just didn't care. As soon as I'd done it I knew it was wrong, so then I was crying even more, and I was scared as well as sorry for having done such a wicked thing. I hid the bits underneath the mattress. And even though I thought, that's it, I'm not angry any more, when I got into bed I was still thinking about how old I would have to be before I could leave home, and how my mum would be sorry if I ran away and left her by herself. It was then I decided to listen at the wall. First I had to tip-toe to the kitchen without putting lights on, then I got a glass so I could put it to my ear. I've seen people doing that on TV. It really does work because when I put the glass on the wall and put it to my ear, I could hear almost everything my mum and sister were saying.

First Pearl said, 'When you left, Momma, nobody told me you were gone, I kept waiting for you to come and see me.' There was silence until she continued. 'Daddy moved in with his girlfriend, do you remember her, that woman called Flo? I had to call her Auntie. Flo was good to me but I didn't see much of Daddy, he was out most days and he never came home till late.'

'I never stopped trying you know,' Mum said. 'First I wrote to the government then to your school. I even hired a private detective but it was as if you'd disappeared. Did you get any of my letters?'

'No, nothing, but I cried every night waiting for you to come and get me. Anyway, it didn't take long before all I heard was Daddy and Flo shouting at each other, then one night Daddy came and told me we were leaving. After that I had more homes and aunties than I can remember. I gave up counting in the end. Each time Daddy got a new girlfriend we moved on. Some treated me good, and the others . . .'

I couldn't hear anything for a while, then there was shuffling and something like coughing.

'Momma, Momma,' it was Pearl's voice. 'Where did you go?'

'Darling, I tried to find you, I did everything I could. Please, don't cry, you're here now and we're together, that's what we should be glad for.'

'Daddy said you were never interested in me. He said as soon as I was born all you wanted was to go back to your studies so you could play around with your boyfriends and read books. He said that's why they put you away in the asylum because he came and found me screaming in the cot, all messed up where I'd been left so long.'

'Listen baby,' Mummy answered, 'I admit, I haven't always been the best way I should, that's the God's truth, and I'm sorry for it. But you have to understand, things happened then, things I didn't expect. After you were born I should have been happy but it felt as if my sky had fallen in. It was never about you, I wanted you so much.' That's when I almost dropped the glass, then my mum said 'C'mon, don't cry. The thing was, I didn't know anything about being a mother. Your Daddy was out all the time and I was so . . . lonely. Sometimes I felt so bad I couldn't get out of bed, I wanted to die, all I did was cry. And there you were, my beautiful baby girl, you were everything I'd dreamed of . . . But then you started screaming and when Daddy did come home he was yelling at me too so in the end it seemed as if everything was screaming and yes, one day, I just walked away. I had to get out. I had to go where no one was shouting any more. I know what I did was wrong, but baby I've been punished enough, and anyway, that's not how I ended up at Pilgrim State, your Daddy —'

'Momma,' Pearl shouted, 'I don't want to hear all that stuff any more; that's between you and Daddy.'

'But you're old enough now to understand what happened . . .'

'No, Momma. I don't have to understand anything. That's about you, not me. When you went away Daddy was all I had, and whatever he did he's still my Daddy.'

'All right, baby. I know, I know. Don't cry any more. I have no bad feelings for your father, not anymore. You tell your Daddy for me, it's time to let the past go.'

'Well, sometimes the past won't let us go whatever we do. I told Daddy I was coming to see you and Teddy. He said that boy had nothing to do with him, but I can see he's wrong about that. Teddy is more like Daddy than I am.'

Then my mother said, 'Alright honey, like you say, it's time to leave the past where it is and look towards the future. When are you due?'

'In September,' Pearl said slowly. 'I'm four months now.'

And it went quiet again and I wasn't surprised because I knew they were talking about Pearl having a baby.

'Have you thought about what you're going to do? I will help however I can, you know that.'

'I'm going to get married Momma. He's got a good job.'

'But do you love him?'

'Momma, I'm having his baby and I'm going to marry him and bring my child up in a proper family way.'

Then my mum was crying, and I was really tired, and my feet were getting too cold, but I still didn't want to miss what they were saying, so I rubbed my feet against each other.

'Sweetheart,' my mother said, and the sound of her words

went up and down as if she was singing. 'I know how it must seem to you now, but there are worse things than bringing up a child by yourself. Stay in England, I'll help you all I can, you'll have your family around you.'

So then Pearl was crying again.

'I can't live with you Momma, there's no room here. There's never been room in your life for me. You already have more kids than you can handle.'

Now my mother's voice was low, as if she was seriously thinking and choosing every word she was saying.

'Pearl, every child I ever had has been nothing but a blessing to me.'

'Except for the times when you left them.'

'What do you mean?' Now Mum was talking and crying at the same time so I couldn't hear what she was saying.

'Momma, it's what you've always done, can't you see? One way or another, you always leave us.'

Mum's voice was choking and that made my heart start thumping and my face was getting hot because I wanted to shout at Pearl and tell her to stop saying those things and part of me wished I'd never listened at the wall, but I did, and now there was no going back.

'I never left my children because I didn't want them,' my mother yelled. 'Life is hard, Pearl, and more complicated than you know. You think you're such a grown-up woman. Your father took you away from me . . .'

And then they were both shouting at each other.

'I said I don't want to hear it any more.'

'All right, that's enough, I'm tired of it all. But you, my Pearl, my girl, I love you so much. Every night I prayed God to help me find you, prayed that he'd send you back to me and He answered my prayers. We're together now and it's our chance, it's my chance to be your mother again. Let me do it child, let me do it for your baby. Don't throw yourself away like this.'

'Momma, it won't be the same for me, my man has a good job and he loves me.'

'Sweetheart . . .'

'You don't have anything to tell me. I'm going home Momma, to my home, as soon as I can book a ticket. Don't say any more, that's the end of it.'

After that there was a lot of crying so I couldn't hear the words, then the front room door squeaked open and there were footsteps along the hall. I ran back to bed and pulled the covers over my head. My heart was beating so fast and all I kept thinking was how I'd felt when my mum had left me and that made me want to cry, so instead of thinking about that, or what I'd just heard, I tried to remember a story from *Doctor Who*. In this one, the Earth is being invaded by aliens that look like Human Beings. What the aliens are trying to do is to get rid of important people like the Prime Minister or a Headmaster or someone like that so they can take control of the Earth because the aliens want to farm Human Beings, keep them like cows, so they can live off their energy. Nobody knew what was going on until people started to act strange. That series of *Doctor Who* made me think, how do we ever really know who someone is, even ourselves, because we can all do unexpected things. I can even surprise myself, I've noticed that especially since Pearl came. I always try to be good, but sometimes it's as if I have no control. So it could happen couldn't it, that someone could seem like one thing and in fact be something else and maybe you wouldn't find it out until it was too late.

Greenwich, London
July 1965

On the last day at Saint Peter's school we emptied the desks and cleared our work from the walls. When we finished, the classroom looked bare, as if we'd never been there at all.

In assembly the Headmaster talked about going into the world and how we should come back to see him. I will miss my friends very much, especially Margaret. She's going to a different school and even though she'll still be living on the Estate, I know it will never be the same between us, things are bound to change.

A lot of my friends were crying when we said goodbye. I took a camera and got them to stand against the wall and smile.

Sometimes I think my mind is like a library with rows of shelves where I stick on labels and store the things I want to remember because most of the time I can open a memory wherever I want, but some things are stacked up too high and they're hard to reach.

The school I'm going to in September is very different to Saint Peter's; it has more than two thousand children and so many classrooms and corridors that it's hard to imagine I'll ever find my way around. I'll have to get the bus in the mornings with my brother and wear a blue blouse and grey gymslip dress but I can't get the uniform yet, I have to wait till my mum gets the Clothing Grant from the Council. My mother says that when the grant comes she will buy me a proper school bag and a pencil case as well.

When I went home after the last day at my school, my mum was still wearing her nightdress and she was wheezing quite bad. She said she wasn't feeling well again because her inhaler isn't working like it used to, she needs the medicine inside it to be stronger.

If I had a time machine I'd go to the past not the future. Last term at school we did a project on Egypt and the pyramids. Some Egyptians had dark skin like me, they believed in more than one god and in life after death. I copied a painting from the tomb of Tutankhamen into my rough book. I did the drawing really carefully, matching the colours and the hieroglyphs so well that my teacher gave me a gold star. Once the body of a person was mummified the priests awakened the soul with sacred ceremonies and a wand called an ankh so the dead could go on living forever. That's why, when Ancient Egyptians died, they were buried with everything they needed to go hunting, or have dinner, or talk with their families and friends.

April 2004

'1965 was our endless summer, or that's how it seemed. There must have been rain some days; memory gives us more blue sky days than the weatherman. The streets baked, the asphalt on the courtyard of our flats blistered like melting cheese. It seemed as if hardly a drop of rain had fallen for a month or more, so by August the grass outside the front-room window had lost all its greens. My mother never talked about what had happened with my sister in the spring. She never spoke of being ill. If she was sad she never showed it, she'd set her sights on the future; the new grandchild that was due in September. She spent what was left of her savings buying things for the baby; I had never seen so many new clothes in our home. Each purchase kept my mother occupied, it seemed to me, for days. Everything was wrapped in tissue paper, tied with a bow, labelled and stacked behind the bedroom door, as if this knitted shawl or cap or those mittens were part of the grandchild she was expecting to see one day, maybe, she hoped, soon. When the stack of baby clothes was large enough, my mother filled a tea chest and shipped it to my sister.

'I was more than happy to forget the spring; it seemed easier that way. We ate our meals around the TV again, there was no more whispering in corners and when the shadows chased me down the hallway at night, I could run to my mother's room without worrying she might send me back.'

Nights with my mother seemed endless that year, hot nights spread out dark and sweet between the long, bright days of high summer. As soon as I ran into her bed Mother would laugh at me for getting chased down the hall by nothing but the darkness.

'Duppy know who fe frighten,' she'd laugh and say, 'you know, those shadows you're so scared of were living people once like you and me. They're only trying to find their way back to the world through your dreams. The more you run, the more they'll chase you; best thing you can do is slow down, let them walk beside you.

When nights were too hot to sleep we'd lay on the bed with the sheets pulled down, talking to each other until even the sound of the river seemed to drift into silence and all we were left with was each other's voices. Then my mother would fill the bed with her stories, talking about the family, of her past, of her childhood on the Island, trailing words through my imagination, the way she said orchids dropped flowers from the trees.

'When I was a child my momma told me that the ancestors of our people lived in the earth, in the roots of the cotton tree. I never forgot what Momma said, and after she died I'd watch for the nights when the moon was big enough to light my way to the gulley; Sister Night was still dark enough to wrap her cloak around me, so then I'd climb out the window, tip-toe my way past the yard dogs till I could run without them chasing me, never stopping once till I got to that old tree. Bats swooped like angels there, hunting moths and fireflies. I'd stand against the tree and watch them soar, then I'd loop my arms around the trunk of that tree and I'd stay there till I felt my mother's heart speaking to me.'

'One of those nights that long hot summer I dreamt of my own mother again; I saw her rising from the roots of a cotton tree, stirring crabs from their nests so they swarmed in a mass as they scrambled from the rocks to dip their claws in the warm, black sea. She raised her arms to the heavens, then she lifted her face. I could see every detail and this time, just like the Virgin, my mother didn't leave her body behind, she was whole, intact, and her head was crowned by stars that had danced in the reflection of the sea.'

Greenwich, London
October 1965

It should have been the first day at my new school weeks ago but I haven't gone yet because my mother's been too sick to go to the shops and buy my uniform. Mother says she'll try to do it sometime this week, maybe after she's been to the doctor about her inhaler.

This morning, when I looked out of the window I saw children from the Estate going to the bus stop. They were laughing, pushing each other and swinging their bags. One of them was Margaret. I didn't recognise her at first because she was dressed in uniform and she had her back to me, so I waved and knocked on the window but she still didn't see me.

After breakfast I went to the shops for my mother. It was strange to go past my old school and not go inside. As I ran down the street I could hear children playing in the yard. I was hoping no one would see me, especially not the teachers. By the time I got back home my mum was out of bed.

'Put the food away Jackie, and come and sit with me.'

We've been doing that sort of thing a lot recently. Ever since Pearl left we've been having talks. Usually it starts with my mum asking a question like, do you know where babies come from? I told her how Margaret had explained it to me, and then I laughed because I hadn't believed a word of what

Margaret had said – as if anyone could believe babies are made like that! My mother said she thought it really was time for us to talk together, like two women should, so I put the food away and went to sit on her bed.

'Jackie, remember when I told you how much I loved your father?'

I raised my head.

'And you know that your father and Teddy's father are not the same people?'

'Yes,' I answered.

But then, instead of telling me about my dad she started to say how I should be careful of men, as if I don't know, that mostly they just want one thing, whatever that is, and if ever I got pregnant like my sister did, however that was, that I should come and tell her and she'd never be angry and she'd help me any way she could. Well, all that sounded like it made sense, but by the end of our talk I still didn't know what she was talking about because then she jumped up.

'Oh no,' she said, 'just look at the time!' and she grabbed her coat. 'I'm going to miss my appointment. We'll talk some more later.'

But when my mother came back she was looking even worse than when she'd left.

'The doctor won't give me a stronger inhaler, even though I told him the old one wasn't working.' She sat on the sofa and pulled off her shoes.

'Never mind, Mummy,' I said and I stroked her face. 'Maybe you can try again in a few weeks' time.'

'I kept trying to tell him, but he just said I needed to calm down because I was getting hysterical and it's not as if people die of asthma these days. Jesus, that man may be a doctor, but he's a damn fool.' Mummy rubbed her feet and lay on the sofa. 'We'll get your uniform tomorrow sweetheart, even if we have to get a taxi.'

But when tomorrow came, my mum still couldn't get out of bed.

Greenwich, London
October 1965

Just like the summer, this year's winter seems to have come earlier than usual because it's cold already, cold enough to have to light the fire every night. My mother says that doesn't usually happen till November.

The fog has come back from the river and the trees are changing quickly now, shaking off their everyday greens, so it seems as if the leaves are flaming, bursting into reds and oranges too. The trees don't keep those colours for long. It's as if they have to wait all year to put their party things on and then almost as soon as they've got dressed up, they have to put their best clothes away to save them for the next time.

Soon, in the park, the conkers will get ripe and fall to the ground. Some of the conkers will get buried and stored by squirrels, a few will get lost and turn into trees, but most will be collected by children like me who will take them home, cook them in an oven till they're hard so they can be threaded with a lace and smashed against each other to see who has the champion conker. The sweet chestnuts will ripen next, then every leaf on those trees will fall, each one in its turn and thousands and thousands of leaves will cover the ground, until you can hardly see the grass any more.

Each year I try to notice the day when the first leaf falls, but it always seems to happen before I see it, and then, once it starts, it's as if all the leaves want to follow. It's like raindrops, first one, then another, then a storm comes, or some great wind blows. Even the leaves that cling till they're curling at the edges will fall when they get too old to hold on any more. In the end the leaves will fall in showers of red and gold, falling on the dried-up grass, making leaf pools on the faded greens. The best time to play in the park is just before the keepers sweep the leaves away because then I can climb to the top of the hill and roll down the slope without being worried about hurting myself when I land at the bottom – that's where the leaves get blown – where the crease of the hill meets the part of the grass that lays flat against the footpath. Sometimes, in a good year, the leaves will stack up so high they reach past my waist and then I can bounce and jump and throw the leaves all over the place, or I can kick them into piles, or dive in and hide beneath them when no one is looking.

Yesterday there was no fog, the air was clear and clean and the wind was blowing hard, whipping such a steam of froth and bubbles on the river that it seemed as if the tide was boiling as the waves hit the piers of the embankment. I put my face into the wind and hollered and ran along the road as the sun went down. No one could hear because the wind was so loud, then I turned the other way so the wind was at my back, pushing me down the street as I ran between the blocks of flats. The wind sent the rain spitting up against our windows, blowing so hard that the front door rattled and it didn't seem to matter what my mother did, the living room was filled with the coming winter.

My mother's not moving very fast again today. She says the effort of going to get my uniform last week really wore her out. When she walks she has to hold onto the walls until she catches her breath. I hear her breathing all the time. Last night, when I lay in bed half asleep, I thought I heard the wind whistling at the corner of our building until I realised it was the air coming from my mother's chest.

Tomorrow I'm going to my new school. My mum will have to show me how to make a tie.

Greenwich, London
October 1965

K idbrooke School is almost new. It has lots of large windows and nice shiny blue and pink tiled floors. The entrance is like a railway station, all glass with doors at each end with the assembly hall in the middle. I had to report to the office on the balcony when I first got there to find out where my class was.

Kidbrooke has lots of buildings and so many classrooms I can't even count them. The playing field is bigger than most parks I've been to with a full-sized running track and still more space for athletics and games. In between the main buildings are large squares of grass called quads, bordered at the edges with pink and yellow roses and every now and then there's a weeping willow or a crab apple tree that bends and dips its branches to the grass.

I had to stand at the front when I got to my new class and everyone stared at me. There are no other coloured girls in my class, but everyone seemed friendly, especially the form teacher, Miss Lewis. She's small and thin with a face like a dried-up apple and little round glasses that sit at the bottom of her nose. You wouldn't think that the class would take any notice of her the way she looks so old but when she speaks her voice is strong and she's always smiling.

I can see why the class like her. Each morning we have to say our number from the register in a different language. Today it was the time to say it in French. My number on the register is trent-et-un.

The first day was very busy, four lessons in the morning and three in the afternoon; that's a lot of walking because in this school the teachers stay in the classrooms and the children move around at the end of lessons. I have to keep my books and P.E. kit inside a locker and remember what lessons and what room I'm going to each day.

When it was dinner-time some girls from my class, who didn't even know me, asked if I wanted to sit with them. There was sausage and mash and for pudding spotted dick with the most disgusting custard. The afternoon went by even faster than the morning. My favourite lesson was English. The teacher said I could take the book home, that it wouldn't take long to catch up with the others. The story is a legend from Anglo-Saxon times called Beowulf. Apparently Beowulf is a prime example of an epic hero. I'm going to have to find out what that means. I was having so much fun that I almost didn't notice it was time to go home.

When I got back my mother was in her nightdress and there was a tea chest beside her in the front room.

'What's that?' I asked.

Mummy didn't answer straight away, even though she wasn't crying. Then she said, 'It's from Pearl,' and she looked at me. 'It's the baby clothes.' My mother pressed her hand on the top of the chest, 'She sent them all back. She never even opened it up.'

I didn't know what to say. I could see my mother was

more than a bit upset, even though her eyes weren't wet. It didn't make sense to me. Why would Pearl do something like that?

Greenwich, London
22 November 1965

The winter has settled all around us now, covering the sky with its thick, dark coat so it's easy to forget there ever was a summer that blazed so hot we sweated just to be in our skins. They've cleared the leaves in the park already, the conkers and chestnuts are all used up and the pond has been drained away. Now the days are short, the night-time starts before I get home from school.

Even though it's supposed to be God's special time, Sunday is always the worst day for me, especially in winter when it's too cold to play outside and there's no school and they put the worst programmes on the TV. This morning my mum sent us to mass so we ran through the park, but for the rest of the day we were stuck indoors, getting on each others' nerves. Later my mother watched *Songs of Praise*, I read for a while and then I tried to see if I could count the hailstones that landed on the window sill before they melted and it got too dark to see.

This evening, when we were in the front room, Teddy had a row with Mum. He went sort of mad, got all upset and the veins at the side of his neck stood out because he was shouting so much. I hate that. My mother says to take no notice when Teddy gets like that because he can't help what his hormones are doing to his emotions. I don't know what their argument was about, I was trying to listen to the TV, but when I told Teddy to be quiet he kicked me on the leg. I started screaming and a big blue bruise came up below my knee and it was really sore. Then my mother started to cry, she said she'd had enough, that everyone might as well go to bed if all we were going to do was fight. I was really angry because I thought it wasn't fair, Teddy started it, but I felt better when my mother said I could sleep with her in the living room.

When I got under the covers I noticed my mother had already fallen to sleep. I had to get up and turn the light off by myself. Usually my mum says goodnight and God bless when I'm going to sleep so on the way to the light switch I said it instead, hoping that would mean we'd all sleep well and have good dreams, and perhaps the next day would be better for all of us. I don't think Mummy heard me.

Soon as I flicked the switch I ran back to bed, but at first I couldn't see anything and I was frightened because even though I could feel my mum lying all warm and heavy beside me, I couldn't hear her breathing and it felt as if I was alone. But it didn't take long for my eyes to get used to the dark and I saw there was some light. In fact the moon was full and bright, moonlight coming through the curtains bright enough for me to see my mother's face, and it was as if she was young again, no lines on her skin or shadows underneath her eyes, and she was so beautiful. I didn't shut the curtains because I wanted to see her face looking like that until I fell asleep.

The interesting thing about the moon is that it's always there, even when it looks as if it's disappeared, the moon waxes and wanes. My old teacher, Mr Springer, told the class that the moon has a cycle like a very slow pulse, growing bigger for half of the month before it gets smaller and finally disappears.

One day, I will open up my eyes in a room like this and it will be morning and the spring will have come and everything that looks like it's sleeping or dead now will have come back to life because the seasons have their own cycle like the moon. I wish it was summer again.

I love my mummy.

Greenwich, London
23 November 1965

It was dark, still dark, not even two o'clock the clock said even though the rest of the night was silent, empty and empty, all the minutes going by so slowly that I could count them on a breath, her breath, each breath taking up to a minute. Or was it an hour? Yes, it must have taken at least one hour for my mother to fall – did I see it?

It was the light that woke me at first, I remember it cutting through my eyes so I had to turn my face from the ceiling as I opened my lids. And it was cold, the shivers were running up and down my back. I remember pulling at the covers. I suppose that's why I didn't see Mummy, but I could hear the breathing and I was thinking that it must be really late, because the fire had gone out and the ashes had fallen through the grate and settled on the hearth in a pile of dirty flakes. Mummy was sitting on the arm of the sofa. I shivered even more as I stood next to her, pushing past the rasping of her throat to reach for the inhaler that was lying on the table right next to her hand. And as I walked I stumbled, tripping on her feet, but Mummy was quiet even then, all I could hear was the see-saw gasping of her breathing, that and the chattering of my teeth. So then I ran and as I opened the door the light went spilling onto the hallway floor that seemed much darker than before, longer than before, the way the light ripped the tiles into pieces. But I wasn't frightened. I pushed on Teddy's door.

'I'll go to the phone box and call the ambulance,' Teddy said, pulling his coat over his pyjamas.

He hardly had time to put on his shoes; I could see the back of his soles as he flip-flapped across the courtyard. Then I rushed back, stared at Mummy who was sitting all hunched up with the arm of the sofa around her and as I watched, it seemed that she was on the floor, just like that, her head by the hearth, her hair getting dusty with the ash from the fire that was landing in her mouth and on her tongue. I didn't move at all because Mummy always said to leave her alone when she was having trouble breathing. But Teddy rushed in, he knew what to do, and he pulled her on her back – she didn't say no, she couldn't say so because she had her eyes almost closed by then, even when he had his lips on her mouth, blowing in the air till the sound of her breathing came out of her chest like water running down from a gutter.

It took endless time for the ambulance to come, or that's how it seemed, the minutes going by slowly enough to give me plenty of time to kick my legs and think of all the things I should have done.

Roy grabbed my nightdress. When the ambulance man pushed past the sofa, I heard Teddy crying. The man put my mother on the stretcher, wrapping her up in a fluffy red blanket while the other man put the oxygen mask onto her face. When I looked again my mother seemed changed, like a hibernating caterpillar or a baby that was sleeping.

This time when the police came they wrapped us in

blankets and carried us to the car as if we might get broken. This time when the police car came to take us away it bumped over the yard and it went along Church Street until it got to the road by the park where we had played, just today, when Mummy had sent us to church. And no one stared this time, even the trees stayed asleep in the hushed winter morning of the night that was happening now, and no one talked, not even us.

When we got to the top of the hill I looked across the Heath and saw how the mist had gathered so it shone in patches like a veil around the moon. And as the car turned I saw that the mist was thicker up beside the pond where it had sunk low onto the ground, drifting like smoke round the bottom of the lights before it floated away and rested at last on the water. Everything seemed so blurred for a moment that I wondered if I was in another dream and then, just as we turned onto the Heath, I remembered this last Easter, my mum and me had been at the fair, there was a hoopla stall, the Heath was dark like this, but there was no mist and the fairground lights were shining so bright that the air seemed sharp when I breathed it into my mouth. My mother had clapped her hands as my hoop had gone around a bowl. Her smile seemed even brighter than those lights, and when I chose a goldfish to take home she said she'd always known I was born with a heap-load of luck inside my mouth, so she bought me toffee apples and candyfloss, as if to prove how lucky I was. And even though I felt sick, I ate everything and a hot dog as well, because that night seemed too happy to say no to anything I could have.

The police car left the Heath and went up the hill and I realised how many things that happened today, or yesterday, or just last month, would never happen to me again ever. I decided to start making lists inside my head, pretend my eyes were a camera, because that would help me store the memories and I wouldn't have to think of what was happening to me right now. Then the car stopped, and the policeman got out, and he went up the steps and rang the bell.

I began the first list as I went through the door, starting with the things in the hall, the blue floor tiles, the pictures on the walls, the lights, the doorknobs, the letters stacked high on the shelf where I couldn't hardly see them, but then I closed my eyes. How can this be normal I thought, and when I opened my eyes a lady had appeared, her pale mouth talking in the light of the hallway, looking like a robot the way she was standing folding her arms around her body. And it was cold. Somewhere a clock was chiming three and Roy started calling 'Mummy, Mummy,' pulling at my skirts so I thought I'd have to push him away till the lady said, 'Hello children, I'm Miss Mackey, is there anything I can get you?' and at last I could stop making the list.

Teddy asked if there were any comics, I needed the toilet and as I went downstairs and shut the door I understood how all this could be normal because everything else in the world has to stay the same doesn't it, even though this is the night my mummy died.

I've never been an orphan before. For a while there will be first times for everything I do and I'll count them and make more lists and then doing that will be normal, even going to sleep when my mother is dead, which is what will happen when I go to bed tonight.

*　　*　　*

I don't know where my mother is, because even if she's wrapped up in that nice red blanket, she isn't anything any more.

I know there won't be any dreams tonight, only the darkness.

Blackheath, London
23 November 1965

Mummy always told me I needed to listen, always said I should learn to hush, slow down my thoughts long enough to listen to what the dark was saying when it looked as if everything was dead. So that night I listened, and I heard, and my mother was right, because even when I thought the world was asleep and the cars had stopped moving, and no footsteps were walking down the street, the wind was still dancing with the moon at its heels, and later, even when there was almost silence, the morning was peeking in through the curtains that were waiting for me to speak. I kept my eyes shut when the light was switched on, listening as the other children woke up, pushing off their blankets, covering their faces with their whispering fingers as they went downstairs. Once they had gone I tried to remember where I was, so I walked around their smoothed-down beds and pulled back the curtains.

It wasn't quite light yet. The sky was like a milky skin, all see through and grey except where the sun was bright and rising at the edges.

At first the street seemed empty, but as the sun got higher, brushing the sky with the morning that was coming quickly now, I saw gardens and cars appear from the darkness. And when I leant across and pressed my nose right onto the glass I noticed that the pavements outside this Home were large enough for girls in scarves to walk together holding hands. I heard them call and laugh as they turned down the alley, talking so fast I could barely keep up with what they were saying as they joked past the postman and the boys who were throwing stones into the trees. I wished it was me walking with them, wished it was me walking and thinking of nothing in particular, laughing at the day with my friends. My eyes followed those girls, chasing their voices till they turned the corner and went out of view. For a moment everything was hushed again, so I screwed up my eyes and looked to try and see if I could find that heaven the priest always talked of because I was wondering if Mummy had reached it already, or was she still floating in Limbo? And if she was in heaven, would she be young again, would she be smiling, would she be a saint, or an angel, or a Goddess sitting by the right hand of the Father with a halo on her head? And would her breathing be easy going in and out now that she was dead? By the time I'd thought of all those questions the sun had climbed onto the rooftops and it was glaring in my eyes, catching the frost that had settled on the tiles so the houses sparkled in the early morning light, but however much I tried I just couldn't see any heaven, the sky seemed empty, not a cloud, or a bird, not even a plane was crossing it, everything from last night had been swept away quite clean and then the door opened.

'Jackie, well done, you're up. I'm Miss Mackey,' she said. 'Do you remember me from last night?'

I shook my head.

'Never mind,' Miss Mackey smiled. 'Your brothers are downstairs already. You must be hungry. Would you like to come with me and I'll show you where they are and you can have some breakfast with them. I've put some clothes out for you. I think they'll fit. When you've finished dressing I'll be waiting outside, all right?'

But I knew it wasn't a question because she went straight out without waiting for the answer of how I was feeling.

As soon as I got dressed I went into the hallway. The clothes were too big so the sleeves kept slipping over my fingers. I rolled them up at the cuffs while Miss Mackey was talking, asking me questions without leaving time for answers, as if she was trying to fill up the space that otherwise might have been a silence.

Miss Mackey smiled again. 'Did you manage to sleep at all?'

I tried to move my face when I answered 'yes' or 'no' but I was still counting floor tiles and pictures. How strange everything looked with the sun streaming through the windows. And then I thought, if everything here looks the same and different from the night before, then our flat, which was my home last night, must seem like a scene from the *Mary Celeste* this morning, with a cup turned over, a comb with hair in it left on the table, because it's empty now, everyone gone, everything cold and turned into ashes, with the mess of the torn-up comic still under the mattress. And I said to myself, anyway, who cares about all those things now, and the answer came back – no one. Those thoughts made me start making lists again so I could eat my breakfast and talk to my brothers as I'd been told to.

The rest of that week at the Home was like a holiday because they kept us off school. All we did was assessments and watch TV. I had to spot the difference in two pictures and do a reading test with a psychiatrist who asked me how I was doing. I told him I was all right, except I wanted go back to school. He smiled and said how nice it was to meet me and he would see what he could do.

The next day I went to a special school that was in a chalet in the garden of the Home. Most of the children were younger than me. I hope to go back to my proper school very soon, but the Staff said I have to stay where I am until after the funeral.

Roy asked, 'Where is Mummy?' only three times today. It doesn't matter how often I answer, he just goes and plays until he asks the same thing the next time. Later, when I was watching the TV, I got upset because the Rolling Stones weren't number one any more on *Top of the Pops*. I couldn't believe it! I know the Stones have been number one a long time but I never thought the Seekers would make a chart hit with that carnival song.

At this Home I'm allowed to stay up till nine o'clock in the week, nine-thirty at the weekend, which is not too bad. There are three girls who sleep in my room and there's no bullying here. Christine is thirteen years old. She's here because her mother is in hospital and her dad can't look after her when he's at work. Linda and Susan are like me because they're never going to live with their parents again, but their mum and dad visit regularly, and they go home at Christmas and other holidays. All the other children have parents. Me and my brothers are the only real orphans. Being called an orphan makes me think of Charles Dickens and Oliver Twist, it's less embarrassing than telling people I don't have parents, somehow, to say that sounds as if I've been careless or that no one ever bothered with me.

Soon the Social Services will decide what to do with me and my family. I know Mummy would want us to stay together. Tomorrow our Social Worker is coming to interview us. I suppose it doesn't matter if I talk to her now my mum isn't here anymore.

April 2004

'What I still don't understand is why I don't remember my mother falling. Everything else is there.' I pressed a hand against my head.

'Maybe you were distracted and you didn't see, or perhaps it was just too painful; Mum, you were just a child.'

'Perhaps; the mind's pretty good at protecting itself and the death of a parent is a powerful thing however old you are. That's why I didn't want to talk too much about it when you were younger; I didn't want you to think of life as being filled with the possibility of such . . . despair.'

Blackheath, London
28 November 1965

I think I understand why Roy keeps asking for Mummy because how can someone be here one minute and gone the next? Even though I'm six years older than my brother I keep thinking how is it that a minute, or a day, can make such a difference to a life? This time last week I was sleeping in bed with my mum and going to school and playing with my brothers whenever I liked and eating dinner on the sofa in front of the TV like a normal person because that's what I was. Now I sleep in a room with children I don't hardly know, and there are laundry baskets and labels on my clothes, and a dining table with jugs and glasses, and staff who look after us but only if they're on duty.

Today we went to the hospital to see my mother. We got dressed as if we were going to church. Miss Mackey took us on the bus. We had to go into the basement which is where they keep the bodies.

Before I went into the mortuary I wasn't sure if I'd get frightened or upset and my hands got cold so I had to rub them together, but when I actually went in, it seemed quite ordinary. Mummy was lying on a table with a green sheet pulled up to her chin. She looked bigger than I remembered and her belly was sticking out, maybe that was because she was laid on a table and it was so high up. She was almost level with my chest. Teddy held my hand and played with my fingers. I knew he was crying, I could hear him sniffing, but I didn't want to look in case I got upset, so I whispered to him that it would be all right because that's what I felt.

I liked that room, the way it was quiet and there were flowers by her head, her favourite red gladioli in a vase, and everything was hushed, which is how it should be when someone's resting.

I had to stand on tip-toes to see her properly. As soon as I did I knew my mum had gone somewhere else. Her face looked empty, and her eyes were slightly open, as if she was only half asleep. And nobody had done her hair, it was all sticking up. In one way looking at Mummy like that made me feel better, but in another way I wished they'd dressed her better, maybe combed her hair and put a penny in her mouth to make absolutely sure that the ferryman would take her soul across the water. And if I did that now, put a penny in her mouth, would she know about Mnemosyne and how to wake from the dream that had once been her life? But then I thought, if I touched her I might get told off, so I decided I'd just look at her face because I knew it was the last time I would see her freckles and the way her mouth was curved like a heart even when she didn't have lipstick on it. My throat went tight when I noticed her teeth were biting her lip. It made me think of how she'd laid in that room by herself until now. And it was lucky, because just as I felt my eyes begin to water the man said, 'We recovered things from your mother that you may want to keep,' and he opened his fingers.

There were two rings, one was plain gold, but the other had rubies and pearls set in a pattern. I could see from his eyes that the man thought my mum was a poor, sad woman but I didn't care, because I knew who my mother really was. They should have wrapped her head in rainbows, made a crown as well, dressed her like a Goddess, with a footstool of clouds for her feet, so I said, 'No, put her rings back because she never took them off.' Then I closed my eyes and that's how I saw her, and that's how I'll always remember her, because whatever she was wearing and however her hair was looking, she will always be just beautiful to me.

Now, when I sleep, my dreams have hardly anything in them, or nothing important enough to remember. Sometimes, when I'm in bed, not quite asleep, I think I hear my mother breathing, but it's just pipes or the wind or a door that's creaking.

Blackheath, London
5 December 1965

This morning we didn't have breakfast because we were going to my mum's funeral mass even though it's Thursday and not a saint's day. Roy wasn't allowed to go because the staff said he was too young.

Miss Mackey took me and Teddy to the Saint John Fisher church at the bottom of the hill. The church is named after an English martyr, but I don't know anything about him, it was our first time there. I hadn't been in that church before and neither had my mother.

As we walked down the street the traffic rushed past, all the people going to work or school and lorries making so much noise that even when we spoke we couldn't hear each other. It didn't take long to get there, I saw the spire first of all. The funeral cars that were parked on the kerb by the door were so big we had to walk around them, that's how I knew my mum was inside already.

Saint John Fisher Church is almost new, it looks as if the builders have only just left. It has white walls, quite bare, and brightly coloured glass made in patterns like a mosaic so the sun that comes from the windows is stained. It sends blue and red rays of light across the aisles and it lands on the new wooden benches before it falls onto the ground.

I like old churches better because they smell of incense and have more statues and pictures.

Apart from us, the pews were empty, except for the undertakers and one lady sitting at the front who had a mantilla on her head, I only had a scarf. The coffin was in front of the altar. For a moment it seemed too sad to see it sitting by itself. I thought I would cry until I remembered that my mum wasn't in that coffin at all, it was only her body, like a dress is only a piece of sewing until someone puts it on. I wanted to go to the front to be closer to her, maybe even touch the coffin, but Miss Mackey took us to sit near the back. If someone had come into the church it might have seemed as if the lady with the mantilla was the only person there for my mother, but I didn't make a fuss, and soon the priest came and the service began.

I'd never been to a funeral before. It was interesting because as the service went on I saw how the scene was similar to the paintings from the ancient tombs of Egypt where the dead pharaoh waits, laid in the sarcophagus, for his spirit to be awakened by the ankh and the priest. It seems that over thousands of years Human Beings, even when they weren't Christians, have believed that similar things happen after death.

First there was an ordinary mass, nothing special, except the priest wore black vestments with a purple lining which represents mourning. Teddy held my hand while we were sitting and we went to Communion which was the nearest I got to my mother. Then the priest stood in the pulpit and said, 'Dorothy Brown leaves three children and although I never met her, we are here to celebrate her life and pray for her soul.'

I have to admit I felt better when the priest stopped talking and I could think of mum for myself. Thank goodness, he didn't take long and then we all stood up as the undertakers carried my mum's coffin high on their shoulders and put her in the back of the car as if she was special, like a princess. I wished I'd bought some flowers because then, when we followed in the other black car, I noticed how the top of her coffin was empty.

We drove very slowly and the traffic had to wait behind us, except for one car that overtook, which made our driver shake his head. There was no speaking again, just Teddy sniffing and no one looking into anybody's eyes in case they might have to see what was going on. It's amazing how often that happens. I stared through the window. As we went up the hill the sun broke out from the clouds and for a moment the day was bright. If I hadn't seen the bare branches of the trees I might have thought it was summer and a lovely day because the street was suddenly filled with light and people smiling, doing shopping and talking, not looking at us and the coffin, because all they wanted was to forget how this could happen, will happen to them, on a normal day like this. That's when I saw the man; I thought he was waiting to cross the road, but he was staring at me. He raised his hat and bowed as our car went past. As I turned I saw he had waited till we'd gone right past before he put his hat on again. That's when the sun went back behind the cloud, brightening the rim so it shone like a halo. And when the car turned into the cemetery, climbing up the little black path, past the gravestones and the hundreds of crosses, past the stone angels with their empty eyes and faces, the coloured pebbles and the dried-up flower vases a line of crows swooped up, leaping to their wings and calling to each other like a choir. When we got to the top we slowed for a moment and I saw how the graveyard was raised like a bed, high at the middle and falling away at the corners. The driver looked this way and that, as if he was searching for where to go. In the end we stopped at the lowest part of the hill, where the land slopes more steeply down towards the hedge. The sun dipped behind the thickened grey clouds and a soft rain began to fall. As soon as we stepped from the car our faces were damp and my hat, and the coffin, and the grass, and every surface got covered with spangles of rain. It was brighter than dew. Then I saw where we were going because by the fence there were workmen standing near a hole with earth piled up on either side. And as we walked towards the hole I noticed that even though it was winter there were still some blackberries clinging to the briars by the fence where the council flats looked onto the graveyard. Then a magpie lifted his tail, pulling at a worm that must have lived in the ground with the beetles and the ants until it had been dug up only this morning.

Last spring at school we had a competition to see who could grow the best nasturtium. For just sixpence we were given a packet of seeds and a pot. The seeds looked all dried up, as if they were old and dead, but then Mr Springer told us how to look after plants – that we had to dig a hole, not mind if our hands got dirty, and if we planted the seed by putting the soil back and tapping it firmly down on the top and then watered the earth regularly so it didn't dry up, then in a while, just a short while, a nasturtium flower would grow. So I did that, and for more than a week it looked as if nothing was happening, even though I put the pot on the sill where it could see the sun and keep warm. It was hard to remember to look after it when nothing seemed to be happening, but I was patient and I waited and watered, and I never forgot it. Then one day, just below the earth, I saw the curl of a shoot, and very soon that curl was pushing its way to the surface, though it still had the shell of the seed case stuck on its tip so it looked as if it was wearing a hat. I was proud that I had done that, made a flower able to grow, even though my nasturtium didn't win the competition.

As I walked towards the fence, I could feel the grass was damp, it sank beneath my feet, as if the whole earth was ready to take my mummy, making it easy for us to lower her body, the ashes of her ashes, into the dust of the dirt that was really happening now to her and me. My lips said 'Amen,' the prayer smoking up like whispers through the sharp biting cold of the morning.

The man gave me earth to put in my hand. The smell was like the park and the leaves in autumn. And as I looked into the hole and threw the earth onto the coffin and rubbed the clay that was clinging to my fingers on the side of my coat, I saw that the ground was full of things, not just pebbles and stones, or worms and beetles, there were roots, small ones that ran in threads and knots, knitting their way through the dirt. The large roots were like broken off fingers and it seemed that the ground was waiting to hold my mother, just waiting to grow around her, while the hole was filling up with water from the rain. I didn't get a chance to make sure that the men with their spades would pat the soil down firmly enough, Miss Mackey said we had to go, but it was all right I thought, because planting is their job not mine, so they must know how to do it. And as I walked away I knew my mother would live in that ground forever, growing and changing, happily watered by the rain, each day becoming more and more part of the earth that would always be at my feet. And in spring the roots will grow around her, the worms will move the soil, the ants will make their nests next to her coffin and all the other things that make the world come alive from the darkness of the earth will be with her and part of her for ever.

Blackheath, London
December 1965

No one in the Home ever mentions my mother or what happened to her. I suppose that's because they never knew her.

Before my mother had been dead two weeks Miss Mackey told us the Council were sending men to clear out our flat. They gave me and Teddy a day to go home and decide if there was anything we wanted to keep, as long as it was small.

When we got to our flat the front door was open and a van was parked on the courtyard opposite the door. There were stacks of sacks folded up against the outside wall. Teddy knocked, we waited, and when no one came out we went through the door and into the hall by ourselves. It was strange to see our home like that, full of people who weren't us, men smoking in the kitchen, drinking cups of tea in the kitchen, moving our stuff around the front room. Every now and then one of them walked past carrying a box or a bag, but it was as if they couldn't see us.

'Excuse me,' Teddy said, 'the Council said we could come and get some things.'

A man called back, 'Well, you'd better take what you want now and do it quickly, we've started already and we have to be cleared by the end of the day.'

It was hard to know where to start because our flat looked like it was ready for a badly run jumble sale with letters stuffed into sacks, dirty footprints on my mother's photographs and the sofa bed in the sitting room turned onto its side. When I went into my mother's bedroom the wardrobe doors were open and the satins and furs and all the happy, matching gladness of her shoes and handbags had been thrown on the bed or the floor. My brother grabbed a few things and put them in his pocket before we left.

We never saw our home after that and we hardly ever spoke of it again, but it didn't matter. Since I'd been little I'd been saving all the times inside me, the good and the bad, so whenever I needed, I could think of the stories my mother had told me. I still wondered where she had gone but I also tried to remember what we were doing this time last year or the year before when I was really small. Every night I replay things that happened to us as if it's a movie so I can think of the things I loved, the things I could have done or said to make it better and then I can relive them again. I retrace every detail of our last day together, the pattern of hailstones on the window sill, the look of the fire that had almost gone out, the drive across the Heath, the only part I can never see is the bit when my mum fell off the sofa, but I keep on trying, keep on picking through the memories as best as I can, hoping one day I'll get back . . . everything.

Blackheath, London
March 1966

This last Christmas everyone seemed to want to give us presents – the Social Services, people from the office where my mother used to work, a charity called the Round Table, they even made a collection at my brother's school, we were so lucky, the staff said, and they were right, we've never had so many things before.

They had an enormous tree at the Home, tall enough to reach to the ceiling in the hall. The whole day was like a special treat and even though there was no snow on the ground, the frost that covered the branches lit up the trees so the back garden sparkled like a Christmas card with the grass tipped with ice and the holly tree heavy with berries. At first, after my mother was buried, we went to her grave every Sunday. We'd talk of home or try and think of what my mother would want us to say or do in our lives.

The earth seemed to wake slowly, it had been such a long winter. It was only when I noticed a crocus flower peeping through the cover of grass by her grave that I realised that the spring was really here. And when we went to see Mummy the next time, in the days between one visit and another, the brambles that ran along the fence had begun to stretch new shoots across the dip and scrub of the grave so I knew the spring had started to push it roots even to the stoniest heart of that earth, I knew that the Earth had started sucking life into the smallest leaf and bud that was waiting its turn to uncurl. And somehow, after that, there didn't seem much point in visiting my mum's grave every week because anything that could be thought about there could be thought about anywhere else.

Case Conference Review, Stonefield Reception Centre, April 8, 1966

    Teddy Brown — 1/2/49

    Jacqueline Brown — 10/04/54

    Roy Brown — 9/9/1960

Summary of Events

Greenwich Social Services has had contact with this family since 1962 when a Protection Order was issued at the Greenwich Magistrates Court after the police were called to the family home.

Pilgrim State

Although the home was chaotic, Mrs Brown appeared to be an intelligent woman, genuinely concerned about the welfare of her children. However, she was seen as unsociable, had no friends and did not get on with her neighbours. Social Services staff often found her behaviour erratic and difficult to handle, particularly as she frequently expressed strong feelings about her colour, especially when she felt her rights were being infringed.

In 1963, when the family were living in Deptford, Mrs Brown expressed concerns to social workers about Jackie's emotional state. She felt Jackie was beginning to show signs of disturbance and said her daughter was often frightened and frequently woke screaming in the night unless a light was left on or she was in her mother's bed.

After becoming unwell in 1964, Mrs Brown gave up work. At that time Mrs Brown appeared to be in an even more agitated state than usual and told social workers she could no longer cope. In September of 1965 Mrs Brown arrived, without an appointment, at the Social Service offices with the youngest child Roy. She appeared to be in a highly excited state, asked that the younger children should be taken into care immediately and demanded help to clean up her home. However, after the NSPCC offered domestic support, Mrs Brown changed her mind.

The Brown family were received into care November 23, 1965 at Stonefield Reception Centre, Kidbrooke Grove, Blackheath, after the death of their mother.

The children are intelligent and appear well adjusted. Teddy assumes a very grown-up role within the family. After the death of his mother he was particularly concerned with the welfare of the other children and suggested that he

323

should go out to work immediately so he could offer the family financial support.

Jackie is a lively child with few problems of communication. However, she appears to share her mother's anti-authority attitudes, this can make her behaviour difficult at times.

Roy has achieved the normal developmental milestones for a child of five.

The children have expressed a wish to be kept together and every effort has been put into achieving this outcome, including placing adverts in national newspapers for foster parents and approaching relatives in America and Jamaica. However, it has not been possible to find one placement which could take all the family. Saint Anne's Roman Catholic Children's Home in Orpington has offered placements for the two younger children and Teddy has been accepted into a young people's unit at Pagoda Gardens in Blackheath. The panel recommends that the Brown family should be moved to their placements by August.

Blackheath, London
June 1966

They have decided that me and Roy will move to a new Home in a few weeks' time. At first I was worried when the Social Worker said Teddy wouldn't be living with us but then my brother promised he'd visit every week, just like Mummy did when she was alive.

The new Home is part of a convent called Saint Anne's in Orpington, Kent. I've been to see it already with my Social Worker, it's run by nuns who come from the order of the Sisters of Mercy from Ireland. It's a very big Home with a church and a school and a great old building that looks like a hospital on the top of a hill where the Mother Superior lives. There are trees around the main convent, some of them big enough to swing or climb in.

When we got to Saint Anne's we went up the drive to the main convent past the statue of the Virgin. We rang the bell by the big double doors. I hadn't seen a nun before, except in a film called *The Nun's Story* that I watched on TV one Sunday afternoon with my mother. In that film the nun is beautiful and she's sent to Africa to save coloured people by teaching them how to wear clothes and believe in the one true God so they'll live better lives than they did as natives. The real nun who opened the door was short and plump, with a big flat nose and fleshy red lips. When she said, 'Good morning, I'm Sister Patrick, come in and wait for Mother in reception,' little drops of spit sprayed from her mouth and landed on her chin.

What Sister Patrick called reception was set out like a living room, except there was no TV and it felt as if no one had ever lived there. The chairs and table, the bookshelf, the little china dishes and the silver cross in the glass-fronted cupboard looked as if they had never been new, never needed dusting, almost as if everything had grown where it was set. The walls were covered with pictures and each corner and every cupboard was crammed full of books and statues. Jesus looked down at this perfect, untouched room from a painting that hung above the marble fireplace and he smiled, as if he knew what I was thinking, and he pointed a finger to his open chest where his heart was still bleeding for my sins. Except for the ticking of a clock on the mantle shelf, the room was filled with silence and the air was thick with the same dark smell of a church. And even though hardly any light could get past the red velvet curtains, the chairs and tables were shiny and there was a glow to the place as if it was holy so I began to make good thoughts in case God might hear me.

When Mother Superior came in she said, 'Hello, my name is Mother Benedict, but you can call me Mother.'

All I could see of Mother Benedict was her face and hands because she wore a long black dress, called a habit, with sleeves to the wrists and a veil on her head that was pinned to a stiff white collar wide enough to lay flat right across her chest and shoulders. Although Mother Benedict's face was pink and looked soft as warm wax, her hands were white and she moved them quickly so they seemed like paper or butterfly wings the way she clasped them together and fluttered them away again. Mother seemed friendly and her face was as calm and empty as the pictures of the saints that hung around the walls because even when she smiled it was with the smallest curve of her lips and her eyes always looked into the distance.

Mother told us that Saint Anne's Home is split into family-size units, each one run by a sister and a lay house-parent. The houses are named after a place where a great saint lived, me and Roy would be living in one of the modern houses at the bottom of the hill called Glendalough and the nun in charge is Sister Kevin.

As we walked down the hill the sun came out. There are playgrounds, each one like a little park, and the six new houses have their own gardens and washing lines so the whole place seems more like a village than a Home. Children were playing in the gardens and every so often a voice called out, 'Good morning, Mother,' and Mother Benedict would raise her head as if she was the Queen and the bangle of keys that hung against the rosary around her waist swished and jangled at her knees.

Orpington, London
January 1967

Ihave to go to bed now, I'm not feeling well, my head is swimming and there's an ache in my belly. I've been here more than six months now and I don't like this new Home, one reason is that I'm always hungry because the boys here get the most food at dinner-time. Sometimes I think that's why I have so many dreams. The next problem is that at Saint Anne's we have to go to church almost every day and at six o'clock each evening we say the rosary in the living room on our knees in front of the statue of the Virgin and before I go to school, it's my job to clean the dining room. At the weekends I have to scrub the floor with wire wool and polish it shiny on my hands and knees. Sister says work and forbearance strengthens the soul. I remember what my mother used to say, I think my soul is quite strong enough already.

Sister Kevin saw me looking at a boy through the kitchen window, she slapped my face and told me I was a dirty slut and she sent me to my room with a book called *Growing Up the Catholic Way* that described how to get dressed without using a mirror.

Last night, after I had been crying long enough to fall asleep, I had a dream. I was in the park at Greenwich and my mother was next to me. We were sitting at the top of a hill, the place I always loved the best. It was a perfect day, like a painting, or a postcard with the sky the same colour as the bluebells that were swarming underneath the trees. Each time a breeze came up the bluebells shook their heads, their tiny little hoods made heavy by the first breath of the spring. In the dream I knew my mother was dead, even though she looked well and happy with her shoes kicked off and her lips all shiny and pink. She was dressed as her normal self, no stars at her head, no shroud at her shoulders, but there was something bright about her, a shimmer as she moved, a glistening at her fingertips, and the world was ours for those moments, hers and mine together. And suddenly, just the way it can happen in dreams, it made sense that my mother was alive and dead at the same time, eating jam sandwiches, stroking my hair and smiling at the day. And there was no difference between how I was feeling and the life that was spreading out between us. Mummy lay on the ground, and there were daisies at our feet. She closed her eyes and sucked in the air as the sunshine shadows of the wind-blown clouds played games across our faces. I told her of the Christmas that had just passed and the presents I'd got and what I'd eaten, talking on and on about everything in particular. And when at last I ran out of things to say and we had stopped eating, my mother took me in her arms, sang lullabies to me, rocking me softly so I knew that I was hers and that we would always be each other's most close and precious thing.

Then Mummy said, 'Listen child, I have to leave now. This is the last chance we will have to see each other for a long time.'

Although I held her tighter and pleaded with her to stay she just smiled and stroked my cheeks, wiping my tears and saying quite slowly, 'Baby girl, you know, it's my time, it comes to us all and this is mine, but you don't have to worry any more, you hear? Everything will come good, you wait and see.'

Even before she had stopped speaking she was floating away, up into the clouds, smiling and waving until she was just the smallest twinkle and I couldn't see her any more. But even though I was crying I was happy at the same time, because I knew Mum and me would be all right, as long as I remembered the past, everything we meant to each other, and all the things that had happened to her and me and my brothers all those once-upon-a-time long moments ago. I had never done that before, been happy and sad at the same time together.

The next morning, when I woke, my nightdress was sticking to my legs and there was a patch of blood that had seeped onto the sheets.

Sometimes, when I used to go into my mother's bed, there'd be a stain like that on the sheets. Mummy told me that's how you can tell when you've become a woman. Then I knew for sure that my mother had come back to say goodbye and that me and my mum will love each other the best always and forever.

When I grow up I want to be just like my mother.

April 2004

I can feel it. Soon the bare-faced summer will return and the sun will stretch back the days. It felt so fine to have that first warm breath blowing through the city, I asked Eleanor if she'd come and walk through the park with me, lope up the hill with the sun on our backs. We passed the places I'd played as a child, the boating pond by the gate, the planted gardens and the ancient oak trees, and she was sharing it with me. We stopped at the Observatory, looking down on the city from the little paved plateau where love-bird couples sat perched and trembling in the sharp spring air. And there it was, our city, spreading its metalled streets and towers from the valley to as far as our eyes could see.

'You know, even though I've never moved away, when I'm in this place I always feel as if I've come home, so much has changed and so much stayed the same. I wouldn't be surprised to turn a corner and hear my mother call me.' Eleanor smiled at me. 'The truth is, I feel closer to her now than I ever did.'

'And in the last few months I've got to know both of you better.'

'Good, because I couldn't have gone through it without you.'

'But they are your memories, you just shared them with me.'

'No, theyr'e our memories, what we are to each other. That's why these conversations have been so important, they've given my mother her voice back again.'

'And mothers before that.'

'Yes, of course, and now I see it; she never really walked away, even now she's here with you and me.' Eleanor took my arm. 'And looking at you, I know that a lot of things have turned out the way she would have wanted.'

And I smiled because I saw it, the beauty of the city, as finely drawn as I'd known it, ever since I was a child, the Heath and the terraced streets that lead to our road, the cars stacked nose to tail, the slender shoots of the cherry trees, the ramshackle order of the little front garden. Eleanor picked up the post as we went into the house and followed me to the kitchen.

'It's a packet,' she said, 'for you.'

I slipped my thumb beneath the flap and ripped at the fold. 'From the United States of America Department of the Interior,' the letter began . . .

Dear Ms Walker,

In response to your request to be given access to documentation held by the U.S. State Department regarding your mother, Mrs Dorothy Walker Brown we enclose the following:

- Record of the Immigration Service Hearings
- Letters relating to proceedings of the Immigration Service
- Divorce proceeding between Clifford Nathaniel Brown and Dorothy Walker Brown
- Deportation Order

I turned the page.

U.S. DEPARTMENT OF JUSTICE

Immigration and Naturalization Service

New York, N. Y.

— — — — — — — — X— — — —X

In The Matter Of   :   New York File No 0300—116510

Deportation Proceedings   :   Central Office File

Hearing Officer   :   Charles D. McCarthy

Stenographer   :   Abe Schwartz

Language   :   English

Date   :   May 22, 1951

Hearing Conducted at   :   **Pilgrim State Hospital,**

                                        W. Brentwood, LI, N.Y.

Against   :   Dorothy Walker

                                     :   Or Dorothy Brown

                                     :   Or Dorothy Rebecca Brown

                                     :   Or Dorothy Rebecca Walker Brown

Counsel or Representative :   None

Present   :   Dr Karen Mallins, Supervising

                                        Psychiatrist

Respondent   :

— — — — — — — — — — — — X

HEARING OFFICER TO PHYSICIAN:

Q Doctor, will you state your name and position?

A Karen Mallins, Supervising Psychiatrist.

333

Jacqueline Walker

Q Are you the supervising psychiatrist here at the Pilgrim
State Hospital?

A That is right.

Q Do you have under your care and supervision at the
present time a patient by the name of Dorothy Walker
Brown?

A Yes, I do.

EPILOGUE
PERSEPHONE

*We are Daughter and Mother, the two that are always one,
our souls sealed together in the promise of new life that rests
in winter.*

*It was me; I was the Maiden, Persephone the Kore and he
wanted me, that's why it happened. Or it may have been
because we were more than Divine, the Corn Mother and the
Daughter, stronger in the love of each other, so happy that
the gods themselves became jealous. Or it may have been that
I was young and foolish enough to forget the wisdom of Her
ways, because the sound of the music was burning in my
head and I couldn't stop dancing with the flowers.*

*I was with the flowers when I felt him rise from the horizon,
his shadow darkening the Earth as he raced towards me,
pulling at the reins, whipping at the flanks of his steel-hoofed
horses when he saw me.*

*The slit of his mouth opened wide as a grave when his
wings enclosed me, his claws took hold of me, his foul breath
burnishing my cheeks and we soared, we soared, not to the*

heavens like the dove-winged angels, we dived into mountains, racing through the winds while Hades set a hell fire burning inside me — inside me!

I gasped when it happened, calling for my Mother, but I knew I had faltered, clutching at the space that was spreading out between us till the void hid her face far from me.

I did what I could to resist him, remembering my life and the things my Mother had told me; I didn't speak or eat at his table, but I have to allow it; something inside me stirred.

As time went on he tried a different approach, stalking my sorrows with sweetness, using the stealth of the Night-Cloaked Hunter, which has always been his way. He told me Beauty breathed her graces around me, that I would be his Queen, that all I needed was to give him my trust and I'd forget all my sadness.

At first I opposed him, but I was hardly more than a child, small chested then, more like a boy than a woman in my ways, so when he brought me to the feast, how could I resist him; can you imagine it? Think how one pomegranate would seem in the middle of a famine, in the middle of an endless desert; it was like an oasis!

Soon as he opened the flesh I saw it, the red juice dripping from his fingers. It was enough; I hesitated, his hands were on me and I forgot everything — until I saw Her again, Demeter my Mother, a shimmer of the morning rising from the darkness, a lash of the dawn brightening Her brow as She stood with the moonlight pulling at Her hair. As soon as our eyes met Her love was all around me and I laughed, I laughed; recalling the days and the dancing, knowing we'd be strong again, standing at the portal of each day. But it was too late, the Death-Headed God had come between us.

She is mine, he said, the meal has been taken, the contract is sealed. I was filled with such shame I covered up my face . . . But Demeter is the Mother, mine.

Hades, she said, Brother Zeus has set this struggle to come between us. We must find a way to sit in peace before I lift the curse. And even though you used your tricks, I agree, my Daughter sealed her fate, so let this be the bond; for one third of the year she will service your will, she'll be your Queen and lay like Death and forget her Mother's ways and what we have been, and the Earth will be as cold and barren as I've left it now, but for the rest you must concede; Persephone comes with me.

And so I was tied to Hades, but as winter's darkest night comes, and Death holds me in his embrace, I watch the horizon. I know she will come.

I love the Mother.

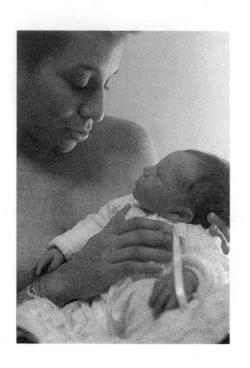

Acknowledgements

Although this book is dedicated to the many women who have mothered me, there are a number of other people I need to thank in particular; people who enabled me, in a more specific way, not just to begin this project but who gave me (even against the odd dissenting voice) the help, support and at times the love I needed to complete it.

The Arts Council of England saved me, buoying both me and my finances back up to a breathable surface when, close to the end, I was left without money or good cheer. My thanks also go to the Arvon Foundation, their Centre Directors, tutors and staff who provided me with much of the confidence and many of the skills I needed to keep going over the more than two years it took to finish *Pilgrim State*. I also have a debt of gratitude to Writers of Our Age (WOA, my local writers' group) whose members gave more than generously of their time and support. WOA also provided regular opportunities for (at times) hilarious and always useful perspectives on the joys and tribulations of being a writer at their fortnightly meetings that I still attend at a number of well-known South London beauty spots.

RAG, the Radical Anthropology Group, the longest running

Acknowledgements

evening class in London, gave me intellectual stimulation and a weekly window on a number of other cultures, past and present. RAG also encouraged me to believe that there's always hope for Humanity (well, most of the time) and helped me to develop a better understanding of the significance of female solidarity, of ritual and myth, not just to contemporary society or for deciphering the clues of our origins, but in a way that enabled me to find the key to narrating *Pilgrim State*, my own story. In this task I was more than lucky to have two friends who agreed to use their diverse talents to be my critical readers; Meegan McGilchrist and the wonderful Ann Bliss who not only read the manuscript almost as much as I did, but gave me a bed and shared a caravan by the sea when times got rough.

I'm glad to say this practical body-and-soul support was also provided by a number of others – thanks for the homemade soup and the soft shoulders: Michelle Laufer, Amicie, Caroline and Carolyn, Lynn McDonald, Clare Schulz, Marcus Fitzgibbon, Camilla Power, Chris Knight, Pauline Marshall, Anne Marie and Paul, Richard and Kate. Of course, I must thank my children, particularly my daughter, who very often during the writing of this book had to wait in line, even though they were so much the reason I wrote *Pilgrim State*. Gratitude also goes to my brothers, especially Teddy, who went through most of what happened in the book with me and is still, as far as I'm concerned, Superboy. Most particular thanks and respect go to Rachel, a special mother to me, who can never be properly recompensed for her good counsel. To Nigel Drew, who always, I have to admit, thought I could do it. To Lynette Owen and my agent Carole Blake. To the staff at the Hodder office, in particular of course, my editor Lisa Highton, her

Acknowledgements

down-to-earth exhilaration kept my feet on the ground and my mind floating free.

And last, but nowhere least, thanks must be given to three special people: Elizabeth Power, a remarkable woman who read the manuscript of *Pilgrim State* as she was preparing for her final journey from this life; Seana Culwin, who died unexpectedly at the beginning of her adult life, just as I was coming to the end of editing *Pilgrim State*. For a time, when we were both much younger, Seana gave me the opportunity to see what having a daughter could be like; and finally I owe much more than thanks to my own dear mother, whose book in truth this is, because whatever has happened or will happen over the remaining course of my life, her love will always be the most important gift anyone could give me. I have been so blessed. Thank you.

All photographs supplied courtesy of the author.